THE MAN IN THE GARDEN

JEFF CARLETON

Copyright © 2016 Jeff Carleton

ISBN: 9780692773468

DEDICATION

To Kiki

CONTENTS

ACKNOWLEDGMENTS

Thanks to Mom and Dad for taking me to church
and teaching me the importance of religion and spirituality.

Thanks to Raby Edwards, Bill Sachs, and Randy Hollerith
for translating the lessons of the Bible to daily life.

Thanks to Kiki for your love and support
while I pursue my dream.

1 THE FAMILY THAT PRAYS TOGETHER

"An angel from heaven appeared to Him and strengthened Him. And being in anguish, He prayed more earnestly, and His sweat was like drops of blood falling to the ground."

Luke 22: 43–44

"Hurry up, kids! Your mother wants to get there early so we can find a good seat up front," James Howard called upstairs to his two children as they scrambled to finish getting dressed for Sunday church.

Two thumps reverberated throughout the two-story brick house from the second floor. They were the Bass Weejuns dress shoes of Billy, the thirteen-year-old son, hurriedly being tossed onto the floor so he could slip them on and run down the stairs to catch up with his parents while they made their way to the front door. Billy's nine-year-old sister Claire was already at the bottom of the steps when Billy started to jump down the staircase two steps at a time.

"Out of the way, Claire!" the boy yelled. "I'm coming through!"

"You're late, slow poke," she countered as she sprinted to

the front door in her kelly-green, long-sleeve dress and black patent-leather flats.

"OK, you two. Slow it down. Let's all get there in one piece," commanded Sarah Howard, the calm, controlled matriarch of the Howard clan. "We're only a couple blocks away, and it's a beautiful day. Save some of that energy for after church."

James Howard waited for his wife and kids to clear the doorway before he pulled out his keys and locked the deadbolt of the front door to his modest house on Grove Avenue in the near west end of Richmond, Virginia. He returned his keys to the well-worn, slightly frayed, front pants pocket of his grey flannel Joseph Bank's suit, which was past the end of its useful life after years of regular service at the law firm of Clark, MacArthur, and Williams in downtown Richmond.

With more than a dozen years as a mid-level real estate attorney and currently as partner for a smaller firm in Virginia's capital city, James was able to provide his family most of the trappings many middle-class families hope to enjoy in life — a comfortable home in a nice part of town, membership in the local pool and racket club, private school for both his children, and an SUV for his wife and a Mercedes sedan for himself.

But to be able to afford all these niceties, the Howards had to make a few accommodations along the way. William's work clothes had to last longer than their optimal lifespan. His Rolex was fake, as evidenced by the ticking second hand instead of the real version's sweeping hand. The Mercedes was bought used with high mileage through a wholesaler. And his wife's jewelry, while still being appreciated for its emotional and romantic thoughtfulness by Sarah, included pieces like a modest gold necklace and a diamond engagement ring that was significantly smaller in carat size than the rest of her friends.

This was all part of the balancing act the Howards knew they had to play. James' work reputation depended on it. He had to look successful to bring in new clients, but he didn't earn enough yet to afford the complete image of an upscale address in Windsor Farms, membership at the country club, and a second house at the beach. To make the connections he needed to get ahead, he had to look, act, and play the part. So far, he had worked hard and done well for himself and his family, but he still looked forward to being able to attain his idea of success, or at least what he thought was his idea of it.

The walk from the Howard's house to church was only three blocks, but it took almost a full block before Billy and Claire stopped running and jumping after each other and slowed down to a relaxing walking pace with their parents. A clear, bright-blue, sunny sky held only a few puffy, white clouds in the distance, so their walk was entirely into the low-angle sunshine of an early-December Sunday morning. A subtle, brisk gust of wind would temporarily chill their faces, but then the piercing white orb of a winter sun fought back to warm them just enough to make the walk pleasant. A few determined, brown and yellow leaves stubbornly clung to the tree branches trying to defy the inevitability of the changing seasons, but except for the evergreen pines, the rest of the trees were bare and empty.

Sarah took a moment to appreciate the beautiful day with all her family together and healthy. She made sure to smell the roses during moments like this whenever she could. She knew how life could change in an instant, and she also knew her children wouldn't stay this age forever.

"Do you two have your Christmas lists ready for Santa yet?" she asked her children. "You know he gets pretty busy right about now, so you don't want to be late."

Claire spoke up first. "I want a new ski coat for our trip to Snowshoe. I saw a pink one at the store with Nanna last week. And the new iPhone just came out. Becky and Julie already have it. I love it."

"Maybe Nanna can get those for her," James whispered to his wife sarcastically before asking his son, "Billy, do you know yet if you're going to be an acolyte for the Christmas Eve service? Nanna and Granddad want to join us for that."

"I don't know yet, Dad. I'll check the schedule today after church."

"If you are, I bet Tricia will be there," Claire teased her older brother. "And after church, you two can be all kissy kissy together, even if it is Jesus' birthday."

Claire held the back of her hand up to her mouth and made loud kissing sounds.

Billy replied immediately, "You better watch out. If you keep talking like that, Santa won't be bringing you that ski jacket or iPhone. Instead, you'll get a plastic rain poncho and an old flip phone."

"What's a flip phone?" Claire asked.

Billy just rolled his eyes, forgetting how young his little sister was.

The Howards waited for a gap in the Sunday traffic and then crossed the last street before the block of the church. The parking lot to their right was quickly filling up with Mercedes, Range Rovers, BMWs, Audis, Jaguars, and every other brand of expensive car and SUV. The grass to the right of the sidewalk was now a summer-like bright green instead of the dormant, brown Bermuda grass from the previous blocks. Bluegrass fescue stayed green all year long, so the church chose to use it even though maintenance was expensive and year-round. Plus, the emerald sheen added a soft, plush contrast to the hard, light grey stone walls of the gothic-designed cathedral building.

Just a few steps ahead were two eight-foot-tall stone columns that, like silent, steadfast sentinels, guarded the stone sidewalk leading to the side entrance of the main chapel. The Howard family turned right off the main sidewalk, headed through the stone columns, and approached the line of people waiting to go in through the side entrance of the church. Billy looked up at one of the giant oak trees just next to the church as a small flock of birds took off in unison from the half-bare branches. They swarmed together for a few seconds, darting up and down and left and right like a small, black, living cloud. Just as the flock turned to shoot up skyward and leave the area, Billy noticed two birds crash into each other head-on and tumble slowly to earth, flailing their wings in vain to try to prevent hitting the ground. After they both landed in the thick, green fescue grass, one of the birds immediately stood up, shook its head, and flew up to rejoin the rest of its flock. The other bird stayed on the ground motionless. As Billy was about to step out of line and go over to check on the bird, it regained its senses and flew away into the clear blue sky.

About twenty feet farther up the main sidewalk past the stone sentinel columns could be seen a black wrought-iron post holding a white metal sign in its center that read simply *St. Andrew's Episcopal Church* with a formal crest adorning the top. But most around town knew this church as *the country club of God*. There were many reasons for this derisive nickname, other than the obvious name of the church itself. The sheer size and opulence of the buildings were impressive. The parking lot looked like that of an expensive restaurant in Los Angeles. And the church's proximity to one of the most exclusive private country clubs in the state didn't help prevent sarcastic jeers either. Just three blocks, or rather a par five, away sat the eighteenth green of the Virginia Country Club. Many parishioners made a beeline straight to the club once the church service was over, especially on a nice day like this in December, which was probably one of the last days to get a round of golf in before the ice and snow of a mid-Atlantic winter would soon begin.

The interior of St. Andrew's contained high-vaulted ceilings with dark wooden crossbeams that seemed to be suspended halfway to heaven, causing churchgoers to strain their necks if they looked up that high for too long during the service. The traditional cross-shaped layout of the building included two side vestibules, one to the right and one to the left, that were usually the last to fill up because of the obstructed views to the pulpits and altar. Ornately carved wooden panels rose up above the choir seated on both sides of the altar, with the organist tucked in behind the main pulpit to the right. At the very front of the church above the white stone altar and a detailed, carved set of wooden panels decorated with paintings of various Christian saints, three tall columns of stained glass overlooked the entire congregation, letting in streams of red and light- and dark-blue sunlight. In the middle stained-glass column stood the image of a strong and resolute St. Christopher fording a stream with baby Jesus on his shoulder.

The overall feeling inside the church was one of strength and solidity. The bare white plaster walls and stone arches weren't adorned with tapestries or paintings. The bare wooden pews curved just right at the bottom and lower back to allow a comfortable hour or two of worship. Clean, polished brick floors contained no cracks or scrapes. No carpets cushioned your steps while walking up front for communion. The austerity and simplicity of the building's design on the audience's side of the pulpit added to the church's aura of prestige without being gaudy.

Yet it was the sheer size of the place that made it seem almost overwhelming. Sure, there were modern mega churches out in the suburbs built like auditoriums that could hold thousands, but St. Andrew's had the atmosphere of one of the classic cathedrals in London or New York, except in a smaller city in the south. Hundreds of mothers, fathers, children, grandparents, friends, couples, and singles filled the pews even on this non-holiday Sunday. And one of the main reasons they were all there was because of who was getting ready to deliver the sermon in just a few minutes.

But right now, 30 minutes into the service, all those eyes were focused on Billy Howard as he cautiously approached the secondary, left pulpit to read a verse from the Bible. He was careful to take each step slowly and surely because the last thing he wanted was to fall face down in front of hundreds of people. When he reached the podium, the Bible was laying open to the correct page with a red sash down the middle seam. He pushed his face forward so his mouth was near the microphone and began to clearly enunciate without any hint of nervousness.

"Today's reading is from the 26th book of Matthew, verses 36 through 46.

"Then Jesus went with his disciples to a place called Gethsemane, and

He said to them, 'Sit here while I go over there and pray.' He took Peter and the two sons of Zebedee along with him, and He began to be sorrowful and troubled. Then He said to them, 'My soul is overwhelmed with sorrow to the point of death. Stay here and keep watch with Me.'

Going a little farther, He fell with his face to the ground and prayed, 'My Father, if it is possible, may this cup be taken from Me? Yet not as I will, but as You will.'

Then He returned to His disciples and found them sleeping. 'Couldn't you men keep watch with Me for one hour?' he asked Peter. 'Watch and pray so that you will not fall into temptation. The spirit is willing, but the flesh is weak.'

He went away a second time and prayed, 'My Father, if it is not possible for this cup to be taken away unless I drink it, may Your will be done.'

When He came back, He again found them sleeping because their eyes were heavy. So He left them and went away once more and prayed the third time, saying the same thing.

Then He returned to the disciples and said to them, 'Are you still sleeping and resting? Look, the hour has come, and the Son of Man is delivered into the hands of sinners. Rise! Let us go! Here comes My betrayer!'"

Billy turned around and deliberately walked back down the same steps he had so carefully ascended just a minute earlier. As he reached the center aisle that would lead him back to his spot in the pews, he glanced up and caught the familiar face of a man dressed in a white robe who was making his way up the steps to the right, main pulpit. The man gave a smile and a sly wink to the boy as if saying without words, "Well done." Billy smiled back and continued to his seat.

Reverend Michael Thomas took one last look at his note card resting in the open Bible on the podium before he gazed out upon the full house. He recognized many of them, especially those in the first twenty or so rows. Beyond that it was hard to make out faces in the crowd. At 42 years old and after decades of reading hundreds of books on history and religion, his eyesight had grown considerably weaker. And his black, rectangular-framed, faux designer eyeglasses didn't help much in seeing the people toward the back of the church, especially with such dim interior lighting.

Thick, jet-black waves of hair were highlighted at the front temples with wisps of grey. A strong, square jawline set off a handsome yet approachable clean-shaven face of a slight olive-toned complexion. Behind the glasses, his blue eyes were warm and deep, contrasting dramatically against his white robe and black shirt underneath. It was easy to see why so many women were in the audience today, even with his wife sitting prominently in the first row. In a deep and commanding voice, his words began to fill the expansive room.

"The passage you just heard, known more commonly as the Agony in the Garden and read so well by Mr. Howard, is one of the most important in the entire New Testament. At first glance, it seems fairly straightforward. This is right after the Last Supper. Jesus and His disciples have retired to the safety of a garden on the Mount of Olives just outside Jerusalem, waiting for the inevitable betrayal by Judas and the arrest of Jesus. Jesus prays a few times, His trusted disciples fall asleep, and then the Romans arrive. In a film or a book, you might even call this a simple transition scene. Give the viewer or reader a rest between the larger scenes so they can catch their breath.

"But there are some key lines in this passage that stand out, the first one being, 'My soul is overwhelmed with sorrow to the point of death.' Now here's where we catch a clue that something serious is about to happen very soon. This is dramatic talk, even for Jesus. He's always been extremely confident about His mission here on earth. He knows He's here for a reason and that God is behind him 100 percent. It's hard to feel more confident than that."

A slight glare from the gold family-crest ring on Reverend Thomas' left ring finger, which also served as his wedding band, caught the corner of his eye as he slightly adjusted his note card.

"Till now, this whole Messiah thing hasn't been so bad. Perform some miracles. Debate some corrupt religious leaders.

Heal some sick people. Turn water into wine. Sure, He's felt strong sorrow for the people in Galilee, Jerusalem, and the rest of Israel, but he's helped them and given them hope. So far, Jesus has done everything perfectly. He's fulfilled the prophecies and God's expectations for Him. Even during the Last Supper, which has just taken place within an hour or so, He speaks confidently and calmly about how He's going to be betrayed and arrested and killed. He prepares His disciples for their lives without Him. Then He goes to this calm, quiet retreat in an olive grove outside of town. All of the disciples fall asleep quickly, and Jesus is left alone with His thoughts. And as the young people like to say, it's about to get real.

"Jesus starts to show weakness. For the first time in the Bible, Jesus exposes His vulnerability. He is overwhelmed. Up until this point, the idea that He would die has always been sometime in the future. But now it's the night before He's to be put on the cross. And that reality is beginning to set in. Hours and hours of beatings, mocking, and pain are just about to start. He's about to go through one of the most agonizing tortures man has ever devised — crucifixion. The pain is so intense, a new word was created to describe it — excruciating, which literally means 'from the cross.'"

"Right here is when the humanity of Jesus shows itself to us. He begins to have some doubt. He asks God, 'If it's possible, can this cup be taken from me?' So here's Jesus, the perfect example of what a human can be. The Son of God. Our Savior. And He has this moment of weakness and asks to be let off the hook.

"So why is this so important? Wouldn't anyone want to avoid such an agonizing death? Wouldn't anyone not want to be crucified. Wouldn't anyone not want to have to endure that much suffering. Obviously yes. And that is exactly the point.

"Anyone would. But Jesus isn't just anyone. He is the Son of God. Throughout the Bible, Jesus would occasionally show some emotion. But most of the time, He is strong and resolute, not making mistakes, almost more like a robot than a human being. But now, He's weak. He says to Peter, 'The spirit is willing, but the flesh is weak.' He's not only talking about Peter falling asleep; he's also talking about Himself. We are reminded that Jesus is not just the Son of God. He has fears. He feels pain. He isn't just a divine vessel living among us. He's also human. And this revelation makes His later suffering even more real for all of us. He's not an invincible deity when he goes through all that torment and pain. He hesitates. He has regrets. He's one of us."

Reverend Thomas took a moment to scan the first few rows of the church to see if anyone was listening. To his surprise, everyone was focused on the pulpit. His eyes stopped briefly at a familiar, middle-aged blond woman in a long-sleeve, burgundy dress seated in the fourth row. Once she realized he was looking at her, she flashed a small, subtle smile. The reverend quickly returned his gaze back to his notes.

"In Luke's version of this part of the story, Jesus sweats blood. That is called hematidrosis, and it's a very real condition that is brought on by extreme stress. So God sends an angel down to comfort and strengthen Him. But regardless of how Jesus was able to overcome his temporary doubts, thank goodness Jesus was strong enough to go through with his fate. It would have been very easy for Jesus, as a man, to simply slip out of the garden, leave His sleeping disciples, and head down the mountain and away from Jerusalem. The Romans didn't know what He looked like. There weren't any selfies on Facebook to give them His description. He could easily have left and never been seen again. Just imagine how different the world would be today if He had just walked away. It's hard to even comprehend it."

The reverend paused for a moment as his left hand started to quiver and shake slightly against the podium. He slid his hand down and put it in his side pants pocket so no one in the audience would see it.

"But obviously He didn't do that. He accepts His destiny and tells our Heavenly Father, 'Your will be done.' He fulfilled the prophecy and became the Savior we needed. And knowing that He suffered as much as any normal man would have makes it all the more impressive. He was the perfect sacrifice for us, and this temporary show of weakness made Him even more perfect."

Once the service was over and the clergy and choir had finished their procession out of the church, each of the three reverends would head to a different exit to thank everyone for attending. Reverend Thomas stood at the side entrance the Howard family had entered through earlier. Some parishioners lined up to shake his hand and say a few words, while others slipped around the line and exited the church directly. The reverend's wife walked quickly by the line, waved as she moved past the crowd, and mouthed the words to him, "See you at home." He smiled back in acknowledgement.

Next in line was the Howard family. Sarah reached her hand out first to shake the reverend's.

"Reverend Thomas, it's always a pleasure to hear your sermons. They make everything so clear and easy to relate to."

"Well, thank you very much, Mrs. Howard. My style may be a little different than that of the traditional Episcopal Church, but I like to think we ultimately get to the same destination of understanding."

He looked down at Billy standing next to his father.

"And Billy, you did an outstanding job with the reading today. You'll have to help out with one of my sermons someday."

"It wasn't that hard," Billy responded. "But thanks anyway. I think I'll leave the sermons up to you."

"Oh, OK. But you just let me know when you're ready. See you all next week. Take care."

The Howards exited the church and stepped out into a bright, sunshine-filled winter afternoon. Dozens more people moved through the line to shake the reverend's hand. Small talk about the upcoming Christmas, the weather, the sermon, and even football continued as the crowd inside steadily thinned out. The blond woman in the burgundy dress, having waited all this time sitting in a pew near the exit, stood up and joined the end of the line. When it was her time to say goodbye to the reverend, she reached out her soft and expensively manicured right hand and shook his.

"The service today was just wonderful. You really have a way with words, Reverend Thomas."

She took her left hand, which bore a round, seven-carat diamond ring on the ring finger, and gently cupped underneath his right hand to secure the handshake further.

"Thank you, Mrs. Woodson," he replied, trying to remain calm and stoic.

"I look forward to the next time," she said as she gently squeezed his hand with both of hers.

The reverend pulled his hand out from her clutch and politely said, "Have a nice day."

"Oh, I will. See you soon."

And she left with a subtle, wry smile.

2 BITE THE ONION

The reverend's office door was pulled closed behind him and locked shut before he made his way to his desk near the floor-to-ceiling window along the back wall. He took out his keys from his pants pocket, unlocked a wooden door in the bottom left side of the desk, tossed the keys on top of his desk, and pulled out a half-empty bottle of Jim Beam bourbon and a previously used lowball glass. He opened the bottle, poured the golden brown liquid so it filled about four fingers of the glass, and put the top back on the bottle and the bottle on the desk.

Still standing and before taking a drink, he walked over to a closet against the side wall and took off his white robe he had been wearing during the church service. As he pulled out a hanger from the closet with his left hand, the quivering returned, and the hanger started to shake like a swimming pool diving board. He quickly grabbed the hanger with his right hand, reflexively looked around to see if anyone was watching, and hung up his robe in the closet. Returning to his desk, he sat down in his chair, and from the desk compartment where the bourbon had been, he pulled out a tin of mints and a Ziploc bag that contained a sliced onion. He placed them on top of the desk next to his keys and returned the bottle of bourbon back inside the desk.

Grabbing the glass of alcohol in his right hand, he slowly swung around in his chair to face the back window and gently leaned back to recline. His office on the second floor offered him a view of a grove of almost-bare oak trees between the church property and the adjoining neighborhood. The exterior tinting on the glass made it so no one on the ground floor could look up and see him inside his office.

The walls of Reverend Thomas' office were lined with bookshelves that were filled with hundreds of books about religion, history, philosophy, science, and even sports. He was a voracious reader, preferring real books made of paper to e-books. In fact, his love of reading about history, religious history in particular, is ultimately what led to his decision to study religion. His diploma from Yale Divinity School hung in a simple wooden frame over in a dark corner away from direct eyesight.

While most priests were focused on the scriptures and what Christianity and Jesus' words really mean, Reverend Thomas was more intrigued by how human history had been shaped and molded by religions, especially Christianity. He was well versed in how Judao-Christian principles had been used over the centuries to influence and govern societies all over the world. From the fall of the Roman Empire to the creation of the United States, religion was a cornerstone of civilization. And even though church and state were legally separate in modern America, he knew they weren't separated in many people's minds around the world, nor had they been for thousands of years.

After a few sips of whiskey from his lowball glass, his left hand tremor began to subside. He exhaled a long, steady breath and looked out upon the trees and the clear, sunny, blue sky. His thoughts drifted back to the blond woman in the burgundy dress, then he took a large swig of bourbon. The last few cars were exiting the parking lot and heading down the side road in the distance past the trees. He wondered where they were going. To Sunday brunch at the club? Back home to watch football? Or maybe even for a leisurely drive in the country? He wished he could be in one of those cars, leaving everything behind with nowhere in particular he had to be.

He finished off the bourbon with one last gulp and returned the glass to its compartment in the desk. He removed the onion slice from the Ziploc bag, took a large bite, and returned the odoriferous remnants back to their concealed home inside the bag. Halfway through his chewing, three knocks on the door rang out.

"Michael, are you busy? Do you have a minute?" asked an older male voice from the hallway.

The reverend immediately recognized the voice of the rector, his boss. He hastily grabbed the Ziploc bag, stuffed it back into the desk, and shut the compartment door without locking it. He continued to chew as he approached the office door, which he unlocked and opened.

"I hope I'm not disturbing you," said the rector. "Are you free to talk?"

"Sure," the reverend mumbled between chews. "Pardon me. I had a little snack after the service. I didn't get a chance to have breakfast earlier. Come on in. Have a seat."

The rector was tall and thin with thick, cropped grey hair; thin-wired, gold glasses; and a weather-worn face from summers in the sun on the Chesapeake Bay. He was still wearing his white robe from the service since he hadn't had time yet to take it off. He sat down in the broken-in leather sofa to the side of the desk and next to the window. His deep, deliberate southern accent was warm but belied his underlying wit and experience. He had heard the door unlock and could smell the onion from a mile away. The smell reminded him of his Baptist grandmother when he was a kid. She would have a drink of sherry in the afternoon and take a bite of onion when friends would drop by unannounced. But he didn't want to talk about that just yet. He had something more important to discuss first.

After finishing his mouthful, the reverend pulled out a couple mints from the tin on his desk and popped them into his mouth. He offered some to the rector, who politely declined. The rector noticed the keys on top of the desk and subtly glanced down at the desk, where he saw the door of the compartment barely ajar by just a few millimeters. But from his point-of-view, he couldn't see what was inside.

"What did you think of the service today?" the reverend asked to break the ice.

"It was nice. People seemed engaged and attentive. And as usual, when you're giving the sermon, the turnout was great. We had a full house today."

"Great. Glad to hear it. So what's up?"

The rector looked around the room and scanned the rows and rows of books on the shelves.

"One of the things that's most impressive about you, Michael, is your thorough knowledge of history. Have you read all these books?"

"Yeah, pretty much all of them."

"That's amazing. So you obviously know a lot about religion and history."

"I like to think I know a little bit about those things. Why do you ask?"

"Well, I thought your sermon today was very interesting. I agree, that passage about the Agony in the Garden is one of the most important in the Bible."

"OK?" the reverend replied inquisitively.

"But I guess I look at it a little differently than you do."

"Really? How so?"

"You talked about the agony Jesus was suffering in Gethsemane as though it were purely based on the physical pain he was about to experience on the cross. And while that might make logical sense to a reader who doesn't necessarily have a very strong faith, I believe his pain wasn't about the upcoming crucifixion at all."

"Hmm," the reverend mumbled. "What was it then?"

"The key to everything is the cup. Jesus asked God if the cup could be taken from Him. Based on your sermon, you believe the cup represents Jesus' destiny to die on the cross. Right?"

"Sure, more or less. Doesn't it?"

"I believe it means something else. I think the cup symbolizes God's wrath."

"God's wrath? At whom? At Jesus? He's about to die on the cross to fulfill God's destiny for Him. Why would he have wrath at Jesus?"

"Jesus' destiny is to suffer for our sins and die on the cross so we can all be forgiven. To accomplish that, Jesus has to take on our sins. And in that garden at that particular time, Jesus drank the cup of God's wrath. Jesus took on all the sins from all the millions of people who had ever lived up until that point, all at once. That's why he was overwhelmed to the point of death and even sweated blood. Michael, this belief is a core tenet of Christianity."

"I've heard that theory from some theologians, but I've read a few scholars, like LeBoule and Dunkirk for example, who agree with me about the anticipation of the crucifixion being the physical cause of the agony. So I could be right. Here, let me show you."

The reverend stood up quickly from his chair and shuffled over to one of the bookshelves, searching for a particular volume. The rector rose up from the sofa and followed over to the bookshelf also.

"How do you know you're right instead?" the reverend continued as he pulled a thick book from the shelf and began flipping through its pages. "The Bible doesn't say exactly what happened anyway. It's up to interpretation. What makes you believe that God just magically dumped all those sins onto Jesus?"

"My faith."

The reverend stopped flipping through the pages of the book and turned to face the rector.

"So you have your faith, but I have mine. Why do you think your faith trumps mine?"

"Michael, I'm not sure you have faith anymore."

The reverend was temporarily shocked by what he just heard and took a moment to compose himself. He put the book back on the shelf. The rector continued.

"This is certainly not easy to say to an ordained Episcopal priest. It may not be apparent to all the people out there in the pews, but it's clear as day from where I'm sitting. Your faith is weakening. I don't know if it's gone completely or if there's some trace of it left that can be retrieved and nourished. But somehow you've got to do some serious self-examination and figure things out. If a priest doesn't have faith, he doesn't have anything."

The reverend stood stunned and silent, trying to take everything in. He wanted to defend himself and deny what the rector had just told him, but he couldn't. He knew he just heard the truth that he had denied himself for a long while now.

The rector continued, "We can discuss it more at another time, if you like. But in the meantime, don't forget the Christmas party next Saturday night at the Woodson's house. They're having everyone from the church office over, plus I'm sure there will be several select and important guests as well."

"Are you sure you still want me to go?"

"Listen, Michael. I and everyone else here at St. Andrew's are here to do whatever we can to help you. You're part of our family, and the Woodson's party is a significant event for the church. I don't have to remind you how important they are to the economic health of this parish. To be blunt, they give us a lot of money, and they specifically requested your presence at the party."

"OK. I get it."

The rector headed for the door. As he was just about to leave the room, he turned around and asked, "Don't you still volunteer over at the St. John's Center?"

"Yes. Once a week."

"I used to work there myself too, but that was quite a long time ago. I believe they still have a lot of great programs for psychological conditions, drug addiction, alcoholism. My grandmother used to bite the onion too, son. St. John's might be a good place for you to start."

The rector closed the door behind him, leaving the reverend in his quiet and now seemingly empty office. He returned back to his chair and stared at the sky through the window. He wasn't ready to go home yet, so he sat alone with his thoughts for a while longer. He really wanted another drink, but he didn't get one.

After a restless night's sleep full of tossing and turning and thoughts of what the rector had told him in his office, Reverend Thomas awoke from what little sleep he had gotten to a splitting headache. It was so intense, he almost considered calling in sick for his teaching job at St. Philip's School, a private all-boys Episcopal school located just a few blocks from St. Andrew's.

The reverend taught one class of religious history every Monday at the school, so he would have felt guilty for skipping. He could tough it out, especially with the semester's final exam coming up in just a couple weeks. He had quite a bit of ground to cover before the exam, and missing just one class would put the students too far behind.

In his shared classroom at the far northern end of the main hall of the upper school at St. Philip's, the reverend stood before a green chalkboard in the front of the room. In bright white chalk was drawn a diagram with "Henry VIII" inside a box at the top with lines dropping down below to six circles that contained the names "Catherine of Aragon," "Anne Boleyn," "Catherine Howard," and the rest of Henry VIII's six wives. Several words were listed down the left side of the board, including "divorce," "Pope Clement VII," "Francis I," "Cardinal Wolsey," and "English Reformation."

On the opposite side of a simple wooden desk from the reverend sat 37 twelfth-grade boys in three vertical rows of metal desks with plastic chairs. The boys' blue blazers were adorned on the left chest pocket with an oval white patch containing a crest made of a red Latin cross, two loaves of bread, and a carpenter's square. Almost every student wore khaki pants, a solid blue or white shirt, and a red and grey striped tie. A few wore grey pants or a striped shirt to mix it up a little. Laptops from Apple, HP, Sony, and Samsung were open on the desks as each student typed in notes at a furious pace, desperately trying to keep up with the reverend's lecture.

The reverend glanced up at the clock above the chalkboard and realized he only had a couple more minutes before the class ended. He put the piece of chalk that was in his hand back in the tray and faced the students to deliver his summary. They knew not to start packing up their computers and bags early because the reverend didn't like that. The semester was almost over, and no one wanted detention right before Christmas.

"The king was never granted his divorce from Catherine of Aragon by Pope Clement. So he did what any self-centered, tyrannical, all-powerful ruler would do. He changed the rules. He declared his own marriage invalid based on the idea that Catherine had previously been married to his now-deceased brother Prince Arthur, and the special dispensation Henry received from Pope Julius II to marry Catherine should never have been granted in the first place. With his kind of logic, I think if Henry were around today, he would be a very good lawyer."

The reverend paused, waiting for a laugh or even a brief chuckle from the students. Nothing happened. He continued his lecture.

"Anyway, no one in the English government was going to stand in Henry's way, for they already saw how easily he had political enemies executed. However, the Catholic Church in Rome and in Spain and in France didn't like what Henry was trying to do. The devout Catholics in England didn't like it either, but to speak up would be suicide. Henry wanted desperately to marry Anne Boleyn and produce male heirs to keep the Tudor dynasty going. Once Henry annulled his own marriage and broke away from the Catholic Church, this marked the beginning of the Protestant Anglican Church, which later became the Episcopal Church here in the United States."

A student in the middle row raised his hand to ask a question.

"Yes, Paul?" acknowledged the reverend.

"So are you saying that the Anglican and then the Episcopal Church were started because King Henry VIII wanted to get with Anne Boleyn, but she wouldn't sleep with him until she was his wife?"

The entire class erupted in laughter.

The reverend fought back a smile at first and then responded, "Well, that's part of the reason. Of course there were also many English citizens who were Protestants and didn't want their country to be controlled by the Pope and the Catholic Church. Which led to the back and forth of the Catholic reign of Mary, known more commonly as Bloody Mary, and the Protestant reign of Mary's sister, Elizabeth. But we'll finish up with all that next week."

The students packed their laptops into their bags and tentatively started to stand up from their desks. The reverend raised his voice slightly to be heard over the sliding chairs and shuffling feet.

"Don't forget, next week is the last class before the final exam. We'll finish up with the rest of the English Reformation. And bring any questions you have from earlier parts of the semester. Oh yeah, and for those who asked me for college recommendations, be sure to give me your information before the Christmas break. I'll be writing them over the holidays, so if I don't have your information before then, you won't get a recommendation. Don't say I didn't warn you."

The reverend sat down in the wooden desk chair at the front of the room and began to pack up his books and computer. After all the other students had left the classroom, one last student approached the teacher's desk and handed him a plain white, sealed envelope.

"Reverend Thomas, here's the information for my college recommendation."

"OK, Paul," the reverend replied as he took the envelope; put it in his bag; removed another plain white, sealed envelope from a separate section of his computer bag; and handed it to the student, all without looking up at the student's face or saying a word.

The student stuffed the envelope into his bag without opening it. He didn't need to. He knew the money was all there, just as it had been every week since the beginning of the semester. He left the reverend sitting alone in the classroom. After a few minutes, the reverend finally stood up, walked out of the room, left the building, and headed for his blue Volvo station wagon in the parking lot. After he started the car and slid the transmission lever into drive, he saw his left hand begin to quiver on the steering wheel. He took his hand off the wheel, shook it a few times in the air in a futile attempt to steady it, and drove out of the school parking lot.

A couple blocks from the school and on the right side of the road, the reverend saw a familiar gravel road. He turned to follow it a couple hundred yards until it led him to an old, rusty, metal maintenance shed. He parked his car behind the shed and turned off the engine.

He pulled the envelope out of his computer bag, opened it, dumped out a translucent blue plastic tube into his hand, and jammed the empty envelope back into his bag. The tube, about six inches long, was opened at one end by unscrewing the black plastic top. Holding the tube with his right hand, he precisely tapped out two inch-long lines of white powder onto the back of this quivering left hand. The tube was carefully turned back to a vertical position so no excess powder could fall out.

He raised his shaking left hand up to his face. He inhaled one line of powder into his left nostril and the other line into his right nostril. He used his left hand to wipe off his nose and mouth first and then replaced the top on the tube, which he stuck back into a zippered section of his computer bag.

After a few seconds, his trembling left hand became steady. He sat quietly for a moment, took some deep breaths, and brushed off his black clergy shirt and black blazer. He looked in the rearview mirror to see if any white residue remained on his nose or mouth. They were clear. He quickly turned away from the mirror so he wouldn't see his own eyes. He couldn't bear to look at them.

3 GIFTS WITH STRINGS ATTACHED

The sunny afternoon was warming up quite nicely, especially for an early December day. The reverend pulled out of the gravel side road onto St. Philip's Lane and rolled down his driver's side window in the Volvo wagon to let some fresh air in as he headed back to his office at the church. He was scheduled for a meeting in about an hour at the St. John's Center, and he needed to pick up some papers on his desk before heading west to the Episcopal rehabilitation and recovery center. Since the clock on the dashboard of his car had been broken for a few years, he glanced at his cell phone to check the time. It read 12:07 p.m. He had plenty of time to grab something to eat before he would have to be at St. John's.

Just as he was about to put his phone away, a text popped up on the screen. It was from Nancy, the church office secretary. The text said that Mrs. Woodson wanted to ride out to St. John's with the reverend so they could both discuss some items before the meeting and to pick her up at her house. Nancy didn't bother including the address because she knew the reverend already had it. The reverend cleared the screen on his phone; put both hands back on the steering wheel; and exhaled a long, deep, sighing breath.

He looked into the rearview mirror and noticed a dark grey

Volkswagen Passat pulling out of a parking spot on the side of the road and getting up to speed about a block behind him. At first glance, he was worried it might have been an unmarked police car, but when he saw the VW logo in the grill, he knew he was safe. The cops didn't drive VWs. If it had been a Chevy or a Ford, he would've felt a lot more nervous.

The Woodsons, 55-year-old Betty and 72-year-old Richard, her husband of 32 years, lived in the very back of Windsor Farms, the most well known of Richmond's upscale neighborhoods. Michael Thomas always felt uncomfortable driving through this area, especially in his old, beat-up car as Mercedes after Lexus after Porsche passed him going the other way. He headed down Sulgrave Road and passed large house after mansion after estate. He had been to many of these houses before since most of the owners were members of St. Andrew's.

Sulgrave Road was a steadily curving street that ran along the back edge of Windsor Farms. The reverend looked back into his rearview mirror again and could barely make out the front of a dark-colored car several blocks in the distance just around the bend in the road so that he couldn't get a clear line of sight on it. He instinctively accelerated and followed the curving road that eventually met up with Lock Lane, a narrow drive that led to a dead end in the back corner of the neighborhood.

He took the left turn onto Lock Lane without even slowing down. Just then he remembered he was heading down a dead-end street. If someone were following him, he had nowhere to go. That was a stupid move. He was boxed in. His mind was racing as he looked back into his rearview mirror. He wondered if he could slip down one of the driveways to find a place to hide. Then he saw the dark grey car continue down Sulgrave Road without turning onto Lock Lane. He was in the clear. The Volvo slowed down as he told himself to calm down.

"It's the cocaine that has you all wired up and paranoid," he tried to explain to himself. "Just relax. Richmond is full of grey cars. Take it easy. Pull it together before you get to the Woodsons' place."

At the end of Lock Lane was one of the largest and most opulent houses in Virginia. The brick, Georgian mansion sat on a 20-acre parcel of land right along the banks of the James River. Due to the geography of the area and how the city was originally developed, riverfront property in Richmond was very rare. Most of it was found on the south side of the river. But in the west end, only a handful of people were able to enjoy waterfront views.

A tall, mature, ivy-covered brick wall extended on both sides of the entrance to the estate, where a 12-foot-high wrought-iron gate automatically opened as the Volvo approached. Just inside the gates, a long oval driveway with giant oak trees lined down the center led to a light grey cobblestone courtyard area just before the front door of the house. The old, partially ivy-covered brick façade of the house loomed three stories in the air, giving visitors the impression as though they were about to meet with a head of state.

The reverend pulled up and parked his old, beat-up, rusty car directly in front of the red front door. He reached into the back seat and grabbed his briefcase to take inside with him because he knew Mrs. Woodson would want to ride in one of her own cars. Just as he closed the car door and turned to head for the entrance to the house, the red front door opened, and Mrs. Woodson carefully walked down the three cement, semicircular steps in her designer high-heeled shoes.

Betty Woodson never stepped foot out of her house unless she was completely put together, and today she was that and more so. Her perfectly blended blond hair flowed down her shoulders to her coal-grey Dolce and Gabbana dress that hugged her curves tightly yet tastefully. She walked the fine line between looking attractive and sexy without going too far and being seen as trashy. At her age, it would have been very easy to go over the line with some of her fashion choices. But her outgoing personality seemed to mesh well with her appearance, so typically conservative Richmonders gave her a pass. Plus it didn't hurt that she and her husband possessed a fortune of at least 2.8 billion dollars. Money like that can help anyone look respectable.

However, she hadn't always been surrounded by this kind of money. She grew up in Richmond in a middle-class family where both her parents worked hard to be able to send her to St. Mary's School, the sister school to St. Philip's, and then later to what was once called Randolph-Macon Woman's College. She was smart and driven, but that didn't always show up in her academic grades. After college, she thought about becoming a nurse, mainly to increase her chances of meeting a doctor. She even took some nursing classes at the Medical College of Virginia.

However, that quickly changed once she met Richard Woodson. Having grown up in Richmond, of course she had known who he was. All the young women in the west end knew of the infamous heir to the Woodson fortune. She had seen him drive around town in his Porsche convertible and once even talked to him for a couple minutes at a keg party. But he went to boarding school at Andover and then to college at Yale. So along with the summers in Martha's Vineyard and the ski trips to Vail, he wasn't ever in Richmond long enough for her to get to know. And whenever he was in town, groups of girls were always hanging around trying to catch his eye.

But one sunny, warm, spring day, Betty and some girlfriends went to the annual outdoor social event of the year, the Strawberry Hill Races held at the state fairgrounds. This collage of high school students, college students, recent graduates, and young professionals was one of the biggest and most popular alcoholic binges in Virginia. Technically, this was a horseracing event with ten steeplechase races spread throughout the all-day Saturday affair, but many patrons had gone for more than ten years and had never even seen the first horse.

The real event took place in the infield of the oval horse

track. Reserved parking spots were sold out every year and hosted elaborate tailgate parties. Most were single or double spots filled with tables behind the open tailgates of Land Rovers and Suburbans with beer kegs and bottles of bourbon and mixers as the centerpieces.

But the Woodson tailgate party was quite different. An open-sided tent covered five parking spots and an array of tables, food displays, and a full-service bar with two bartenders. An invitation to this spot was coveted, but an attractive young woman like Betty didn't have any trouble getting in.

Betty and Richard first really met when he saw her standing alone with a martini in one hand and a racing form in the other. She intentionally had separated herself from her friends because she thought he would be more likely to approach her if she were alone instead of surrounded by a gaggle of women. And she was right. He took the bait and started a conversation with her about which horses to bet on. That led to small talk about gambling in Vegas and playing baccarat in Monte Carlo and then more martinis, which led to talk about skiing in Switzerland and how strong your thighs have to be to ski well, which then led to the folded-flat back seat of his Range Rover.

One of her talents was knowing exactly what powerful men like Richard wanted — a lady in public and a whore in the bedroom. And she was sure to give it to him. After a couple years of dating and satisfying him in every way possible, she received the proposal she had dreamed of. She had achieved her lifelong goal and was happier than ever. Richard eventually took over his family's investment firm and settled into a stable family life. They had two children together and seemed like the perfect couple.

But as time went by, Richard's responsibilities as the head of a huge financial business and the father and husband of a well-respected family started to weigh heavily on him. Betty was willing to expand their intimacy and try anything new that Richard wanted. But he had grown up with endless options and opportunities. Years of the same thing, no matter how many different experiences and experiments they tried together, got old quickly for him. He found it harder and harder to fend off the advances of attractive younger women trying to get a piece of a rich, handsome man. His eyes began to wander.

So the two of them worked out a deal. Richard didn't want the scandal and notoriety of a divorce, and he wanted his children to grow up in a home with two parents. Betty was used to her extravagant lifestyle, but she had signed a prenuptial agreement and wouldn't get very much if they divorced. Plus, she liked being known as Mrs. Woodson. Sure, she could keep the name if she got divorced. But to her, it wasn't the same thing as being Mrs. Woodson.

They agreed to stay together legally but live their own lives separately, even if they did share the same roof. Richard has his own bedroom in the house but never brought home any of his mistresses. Betty could do as she pleased also, but the social scene wasn't quite as easy for a 55-year-old woman as it was for a 59-year-old playboy. Still, they each got what they needed out of the arrangement — he kept his flings and reputation, and she got her money and status.

On this sunny winter day, her gold Gucci sunglasses matched impeccably with her gold watch, necklace, bracelets, and rings. A tan Louis Vuitton purse coordinated with her tan Christian Louboutin pumps. Her soft, slender face showed slight traces of weathering from years of sunbathing in Hawaii and Monte Carlo. A recent facelift from the best plastic surgeon in Miami kept her skin tight and firm, while 10-year-old breast implants from the same doctor were still holding up very well. Bright red lips and nails completed her "I want to look hot but not like a hooker" look.

"Well hello there, darling," she flirted. "Don't you look all professional and serious in your preacher outfit?"

"Hi, Betty," the reverend responded casually, knowing that the pretense of calling her Mrs. Woodson wasn't necessary. "You look all glammed up, as usual."

"Oh Michael, don't you know how to make all the ladies

swoon with your sweet talk? It's nice to see you too. Thanks for stopping by to pick me up."

She approached him closely and wrapped her arms around him in a tight, warm hug. He hugged her back politely with gentle pats on her back, trying not to get too personal. But he was only fooling himself. She felt wonderful in his arms, soft and sensual, and her perfume was intoxicating the restraint right out of him. She pulled away slowly after the hug and flashed him a huge, happy smile. Even though she was over 10 years older than him, he found her exciting and beautiful and incredibly sexy. Yet, he still felt the need to put up a shield and treat this as a business meeting.

"No problem. Are you ready to go?" he asked, gesturing to his car in the driveway.

"Oh, dear. Not that old thing."

She teetered in her shoes across the cobblestones to a row of six garage doors on the left side of the house. She pulled a remote control out of her purse and pressed the button while pointing it at the far left door. It slowly raised open.

"Let's take this old thing," she proudly announced with a gleaming white veneered-tooth smile.

When the garage door reached halfway open, the sunshine reflected off a shiny chrome bumper. Michael recognized the unique front end of the classic car immediately. He was in shock as chill bumps rose up on his forearms under his shirt and jacket. After the garage door opened completely, there sat a pristinely restored dark green Jaguar XKE convertible. The sunlight danced across the long, curved, sloping hood and sparkled radiantly off the bright silver wire wheels.

"So, what do you think?" she asked him.

"What do I think? I think this is the most beautiful thing I've ever seen. That's what I think."

"Most beautiful thing ever?"

"Thing, not person," he clarified.

He entered the garage and slowly walked around the car, almost afraid to touch it.

"Go ahead. It won't bite," she said playfully.

"This is amazing. I don't know if I've ever seen one this well restored before. The paint looks perfect. How many miles are on it?"

"I don't know. Take a look."

He peered through the driver's window to read the odometer. The five numerals in the gauge read 24,293. By the condition of the car, he knew that didn't mean 124,293 miles.

"It's a 1966 series 1 with the 4.2 liter inline six engine and covered headlights. This is exactly the model I was telling you about last summer at the church car show. Where in the world did you find this, especially with such low mileage?"

"I have a friend down in Florida. He can get just about any classic car you want. However, he did say this particular one was very tricky to find. But once you take a closer look at it, I think obviously it was worth it."

He knew it was none of his business, but he couldn't help himself and asked, "How much?"

"Two seventy-five."

The reverend gasped at her response. His jaw dropped slightly. That was almost as much as his house.

"Like my mother used to tell me when I was a little girl, beauty always has its price."

He paused for a moment to reflect on what she had just told him. The truth of this statement struck him profoundly. He imagined it probably wasn't easy to be beautiful, and he knew that to surround oneself with beauty certainly was not easy.

She walked around the car to the passenger door and opened it.

"Let's get going. We don't want to be late."

He was still in shock that he was about to drive his dream car. He opened the driver-side door and slid down into the low-slung, dark tan leather seat. The smell of the interior was rich, old, unfamiliar, and magical, all at the same time.

"It's such a beautiful day," she said. "Let's put the top down."

He reached above the sun visors, unlocked two metal

latches, grabbed a leather handle in the middle of the top just above the rearview mirror, and pulled the top down behind him. He scanned across the dashboard at all the classic gauges and dials. They looked brand new. Then he turned to look at Betty and noticed her blond hair perfectly styled.

"But what about your hair? It'll be a mess by the time we get there."

She reached into her purse, pulled out an Hermès scarf, tied it over her hair, and smiled back at him.

"OK, ready to go."

He pressed the accelerator pedal a couple times to prime the carburetors, turned the key in the ignition, and pressed the accelerator again slightly to fire up the engine. The sound of the exhaust note echoing off the walls inside the garage was intoxicating to his ears. He revved the engine gently just to hear that wonderful noise more loudly. He precisely slid the stick shift into first gear, smoothly let out the clutch, and carefully pulled the car out of the garage and down the driveway toward the gate.

The precision of the steering, the smoothness of the engine, and the silkiness of the ride all combined in a way he had never experienced before. He went to the end of Lock Lane and turned right onto Sulgrave Road. Now driving down this street didn't make him feel so bad anymore. The mansions and estates didn't seem as intimidating. A Mercedes sedan passed going the opposite direction, and he chuckled to himself knowing he was driving a much nicer car.

After a few more blocks and a couple turns, they were on Cary Street heading west to the St. John's Center. It would be about a thirty-minute drive, but the reverend didn't care if it took eight hours. He didn't want this drive to ever end.

They passed the Virginia Country Club and more old mansions and estates as the two-lane, curvy road became River Road and led them farther west away from town. The homes soon began to become more and more separated by land as the distances between each one increased. Eventually the houses seemed to end completely with only fences, woods, and blind driveways being visible from the road.

They rode in silence since they had left the Woodson's house. No radio, no chitchat, no cell phone calls. The only sounds were the deep humming growl of the exhaust and the wind whooshing around and over their leather-lined cocoon. Finally she broke the silence.

"How do you like it? Or should I even bother to ask?"

"I don't know what to say, Betty. I can't describe how wonderful this is."

Knowing how honestly happy he was made her smile. She looked forward above the long sloping hood at the curving road ahead; then back up at the sunny, blue sky; and finally back at him. She could feel his excitement all the way from the passenger's seat, which gave her a sense of contentment she hadn't experienced in a long, long time.

The reverend slowed down the Jaguar as he approached the entrance to the St. John's Center. He turned off River Road and followed the tree-lined driveway about a half mile until he reached the front entrance of the facility. The 1960s-modern architecture with blue and white one-inch tiles; floor-to-ceiling glass walls; and retro-looking, white-lined fountains seemed extremely out of place in the heavily wooded surrounding area, and in Richmond in general.

He parked in a guest spot, got out of the car, hurried around to the passenger side, opened the door, and helped her out of the car. She removed her scarf and left it on the passenger seat. They turned together to head toward the front sliding glass door of the building when Mrs. Woodson looked up at the 50-year-old exterior design elements.

"My goodness," she exclaimed. "It's hard to believe this building and that car were both made at the same time. We've got to do something about this place. It's so… retro no."

"Be nice, Betty."

"Oh, I'm about to be very nice to this place. I think they can take a few words of criticism in the meantime."

A few steps before they could reach the front door, a man and a woman exited the building and rushed to greet Betty and

Michael. The man was in his early 60s with a portly midsection, a bald strip down the middle of his short grey hair, and plump facial features, including a sagging chin and puffy cheeks. She was in her late 50s and extremely thin with short brown hair and black-framed oval eyeglasses. They were eager to meet their honored guest for the day.

"Mrs. Woodson, I'm Ted Sanders, the general manager of St. John's," the man said, reaching out his hand and shaking hers. "And this is Phyllis Burns, our head of development."

All four shook hands and exchanged pleasantries before going inside the building. They turned left past a wide, white welcome desk in the sundrenched all-white lobby and entered a long, open room that was four stories in height. On the left side, floor-to-ceiling windows allowed a tremendous amount of sunlight to engulf the bright orange carpeting and fabric-covered sofas and chairs. On the right side were tall, white walls with rectangular openings at the upper levels where staff in white coats observed subjects on the ground floor below.

A white center aisle dissected the room down the middle, with groupings of orange sofas and chairs and white tables laid out on both sides for what seemed like the length of a football field. Almost every seat was occupied by someone wearing white pants; a white, short-sleeved polo shirt; and white socks and sneakers. There were at least a couple hundred people in the room. Old ones, young ones, white ones, black ones, Asian ones, males, females. Most of them sat peacefully reading a book or a computer or a tablet, while in some cases a few knelt down on the carpet while drawing or writing on paper pads on the tables.

"As you can see, we're completely full here at St. John's," Mr. Sanders pointed out as the group continued walking through the room. "If we had a no-vacancy sign out front like a hotel, it would be lit up right now."

Ms. Burns picked up the conversation where her boss left off.

"We are proud to be able to serve hundreds of guests from all types of backgrounds and with a wide range of conditions and disorders."

"What kinds of conditions?" asked Mrs. Woodson.

Ms. Burns answered, "Some of the more common ones are addictions like alcohol, drugs, gambling, even sex. We also treat mild forms of disorders such as multiple personality, schizophrenia, bipolar, and obsessive-compulsive. We aren't equipped to handle the really serious problems here because, as you can see, we like to maintain an open environment with interaction among our guests. We focus on those who aren't physically dangerous to themselves or others. But unfortunately, we don't have the resources or the room to help all those who need it."

"How about depression?" Mrs. Woodson inquired.

"We rarely see depression strictly on its own. Usually it's tied to other problems like the ones I just mentioned. So while there are no doubt many here who are clinically depressed, we feel that finding and treating the main problem will alleviate the side effect of depression."

"Interesting. I've never heard depression referred to as a side effect," Mrs. Woodson challenged.

Before Ms. Burns could offer a retort, a 12-year-old blond girl jumped up from a table nearby and brought over a piece of paper she had been drawing on for over an hour. She handed it shyly to Reverend Thomas, smiled and giggled coyly, and ran away in an instant. The reverend held up his new gift and took in the detailed black and white pencil drawing of a man, viewed from behind, wearing a dark-shaded robe and walking down a dirt pathway along the side of a hill. The nighttime scene was highlighted in the upper right corner of the drawing by a full moon, which created shadows on the rock outcroppings and shrubs to the man's right and on the short, thick, bristly trees to his left.

"You seem to have an admirer," Mrs. Woodson needled the reverend.

"That's Amy. She's a very special person."

"How do you know her?" Mrs. Woodson inquired.

"I've counseled and worked with her many times here. She

has an interesting form of autism, and she loves to draw and paint."

"So you volunteer here? I had no idea."

"Yes, but only once a week. I wish I had time to do more."

The group of four continued their walk to the conference room, and the reverend threw out a thank you to Amy as he walked by her. She smiled softly and put her pencil to work on a fresh new piece of drawing paper. Mrs. Woodson looked over at the young, blond girl and then back at Michael before returning her focus to the two guides from the center.

At the end of the long room, they took a right turn and entered a short, white corridor, which led to two side-by-side doors that opened into the formal conference room. Medium dark wood paneling lined one side of the room, and floor-to-ceiling glass on the other side offered an expansive view of a lake with two fountains in the foreground and the James River off in the distance.

The two center staff members offered their honored guests two seats facing the large windows so they could enjoy the scenery. In the middle of the table, three large, white schematics were spread out side-by-side. Mr. Sanders sensed some underlying tension between the two women, so he led off the business portion of the meeting.

"So as you can see, Mrs. Woodson, your generous gift to the St. John's Center will go a long way toward helping thousands of people get the help they need. Here are the diagrams of the new wing," he pointed out as he rotated one of the schematics and started to indicate particular areas with his index finger.

"The new guest rooms will be here, lining the top sections of the building. And the meeting rooms and treatment centers will be here, down at this end of the complex. The open atrium and sitting areas will be over here at the opposite end, facing the lake and the river. We think this will make for a beautiful and peaceful place for our guests to convalesce and recuperate. And of course, there will be a large plaque right here to commemorate the name of our new addition — The Woodson

Wing."

Three of them turned their attention to Mrs. Woodson to see her reaction. She stretched both her hands flat out on top of the diagram.

"I am so glad I was able to come here and see how this place operates in person. The people you're helping here are very lucky to have such great care. And I can only hope our contribution will give these same opportunities to even more people. It's easy to see why Michael enjoys volunteering here. It must be so fulfilling."

She paused for a moment and looked over at one of the other diagrams that had drawings of the exterior design of the new addition. The small tiles and design elements matched the older architecture of the original building. She pulled the schematic over and held it up to get a better look.

"Is this what the exterior will look like?"

Mr. Sanders answered, "Yes, Mrs. Woodson. It will match the main building. Is there something wrong?"

"Hmm," she sighed gently. "I guess you couldn't build the wing in a different exterior style as the main building. That wouldn't look right at all."

She reached into her purse and pulled out a Louis Vuitton leather-covered checkbook and a black Mont Blanc rollerball pen. She wrote out a check as she told them her new idea.

"I know I said we would give five to cover the cost of the new wing and help with staffing. But I think the exterior of the addition and the main building need to be a little more up-to-date. I was thinking less tile and more metal. You know, more stainless steel, more 21st century."

She handed Mr. Sanders the check. He looked it over and saw that it was made out for seven million dollars.

"Don't you agree?" she asked.

"Why, this is, uh, very generous, Mrs. Woodson. I'm sure we can take another look at the exterior design of the original building and make it more in line with the newer facilities."

"I'm glad you see it my way."

Mrs. Woodson put her pen and checkbook back in her

purse, stood up from the table, and turned toward the door. The other three rose up quickly from their seats and followed her to leave the room.

"If that's not enough to redo the entire exterior of the old building," Mrs. Woodson said while pausing at the door, "just let me know. I'm going down to Palm Beach after the holidays, so feel free to email me some new sketches of the design when they're ready. I can't wait to see them. Oh, and don't bother showing us out. I'm sure Michael knows the way. Ta ta."

And with that cheerful goodbye, she and the reverend left the two St. John's staff members in the conference room, dumbfounded at what had just occurred. Mr. Sanders looked down at the check and smiled. Ms. Burns simply shook her head in disbelief.

As they exited the building and walked together toward the parking lot, Betty looked up at the exterior one last time and commented, "Just looking at that is enough to make anyone sick. How can you get better if you have to see this every day?"

"You're a piece of work, Betty," the reverend affirmed.

He wanted to ask how much the final check she wrote was for, but he thought twice of it and bit his tongue.

"Thank you very much for that extremely generous gift. It's a great cause."

"If you're involved with it, I'm sure it is."

As they approached the car, Michael politely but also selfishly asked, "Do you want me to drive back?"

"Of course. You know you want to."

He was happy to hear her answer, and he sure wasn't going to argue with her.

The green Jag pulled out of St. John's and accelerated briskly until it was hurtling down River Road well above the 45-mile-per-hour speed limit. Still a couple hours remained until rush hour, so the road was clear ahead. She watched him shift up and down through the gears and guide the large, wood-rimmed steering wheel, feeling his excitement with each gear change and curve of the road.

At an intersection just ahead on the right, a silver Cadillac slowed to a rolling stop on the side street and was about to pull out in front of them. Michael hit the brakes and slowed down abruptly. The Cadillac driver finally saw the speeding sports car and jerked to a stop before entering onto River Road. The convertible propelled itself back up to speed and continued on.

"Whew!" exclaimed the reverend. "That would not have been good. Besides the safety of the precious cargo in here, I definitely don't want to bend up your husband's new prized possession."

"Don't worry. This isn't his. He doesn't like classic cars. He calls them antiques. He prefers his Mercedes. You know, he buys a new one every year, and he always gets the same model in the same color because he doesn't want anyone to know he got a new car. But if it's not the newest model, he doesn't want to keep it."

Michael understood what she really meant about her husband and remarked, "That's his loss."

She changed the subject quickly so as not to dwell on her husband and ruin the moment.

"Now that you've driven it for a while, what do you think of it?"

"It's as close to a new 1966 XKE as I can imagine. The steering is tight and direct. The shifter is smooth and precise. The engine feels like velvet. I can honestly say it's the most fun car I've ever driven. But it's your car. How do you like driving it?"

"I haven't. I don't know how to drive stick."

"It's easy to learn. My cousin didn't know how, and I taught him on my old Volkswagen Beetle. This is a much nicer car, obviously, but I can still teach you how to drive it."

"That's OK. I don't need to. With heels like these, I'll stick with an automatic."

"Yeah, but then how will you ever drive..." he said and then paused, letting the reality of what she had just told him sink in.

He flashed back to the previous summer when St. Andrew's had a classic car show in the parking lot. He ran into Betty there, and she asked him about some of the cars on display. They stopped at a Jaguar E-type convertible, and his eyes lit up as he went on and on about the car. She asked him which model was his favorite, and he described the 1966 green Jag he was currently driving. She had remembered and found that exact, particular version.

"You look great in it. It suits you perfectly," she remarked with a sly smile.

"Betty, I can't accept this from you. It's too much. If I pull up to my house in this, what are people going to say? I don't even have a garage to keep it in. This car deserves to be covered and protected whenever it's not being driven."

"Oh, don't be such a worry wart. It's just a car, after all. Listen, it'll be in my garage, and you can come by anytime you like and take it out for a spin. Just don't wear these preacher clothes. Put on a sweater or a polo shirt and a baseball cap. Plus, you'll be driving so fast, no one will be able to see who's behind the wheel anyway."

How he wanted to do exactly what she had just proposed. He could have his dream car without the hassles of paying for it or maintaining it or having to explain it to members of the church. It wasn't technically his, but it would be his to enjoy. The temptation was just too great.

"Alright, we'll see. I'll think about it. But thanks either way."

He looked over at her in the passenger seat, and his personal shield protecting himself against her started to crack and break away. There was something about her he had never been able to resist. Of course she was beautiful, but it was more than that. She was determined, headstrong, and relentless. Maybe that was part of her appeal. Whatever it was, try as hard as he could, he didn't have the strength to fight it.

She crossed her right leg over her left, spreading open the front slit in her dress and revealing her upper thigh. Her left hand lightly stroked the smooth, tan skin of the inside of her right leg, which drew the driver's attention.

"Eyes on the road there, mister," she teasingly admonished him.

"You're going to cause an accident."

She responded with a sexy, naughty laugh and then leaned over to his side of the car. Her left hand was placed softly on his right thigh. He reflexively jerked his right hand off the steering wheel and gently grabbed her intruding arm. She pulled her arm away and put his right hand back on the steering wheel.

"You focus on driving the car," she said. "I'll take care of everything else."

She put her hand back on his right leg and slowly slid it up toward his waist. He left his hands on the steering wheel this time and didn't try to stop her. Her hand went higher and higher, and then she abruptly pulled it away.

She casually leaned back over to the passenger side and asked, "Is that because of me or the car?"

"It's definitely you."

"We'll see for sure when we get back."

"One of these days I'm going to be able to say no to you."

"I certainly hope not."

She smiled seductively at him, admiring his attractive looks and the strength of his features. Then her gaze slid down temporarily to his neck and the white collar of his clergy shirt sticking out from under his jacket. Her smile leveled out, and she turned away to watch the houses pass by on the right side of the road.

Her affair with the reverend had been going on for almost a year now. It all began when she came back to Richmond from Palm Beach for a long weekend the previous winter. She and her husband Richard spent the winter in Florida each year because his family had a large compound on the ocean in the Juno Beach section of Palm Beach. He justified going down there for so long by telling everyone his clients were there in the winter, so he had to be there also. But in reality, he just wanted to enjoy the warm climate and play golf at Seminole Golf Club every day.

Many of the Woodson Group's clients had been with the firm since before Richard's great-great-grandfather had taken over control of the company. And after decades of continuously strong financial performance for his customers' investment portfolios, Richard didn't need to worry about losing his clients. Short of a crash on Wall Street, everything related to the financial performance of the company was going well and on cruise control.

But what Richard did have to worry about was the board of directors of the Woodson Group. Even though his family's name was on the front door, the board controlled the company. As long as everything continued to run smoothly and there weren't any personal scandals, Richard was allowed to remain as Chairman of the Board. But all 12 members of the board, including four of Richard's cousins, were conservative-minded people from families with sterling reputations. And the last thing they wanted was any type of personal scandal related to them or their company. If it came to light their chairman was involved in multiple extramarital affairs, for example, then he would be voted off the board entirely.

But Betty was smart and would go down with Richard to play the role of his dutiful wife so that everything looked normal. Of course she met several men in Florida who were fun to play around with, but she knew it was in her own best interest to be very careful what she did and with whom she did it. With all the famous, rich, and beautiful people in Palm Beach in the winter, the press was always looking for a juicy and scandalous story to run.

In addition to feeling limited in her options for fear of the truth of her marriage being exposed, she didn't meet any men in Florida who were truly interesting to her. She had always been drawn to men who could hold her attention with scintillating conversation about significant topics like philosophy or global history, not ones who were only full of boring bloviations about the size of their new yacht or which

Gulfstream jet was the best. As she got older, she began to appreciate the quality of the man more than what he could give her.

Going to church at St. Andrew's introduced her to an amazing man she instantly felt attraction toward. Michael's smile and demeanor drew her in at first, and then when she heard his sermons and about all the volunteer work he did for people in need like the homeless and the poor, she fell for him completely. There was just one problem — he was married.

But Betty Woodson didn't let a small thing like that ever get in her way. Quite a few married men in Florida had overlooked their wedding vows to be with her. She had the gift of being able to know what different men wanted, and she gave it to them so that she could get what she wanted. It wasn't hard for her to figure out what the reverend wanted.

She left the public eye and media buzz of south Florida and headed back home alone for a long weekend in the middle of winter to the relative safety of Richmond. The Woodson family had been one of the largest donors to St. Andrew's Church for decades, so when she asked for a private meeting at her home with the reverend to discuss possible charitable contributions, it didn't raise any eyebrows.

They began the meeting talking about ways to help fund the church's programs for the homeless and to provide food for underprivileged families in Richmond. A donation with a significant dollar figure was agreed upon, and they celebrated with a glass of wine. One glass led to many glasses, and the reverend was too weak to resist Betty's advances. But deep inside, he didn't try particularly hard to fight her off. Even if no one else knew it, Betty could tell the reverend had been attracted to her as well, which is probably why she didn't feel guilty or hesitant about going after him.

But now almost a year later as she rode in the Jaguar convertible with him on a beautiful, sunny, early December day, guilt about the affair was beginning to creep into her mind. At first, things weren't complicated in her mind because it was just a fun fling she could enjoy and walk away from when necessary, just like all the others had been. However, she was beginning to feel real emotions for this man, even though she knew about his problems with cocaine and alcohol. If anything, those addictions made him even more attractive to her because they made him less of a perfect, religious figure and more of a flawed man who needed her, unlike her husband. As the wind rushed around and over the windshield of the open car, she wondered if she was in over her head this time.

The classic, green sports car wound its way back through Windsor Farms and down the private driveway of the Greenlock estate. The reverend pulled up to the red front door of the main house, parked, and turned off the ignition.

"This is fine right here," she instructed. "I'll have Manuel pull it into the garage later."

The sun had fallen below the tree line by now, and shadows covered most of the brick façade of the estate house. Only at the very top along the black slate roof could any sunlight still be seen. Betty removed her sunglasses and started to put them away in her purse. Michael interrupted her by reaching over and gently cradling her cheek in his hand and looking into her now unshielded eyes.

"It's been an amazing day, and you are an amazing woman," he whispered, leaning over and pulling her face toward his.

He took one last long look into her brilliant blue eyes before he closed his and kissed her firmly. She wrapped her arms around his shoulders and pulled him closer still. They continued to kiss each other passionately for a couple minutes until Betty finally pulled back to catch a breath.

"This amazing day isn't over yet," she told him. "Come on in."

She opened the car door and slowly teetered up the steps to the front door of the house. He knew that since she was inviting him inside the house, her husband must not be home. And he didn't want to ask and bring up his name, especially now. He climbed out of the low-slung sports car and grabbed his briefcase out of the back seat.

"Let me put this away first," he said as he made his way across the cobblestone driveway to his Volvo.

He opened the driver's door, tossed his briefcase onto the passenger seat, reached over to the passenger footwell and dragged his computer bag onto the driver's seat, unzipped it, fished out the blue plastic tube, and slid it into his inside jacket pocket. She waited for him to reach the front door before she turned and went inside. He gently put his hand on her butt and gave it a little squeeze. She let out a playful giggle in delight and softly swatted his hand away.

4 BACK TO REALITY

The winter sun had set more than an hour ago, leaving Betty Woodson's second-story bedroom in almost total darkness except for a small sliver of light from the outer hallway reflecting through the bottom crack of the closed bedroom door. Thick, white silk drapes remained pulled open and revealed the panoramic windows facing the James River, now shrouded in darkness. The only lights visible through the windows were small dots of yellow and white coming from houses, cars, and streetlights far off in the distance. The sense of privacy on the estate was enough to give one a feeling of impenetrability.

A couple hours of lovemaking had turned the Egyptian cotton sheets into a twisted pile. Many pillows had been thrown on the floor, but several still remained folded and cockeyed on the bed. Michael woke up from a short nap, leaned over, and flipped on a bedside lamp, much to the dismay of Betty. She shielded her sensitive eyes with her hand and grumbled in disapproval.

"It was so nice before you did that," she complained.

Betty's eyes were slowly adjusting to the bright light when she saw him get out of bed and start to put his clothes on, which had been strewn across multiple pieces of antique furniture. Her bedroom was the equivalent in size to at least three large, five-star hotel suites. The California-king mahogany bed anchored one end of the room, and multiple sofas, chairs, and love seats divided the rest of the space into subsections. An ornately carved wooden desk; a leather-clad, high-backed chair; and a tall, frameless mirror grouped together near the windows served as her place to apply makeup and touch up her hair. At least six oriental rugs were spread out around the room on top of white, wall-to-wall carpeting. White and gold silk wallpaper and gold-plated lighting fixtures covered the walls, while three crystal chandeliers, evenly spaced out lengthwise, hung from the ceiling.

"Stop that and come back to bed," she commanded.

"As much as I'd like to stay, I need to get going."

"Richard won't be home tonight," she explained to him while sitting up in bed on one elbow. "We have the place all to ourselves. I'll tell you what. We can order your favorite, tenderloins with Béarnaise sauce, from the club, and we'll eat in. I'll even watch Monday night football with you. How's that sound?"

"That would be wonderful, but I really do have to go."

He paused for a moment, realizing how lonely she would be in that large house tonight all by herself.

He continued, "I'll stop by later this week. How about Thursday afternoon? Are you free then?"

Frustrated he wasn't staying longer, she replied, "I think so. Whatever. We'll figure it out."

She leaned over to her bedside table and pulled out a pack of cigarettes and a gold lighter. She put them on top of the table for after the reverend left the room. She knew he didn't want her smoke to get on his clothes, which would be a major red flag to his wife that something was going on. Betty didn't dare cross that line for fear this illicit affair would be over forever if Michael's wife knew the truth.

Every once in a while she wondered if it would be to her advantage for the wife to find out, thereby breaking up the marriage. Then she could be with Michael for real, even without all the money and prestige of being married to Richard. She would get enough money to live very comfortably in a divorce settlement, especially using what she knew about her husband's situation as leverage. Michael was the first and only man she would ever consider leaving her current life for. But forcing things now by coming out in the open about the affair would be a very dangerous move. She wasn't ready to go there yet.

Now fully dressed, the reverend walked over to her side of the bed and gave her a long, deep goodbye kiss on her lips, from which her lipstick had been smudged off for a while now.

"See you in a few days," he tried to reassure her.

She mustered up a fake smile to hide her sadness and loneliness. He left her bedroom and made his way downstairs, out the door, and into his car. As he pulled out of the driveway and headed back home, his Volvo now felt like an old, worn-out, sloppy, heavy, slow, unwieldy bucket of bolts. This dark, dreary, depressing drive was in stark contrast to the bright, sunny, dreamlike ride he had enjoyed earlier in the day.

About 20 minutes after he had left Greenlock, he pulled into his own gravel driveway, which led to his two-story, 1800-square-foot, wood-sided, Dutch colonial house located just a few blocks down the side street from St. Andrew's. Before he got out of his car, he inhaled deeply to smell if there was any incriminating trace of Betty, including her perfume, on his clothes. He didn't smell anything obvious, but he had a plan just to be sure.

He entered the house, as he always had before, through the side door that opened into the utility room next to the kitchen. He could hear his wife, 38-year-old Beth Thomas, preparing dinner just a few feet away around the corner.

"Michael?" she called out.

"Hi, honey. I'll be right there," he answered as he slipped up the back stairs to the second floor.

Once in his bedroom, he laid his computer bag and briefcase on a small chair in the corner; took off his jacket, pants, and shirt; and kicked off his shoes. He pulled a burgundy sweatshirt, a black t-shirt, and a pair of blue jeans out of the dresser drawer and threw them on quickly. His pants and jacket were carefully hung up on a wooden hanger in the closet. He took a deep whiff of his dirty clergy shirt as he carried it into his bathroom. A bottle of Acqua Di Gio cologne sat on the counter near the sink, which he opened and sprayed lightly over his entire clergy shirt before balling it up and tossing it into the dirty clothes hamper. He turned on the cold water in the bathroom sink and washed his hands and face with soap. But as he dried himself and saw his reflection in the mirror, no amount of soap could have cleansed away his guilt. He threw the towel down on the sink in disgust and went back downstairs to the kitchen.

Beth Thomas was finishing up the final stages of browning the ground beef in a pan on the electric stovetop when she poured in a bottle of spaghetti sauce.

"Michael, it's almost…" she started to say as he rounded the corner and joined her in the kitchen.

"It's almost ready?" he said, completing her sentence for her.

She let out a small chuckle. He gave her a quick peck on the cheek before he opened the cabinet and grabbed two white, ceramic pasta bowls.

"Do you want any wine?" he asked.

"No, not tonight. Iced tea is good."

He set the wooden kitchen table with pasta bowls, silverware, napkins, grated cheese in a can, a pitcher of iced tea, a couple of glasses, and a half bottle of previously opened chianti. Beth brought over a striped, ceramic serving bowl full of spaghetti with a large, wooden serving spoon and fork stuck into the pasta. They both sat down at the small, oval-shaped table; served themselves spaghetti; and began to eat dinner together.

The two had originally met each other in Atlanta 13 years earlier. Michael was working in a small Episcopal church in

Buckhead, not long after having been graduated from divinity school, while he also taught religious history at Pace Academy high school, a prestigious private school in Atlanta. Beth Anderson, as she was previously known, taught fifth-grade homeroom at Pace Academy's lower school.

But ironically enough, they didn't meet at a school meeting or function. Instead, they met through friends at a bar. In early October, Beth was talked into going out with some friends to a large outdoor sports bar in Buckhead called the Three Dollar Café to watch the final, deciding game of the National League Division Series of the major league baseball playoffs. It was a nice, warm, early fall evening, so Beth reluctantly agreed, even though she wasn't a big baseball fan, and it was a school night.

The Atlanta Braves were playing against the Chicago Cubs, and it seemed like all of Atlanta was out this Sunday night to watch their home team hopefully make it to another World Series. The large outdoor deck at the Three Dollar Café was packed with tables of groups of friends watching the game on a giant projection TV screen. In the middle of the fifth inning, Michael bumped into Peter, a friend who also worked at Pace Academy. Knowing Michael only taught one class at the school and probably didn't know many other people who worked there, Peter brought him over to meet his group of work friends, one of whom was Beth Anderson.

The moment he first laid eyes upon Beth, Michael felt a physical, electrical charge go through his chest, something he had never experienced before in his life. And it wasn't because of her looks. Of course she was attractive, but she didn't have the raw sex appeal of a supermodel or a movie star. Instead, she had an almost angelic aura around her face. She radiated happiness, goodness, contentment, and peacefulness in a way he was seeing for the first time ever.

Her dark brown hair dropped straight down to her shoulder, where it gently curled underneath into a soft roll. Brilliant blue, piercing eyes contrasted her pale, soft white facial features, including a tall, thin nose. Her small, narrow lips were covered by a light red shade of lipstick that blended inconspicuously with the rest of her subtle makeup. Her medium build and height of five foot, six inches helped convey the rare and attractive combination of being feminine and strong at the same time.

She also saw something special in him at first glance, but she had just gotten out of a bad relationship and didn't want to get right back into dating someone so soon. They spent the rest of the game together, and the conversation flowed effortlessly. She teased him about being a "preacher teacher" and whether it was a sin for him to drink beer or be out in public at a bar and watch baseball. She even asked if he was allowed to talk to women. He fired back by explaining every simple and obvious detail of the baseball game to her. He told her things like, "The man with the ball throws it, and the guy with the wooden thingy, that's a bat by the way, tries to hit it," and "If the guy swings and misses the ball, that's bad; if he swings and hits it, that's good."

After a few group outings over the next month, he finally got up the nerve to ask her out on a date. He loved movies and wanted to take her to *The Matrix Revolutions* and dinner afterward at his favorite restaurant, Houston's. She liked him and wanted to say yes, but she still wasn't over her previous boyfriend, so she reluctantly declined the offer. A few months later, he took another chance and asked her out again, but she still wasn't ready and just wanted to be friends.

Having decided it was probably best not to keep pursuing her, he resigned himself to the friend zone. Beth just didn't seem to be in the cards for him. In the past, he had usually dated girls from wealthy families, so he moved on and went out with a couple of rich girls, neither of whom developed into a serious relationship. He even tried to introduce some of his friends to Beth as possible dates, but she wasn't interested in them either.

Yet everything changed for Beth and Michael the following summer when she had a flat tire on Interstate 285, the infamous Perimeter highway around Atlanta, during rush hour. Her tire blew out at 70 miles per hour, and she managed to weave through all the continuous, speeding traffic and safely make it over to the shoulder. She didn't have AAA or any family members or other guy friends locally who could come help her out. So she called Michael.

He took the back roads and drove down the shoulder past stopped traffic to get to Beth's car right away. He parked his old Jeep a little ways behind her car to protect her from anyone trying to drive up the shoulder. And in only a few minutes, he had the tire changed and everything ready to go. While waiting in her car for him to finish up, she finally realized he was the one person she could count on to help her out. She found him attractive, interesting, intelligent, and reliable. She asked herself why was she being so stupid by not going out with him? And she couldn't come up with an answer.

So when he got back in her car to tell her the tire had been changed, she quickly leaned over across the armrest and gave him a deep, hard, passionate kiss. He was quite shocked for the first second or two, but then he pulled her closer and kissed her back just as strongly. When it was time to take a breath, she tilted her head back slightly and told him that she thought it would be a good idea for him to ask her out again. He was no dummy, so he did exactly that.

After about a year of dating, they got engaged, then married, and they eventually moved to Richmond so Michael could take the job at St. Andrew's that would be the next step in his career. Beth got a job at St. Philip's teaching fifth graders, which completed the parallel transition of their lives from Atlanta to Richmond.

After finishing her first bite of pasta and taking a small sip of iced tea, she broke the unusual quiet in the kitchen and inquired, "How was school today?"

"It was fine. Only one more class until the exam. I've got to finish up with the English Reformation and Queen Mary and Elizabeth next week."

"That's a lot of stuff to cover in just one class."

"I know. I wish I had more time, but what are you going to

do?"

He twirled a large bite of spaghetti with his fork and spoon and asked her back, "How was school today for you?"

"We're going over long division now. Even the kids who are normally very good in math are struggling with it. And of course they're asking me why they have to learn it when they can just use their phones to divide numbers instead."

"That's a great point. What do you say to them?"

"I try to make up something good like they won't always have their phones with them, and it's important to understand how numbers and math work. It's hard to convince them, especially since I had the same questions when I was a kid. Except we had calculators instead of cell phones. You wouldn't believe the phones and computers these kids have now. They could hack into NORAD with these things, but they don't want to learn how to divide 12 into 144."

Michael took in what his wife was telling him about her day, but he wasn't fully engaged in the conversation. She sensed his distance and even a trace of trepidation. It was obvious to her that he wanted to talk about something but was hesitant to broach the subject. She waited a few moments to see if he would talk to her, but after an uncomfortable period of silence, except for the sound of silverware clinking against the ceramic bowls, she couldn't wait any longer.

"Honey, something's obviously on your mind. What is it?"

He wasn't surprised she knew he had a lot of things on his mind. He just wasn't sure how much she knew and what she suspected him of.

"You know me so well," he replied. "I can never hide anything from you. I'm just going through a lot of things right now, and I'm trying to make sense of it all."

She reached across the table, took his hand in hers, and reassured him, "Tell me what's going on. I want to help."

"Well, I'll just come right out and say it. I'm not sure I want to be a priest anymore."

He paused for a moment to watch her physical response. She kept holding his hand and looked directly into his eyes.

"Why not?" she asked sincerely.

"I've been doing this for over 15 years now, and I don't have the same passion for it like I used to. When I first started out, I was anxious and eager to learn as much as I could about religion and Christianity and the Bible. I wanted to spread the gospel and help people feel the grace of the Holy Spirit. But somewhere along the way, I began to lose not only my passion, but also my faith."

"Is it completely gone? Do you think you can get it back?"

"I don't know. Unfortunately you can't measure faith like someone's blood pressure. I don't know how much I have left, or even how much I had to begin with. I always wanted to help people. And I saw religion as a way to do that. Maybe that was a mistake."

Beth took a moment to absorb the shocking admission she had just heard. She wasn't worried about him quitting his job and being out of work for a long time. He was smart and determined to succeed in whatever he did. She just wanted him to be happy.

"So what would you want to do instead of being a priest?"

"I haven't thought that deeply about it yet. This is all still new to me."

"You enjoy teaching at St. Philip's. Maybe, beginning next fall, you could teach other history courses there too, like American history or even ancient history. With your history major from college and all the books you read about ancient Rome and Greece and Egypt, I would think it'd be easy for you to teach any period of history."

He replied, "That's a good idea, but I was thinking about something that would make more money. I mean, look at this place. Look how we live. This small, ugly house is falling apart. We've got two old, rusted-out cars. We don't get to go on trips anywhere unless it's with the church. Instead of spaghetti, we should be eating steak, at least once in a while. It's ridiculous. All our friends and everyone we know have so much more than us."

Beth reached over to hold Michael's hand and affirmed, "I

don't mind. I like our life the way it is."

Michael pulled his hand away from her and shot back, "Yeah, but we can do so much better. Beth, you deserve more. Tomorrow I'm playing golf with the guys. I think I'll talk to Erik about the insurance business. He's doing very well with it, and I know he would help me get started. It also pays well.

"If that's what you want to do, then I'll support your decision. But you could still have time to do your charity work and counseling at St. John's. Right?"

"Definitely. Insurance guys have great schedules. Listen honey, I know it sounds like a major change right now, but things will work out for us. I'm going to take some time over the holidays to think things through. I don't have to do anything right away. Don't worry, honey. We've got time."

"Yes, we do," she said, reaching back over to squeeze his hand in support. "You know what I always say. Things work out for the best. Maybe not exactly the way you want or expect them to, but they always happen for a reason. If you work hard and do the right thing, life works out. We just have to trust in God's plan."

Michael had always admired Beth's faith in God. From the first day they met, she was open and proud of her religious beliefs. She didn't try to force them on anyone else or shove them in people's faces. That wasn't her style. Instead, she tried to live a just and honorable life. Whenever she reached a point in her life that required a difficult decision, she would ask herself, "What would Jesus do?" To her, that was more than just a cliché on a wristband. It was a guiding principle in how she conducted herself. She knew she would never be perfect like Jesus. Nobody could. But she could certainly try.

The reverend continued eating his dinner and tried to engage in small talk about their holiday schedules, what parties they would attend, and if they could find the money somehow to take a vacation after all the Christmas activities and New Year's Eve were over. Every time he looked at his beautiful wife's face, a jolt of guilt shot threw him, so he tried to minimize eye contact. He didn't know why he was cheating on her or why he couldn't seem to stop. In moments like this, sitting around the dinner table sharing their life stories, he should be content and happy. But he felt like there was a hole inside his soul. Something was missing, and he was trying to fill it with whatever he could find to make himself whole again.

The more he thought about it, the angrier he got at himself. When he finished his meal, he cleared the table and started washing the dishes in the kitchen sink. He grabbed the pasta fork to clean it when he noticed the tremor in his left hand again. The fork started shaking up and down in his hand like a seesaw on fast forward. He sped through the rest of the dishes and rushed upstairs to his computer bag. A couple snorts of cocaine later, his hand calmed down for the rest of the evening.

5 19TH HOLE

Tuesday was Michael's official day off from work. As a reverend, he didn't get weekends off like most people. And with his commitments on Mondays to St. Philip's and Wednesdays to St. John's, Tuesday was when he could take time to recharge his batteries. His favorite way to do that was playing golf with three of his college buddies who had all moved to Richmond after being graduated from Virginia Tech.

The unusually mild early-December weather was still holding on for a little while longer. A cold front was expected later in the week with possible rain or even some snow. But that didn't matter now because the sun was shining and the golf balls were flying all over the course at the Virginia County Club.

Michael rode as a passenger in the golf cart with John McDonald, his old roommate who always insisted on driving the cart. John was an investment manager at an old, well-respected investment firm downtown that managed stock and bond portfolios for private companies. John had short, red hair; a trimmed, red beard; and thin, gold-wired glasses. And while he wasn't the best golfer in the group, he told the best jokes. He didn't care if his friend was a priest. He had known Michael since long before he joined the ministry, and he wasn't about to treat him differently just because he spoke in church on Sundays.

Dan Lee was a dentist and drove the other cart. A tall and thin Korean man with salt and pepper hair and horn-rimmed glasses, Dr. Lee was the respectable one in the group. He had always studied hard and worked even harder to become a doctor. But these Tuesdays on the golf course with his friends were his opportunities to relax and cut up for a while, away from the responsibilities and pressures of the office.

Erik Majors rode in the passenger seat in the cart with Dr. Lee and was a Nationwide insurance agent. In fact, he was the agent for the three friends playing golf with him and for most of the west end elites. He possessed a short and stocky build, and his dark-brown hairline was receding into almost a full strip of hairless scalp down the middle of his head. He was the brash, outspoken, heavy drinker of the group. The only reason he let Dr. Lee drive the cart was because he had crashed one himself a couple years earlier after having a few too many during the round. Since he would let Dr. Lee drive the cart, and John would drive him home afterward because John and Erik both lived in the same neighborhood off of Cary Street, Erik had free reign to enjoy himself on the golf course without worrying about getting a DUI.

Michael's three friends were all members of the club, so he was their guest each week. Sometimes they would pay his greens fees, but most of the time the club would just comp him because of his affiliation with the church. Nobody in the pro shop wanted to be the one who charged a priest to play golf. That was bad karma not just in general, but for their own golf games as well.

"Nice shot, Mikey," yelled Erik from across the 16th fairway after Michael's shot into the green landed three feet from the hole. "I've gotten really tired of saying that today. I think I'm going have to buy a tape recorder and record 'Nice shot, Mikey' on it so I can just replay it over and over and over. That would save me a lot of energy."

"Yeah, Michael, you're on fire today," Dan complimented

his friend. "You're playing lights out like the bishop in *Caddyshack*."

"But fortunately you don't have to worry about getting struck by lightning today like he did in the movie," added John as he looked up into the clear blue sky.

"Even a blind squirrel finds a nut every once in a while," Michael retorted. "But if I don't make the putt, it won't matter how good that shot was."

"The way you're playing today, I'd almost think a higher power was involved," said John.

"Or you made a deal with the devil," joked Erik.

The foursome made their way to the green and finished out the hole. Michael had sunk his putt for birdie, so he was first to tee off on the par-3 17th hole. True to form, he knocked it close to the hole, leaving himself a 10-foot putt for another birdie. His friends just stood in awe and appreciation for what they were seeing.

"What in the world is going on with you today?" asked John. "Even with my stroke on this hole, you're still going to win it. The Lord certainly works in mysterious ways."

Since it was a short hole, Michael grabbed his putter from his bag and started walking from the tee to the green. Dan grabbed his putter also and told Erik to drive the cart himself, feeling confident he could make it 150 yards without crashing. The dentist wanted to talk to his friend some more before the round ended. They strode down the center of the fairway together like a couple of professional golfers in a tournament, except the only gallery here was two jokers in golf carts heckling them.

"So how's everything going now?" inquired Dan.

"Oh, fine, I guess."

"Come on, Michael, you know what I mean. How are you doing? Are things getting better?"

Dan was one of the few people Michael felt comfortable confiding in about his personal problems. Maybe it was because he was a doctor, or because they had known each other since they were in kindergarten together in Richmond, or maybe because Dan was one of the few people besides his wife who ever seemed to care enough to ask how he was. But whatever the reason, Michael always felt comfortable talking to Dan about his problems.

"I think they're getting worse," the reverend replied after a pause.

"OK, am I going to have to pull it out of you like one of my patient's wisdom teeth? How are things worse?"

"The tremors in my hand are more frequent. The doctor did tests and said I didn't have Parkinson's or signs of seizures or a stroke. So it's probably neurological. When they flare up, alcohol helps take the edge off temporarily."

"Are you still doing cocaine?" Dan asked.

Michael didn't even try to lie to his friend and answered honestly, "Yes. It's the only thing that keeps the tremors away for any length of time."

"Don't you see, Michael? The alcohol and the cocaine aren't solving the problem. They are the problem. The tremors aren't because of some neurological disease. You're an addict. And the tremors aren't tremors. They're the shakes. The only way you're going to get better is to quit drinking and snorting. You need a professional detox program so you can quit cold turkey. It's the only way you'll be able to stop for good. Obviously you can't quit on your own."

"Don't you think I already know that?" Michael snapped back at his friend, practically yelling at him.

Michael stopped walking in the middle of the fairway and turned away in disgust. After taking a few moments to compose himself, he turned back and continued walking.

"Dan, I'm sorry about that. I know you're right, and I've known it for a long time. I just can't seem to do anything about it. Everything in my life is falling apart, and I feel powerless to fix it."

"There are some great addiction programs out there for people like you. I'll get some information together so you can take a look. I think they would help you out tremendously."

"Thanks, buddy. But the coke is just part of the problem."

"Are you still messing around with Betty?"

"Uh-huh. Yep. That's a whole 'nother mess. I can't seem to quit her either. She makes me feel things I've never felt before with anyone else. She's like cocaine to me."

"Do you still love Beth?"

"I know it's probably hard to believe this, but yes, I do still love my wife. I just wish she had some of Betty in her to spice things up."

"Is it Betty? Or is it all the stuff that comes with Betty? You know, the big house, the fancy restaurants, the money?"

"Probably a little bit of all that."

"I feel for you, Michael. From what you've told me about her, she's attractive, she's loaded, and she's a freak in bed. What's not to like. Too bad you're both married."

The two golfers in the carts had arrived at the green and were waiting on Dan and Michael.

"Whenever you two ladies are finished gossiping," Erik called down the fairway to them, "feel free to join us for a round of golf."

After the foursome of college friends finished their round of golf on the 18th hole, they made their way to the 19th hole for a round of drinks. The bar at the Virginia Country Club, affectionately known as the 19th hole, was famous for it's raucous happy hours, especially Friday and Saturday after work. But even on a Tuesday evening, there were still quite a few regulars enjoying the low-priced drink specials and beautiful panoramic views of the golf course.

The four golfing buddies were at a table right next to the large window and were finishing up their only round of drinks. It was a weeknight, after all, so they didn't want to get plastered on a Tuesday. They wound up the afternoon's affairs by finalizing plans for their guys' summer trip to John's family's house on the Chesapeake Bay.

Depending on the year, every summer eight to 10 college friends from Virginia Tech would meet up at the McDonald's house on the bay for a long weekend getaway. No wives, no kids, just the guys. This way the group of 42- and 43-year-old friends could act like they were still in college without worrying about their families. Activities for the group included water skiing, innertubing, skeet and target shooting, fishing, poker, fireworks, cigars, and plenty of bourbon. They had all aspects of alcohol, tobacco, and firearms covered.

"So it looks like the second weekend in June and the third weekend in July are our best options," John announced while looking at the calendar on his cell phone. "I'll send out an email to everyone so we can get a final date confirmed."

"And I'll email Mark to make sure he remembers to pick up the steaks from that butcher shop near his office up in D.C.," added Michael. "I've been looking forward to those New York strips since last summer."

Erik interrupted and said, "I found out about a great little distillery in Kentucky from a friend at the office. I'll get a few bottles to add to our repertoire for the taste test."

"Oh no, another taste test," joked Dan. "After the first five or six swigs, no one can tell the difference anyway. This supposed blind tasting of exceptional whiskies is nothing more than an excuse to drink a whole lot of bourbon all day and all night and then claim it was done purely in the name of scientific research."

"I'm dealing with a bunch of amateurs here," Erik fired back. "Dan, you're going to have to work on your drinking stamina this winter. We can't have a repeat performance of last year. Remember? You only tried about five or six bourbons and then you went out onto the porch to lie down for a nap. We didn't see you again until the next morning."

"Is that where you went, Dan?" asked John. "I remember looking all over the house for you, but I didn't think to look outside. I assumed you got fed up with Erik and me and went out to the guest house to get away from everybody."

"I probably would have gone to the guest house, if I could've made it all the way there," responded Dan, which caused an eruption of laughter from the foursome at the table. "The porch was as far as I could get."

A deep, authoritative voice from an unknown source approaching the table pierced the laughter and said, "You guys are having way too much fun. We can't have this kind of noise at the Virginia County Club. Do I need to call security over here?"

The foursome all turned in unison toward the location of the voice to see Richard Woodson just a few feet away confidently striding toward their table. Once they recognized who it was, they realized he was just joking them about making noise and calling security. Richard arrived at the table and stood directly behind Michael's chair, blocking it so the reverend couldn't slide his chair out and stand up.

Michael started to try to stand up to shake his hand, but Richard put his hand on the reverend's shoulder, essentially holding him down in his chair, and told him, "No, don't get up. Please, all of you, I just wanted to stop by and say hello. I heard the laughter and figured I was probably missing out on some fun."

Having seen that their friend wasn't getting up to shake Richard's hand, the other three guys at the table stayed in their seats as well.

Richard asked, "Did you guys have a good round out there? It was a beautiful day for it."

Erik answered first, "The three of us played like crap, as usual. But Michael here had a great day."

"Oh yeah? What did you shoot?" Richard inquired condescendingly.

The reverend hesitated because he felt uncomfortable talking about himself.

"A 68," Erik interrupted, knowing his friend wouldn't brag. "He was en fuego."

Richard replied, "Very nice. Someone up there must be watching out for you."

"I certainly hope so," the reverend responded.

Richard continued, "Sure wish I had free time to work on my game so I could shoot that low. Must be nice."

Before Michael had a chance to respond to Richard's

sarcasm, an attractive blond woman in her late 20s with long blond hair and a tight, short, low-cut dress rushed over in small, quick steps in her high-heeled shoes and caught up to Richard at the table. With his back to her, Michael didn't see her arrive, but the other three guys did and stood up to meet her.

"When I got back from the ladies' room, I couldn't find you," she complained in a concerned tone to Richard.

Michael knew it wasn't Betty, but after hearing a female voice behind him, he forcibly pushed his chair away from the table and into Mr. Woodson, pushing him back a couple steps and almost causing him to fall over an empty chair at another table behind him. Dan instinctively reached over and grabbed his upper arm. Richard caught himself and steadied his balance.

She continued, "I thought you left me," and grabbed his other upper arm firmly.

"Of course not, darlin'," Richard reassured her after he regained his balance and composure. "I saw some friends here and wanted to say hello on the way out. Here, let me introduce you. Heather, this is John McDonald, my investment guy. Erik Majors, my insurance guy. Dr. Dan Lee, my dentist. And Reverend Thomas from St. Andrew's church. I guess you could call him my God guy."

As he said each name to the young woman, each man reached out and shook the lady's hand and said, "Nice to meet you."

Michael ignored Richard's last sarcastic jab.

"Richard, we need to get going," Heather said. "I have to stop by the office before our dinner reservations."

She then remembered her business training and pulled a handful of business cards from of her purse. She passed one out to each of the guys.

"I'm a realtor at Nelms and Bonville over on Grove Avenue. If you're ever in the market, I know the entire west end. Just give me a call on my cell. The number's right there on the card."

"OK, guys," Richard said, trying to wrap up the

conversation and slightly embarrassed at her lack of business couth. "Good seeing you all again. Let's go, Heather."

Richard put his hand on her lower back and directed her toward the door.

He stopped, paused, turned back around, and told the guys, "I guess I'll see you all this Saturday at our Christmas party."

John, Dan, and Michael responded in unison, "See you then," and Erik said, "Wouldn't miss it."

Then Richard leaned in closely toward Michael and muttered softly, "If not before."

"Take it easy, guys," Richard called out to all of them as he turned his back and walked away.

Watching Richard and Heather exit the bar, Michael reflected on what Richard had just whispered to him. He wondered to himself if Richard somehow knew about his affair with Betty. Had Betty told him? Did Richard know that Michael was planning to go over to see Betty this Thursday afternoon? Was their marriage so open and screwed up that Betty would admit to something like that?

His paranoia caused him to break out into a sudden, cold sweat. But his friends didn't notice.

"With a body like that, I bet she does know the entire west end," John joked.

"That guy is my hero," added Erik.

"Isn't he married?" asked John.

Breaking out of his daze, Michael finally turned around and answered, "Yes, he is."

The reverend's blue Volvo wagon sat motionless waiting in a line of cars trying to exit the club's parking lot and make a right turn out onto River Road. It was now rush hour and very dark outside, and he was fifth in line. Each car in the line had to wait minutes for a suitable gap in traffic to get out. Whenever a gap did appear because of a changing traffic light a couple blocks away, usually only two cars could safely make it out onto the main road. A left turn was virtually impossible this time of day, so the reverend knew he would have to turn right and then make a U-turn a few blocks down River Road.

With lots of time to reflect about the day, Michael regretted he hadn't spoken with Erik about helping him get into the insurance business. But with his other friends constantly there, Richard's uninvited appearance, and the subsequent shenanigans at the 19th hole, an opportunity to speak with Erik alone never really presented itself. He wasn't worried, though, because he knew there would be plenty of time to reach out to Erik after the holidays.

Finally it was his turn, and a small gap in traffic appeared. He accelerated out onto the road. A few seconds later, he heard a sustained, piercing car horn a little ways behind him. He instantly glanced in his rearview mirror and caught a glimpse of a dark grey sedan pulling out of the club driveway and cutting off a car two-cars back that had been traveling quickly down River Road. The reverend wondered what kind of idiot would pull out into traffic like that just to save a couple minutes.

But then he remembered the dark grey Volkswagen Passat he thought was following him the day before in Windsor Farms on the way to Betty's house. He tried to look more closely at it in the rearview mirror, but he couldn't tell what kind of car it was since it was partially blocked by the car directly behind him and the headlights and growing darkness made it difficult to see. A couple blocks down the road he pulled into the left turn lane at a stoplight and waited for the red light to turn green. All six cars behind him, including the dark grey one, were waiting to turn left also so they could make the same U-turn and head the opposite direction.

Once the light turned green, the reverend started his turn and soon realized he would have to wait until he finished the turn before he could get a good look at the grey sedan behind him. Otherwise, he wouldn't be able to see where he was going, and he might run into the car in front of him or even a parked car on the right side of the road.

With his U-turn now safely completed, he looked into his left side mirror and recognized the lengthwise, shadowy silhouette of a Volkswagen Passat as it made a U-turn behind him. His pulse started to quicken, and his cold sweat returned. He tried to rationalize to himself that there were lots of grey Passats in Richmond. But it was too much of a coincidence. He wondered why else someone would dart out into traffic like that if they weren't trying to follow someone.

He continued driving down River Road, glancing every few seconds in his rearview mirror. The Passat was still there, two cars back. He thought again about what Richard had said regarding maybe seeing him before Sunday. Was the person in the Volkswagen hired by Richard to follow his wife and keep tabs on her? Did the driver of the VW know about the affair and decide to follow him too?

Michael looked down at his left hand and saw it trembling while holding the steering wheel, so he clenched the wheel tighter. He was approaching his left turn at Libbie Avenue and decided to take it to see what the VW would do. After he made the turn, he looked in his mirror again and saw the car directly behind him and the grey VW both turn left onto Libbie Avenue. After a couple more blocks, he arrived at the intersection of Libbie and Grove Avenues. He would normally stay straight here and continue on Libbie, but this time he wasn't sure what to do. Should he keep going straight and go home? Or should he turn left and see if the car still follows him. The light ahead was green, so he had to make a quick decision. He went straight and didn't turn. He looked through his rearview mirror and could see the grey VW turn left onto Grove Avenue and continue out of sight.

Five minutes later, the blue Volvo wagon pulled into the gravel driveway of the Thomas' residence with the sky now almost completely black. He shut off the car and sat alone in the darkness for a few moments with only the distant streetlights and house lights projecting faintly into the car. Once he got out of the Volvo, he looked up and down the street. There were no visible car headlights or sounds of any vehicles driving nearby. The neighborhood was quiet and still. He tried to see if a Passat was parked close by, but it was too dark to see past a few cars in either direction. He told himself he was probably just being paranoid about the whole thing and tried to calm down. He looked down at his left hand, and the trembling had stopped. Having decided to leave his golf clubs in the back of the Volvo and bring them in another time, he walked directly to the side door of his house and went inside.

6 OPEN UP

Even though the St. John's Center had been around since the 1960s, it was always kept in great condition with routine maintenance performed regularly and any needed repairs taken care of right away. And while Betty Woodson didn't particularly care for the dated architectural design of the building, the facilities were comfortable and offered a warm, pleasing environment in which the guests could get treatment.

Reverend Thomas spent every Wednesday at the center to help counsel and treat some of the more longstanding guests. No, he wasn't officially licensed to provide certain types of treatment for specific cases or disorders. But this was a religious-based organization funded and managed by the Episcopal Church, and most of the residents had strong faiths, even if they were dealing with serious personal and health problems. And speaking regularly with an ordained priest helped many of them feel better.

On this particular Wednesday, the reverend was speaking with one of his favorite patients, Joseph Atkinson, a 34-year-old man originally from Lynchburg, Virginia, who suffered from schizophrenia. Because he stayed on his medications consistently, Joe was able to live a simple, carefree life at the center. He had friendships with many of the other guests and would have great conversations with some of the staff members about philosophy, religion, and science. Reverend Thomas was one of the people he most enjoyed spending time with.

Along one of the sides of the main building at St. John's that faced the James River, a row of individual rooms with white walls and doors provided secluded spaces for counselors to have private discussions with guests. Each of these counseling rooms had a couple of comfortable, overstuffed chairs and a leather sofa facing toward a wall of glass that offered beautiful views of the river and the horizon beyond.

In room number eight, Joe sat on the sofa at the end nearest the window with his legs folded underneath him. On his thin, spindly body, he wore a white, long-sleeved polo shirt; white pants; and white socks. His white sneakers were neatly arranged side-by-side on the orange carpet directly below where he was sitting. Black Ray-Ban aviator sunglasses covered his bright blue eyes and part of his pale, white face. His blond hair was cut very short, almost into a crew cut but not quite that tight. The top of his head looked like little, sharp bristles from a yellow brush. A few red splotches on his face were caused by the dryness of winter and his skin's reaction to even allergy-free soap.

Michael had on a dark grey suit and his black clergy shirt with a white collar and sat in one of the overstuffed chairs directly across a small, white coffee table from Joe. The reverend glanced at his watch to check the time and noticed there were about 10 minutes left in their session.

"Joe, in all the time I've known you, I've never asked you about your sunglasses," Michael commented. "Is it too bright in here? Do you want me to close the curtains?"

"No, I'm fine," Joe replied. "I just feel better with them on."

"May I see them?"

"No, not now."

"OK, no problem. I like the way they look. I used to have a pair just like them, but you know how it goes with sunglasses. I lost them somewhere along the way."

"I've had these for 22 years. I'll never lose them."

"How do you know that for sure?" Michael asked.

"I only take them off when I sleep or take a shower. Otherwise, they're always on my face. So you see, I can't lose them."

"I guess that does make sense, in a roundabout sort of way. Do you have a cell phone?"

"Yes. And an iPad," answered Joe.

"Have you ever lost them?"

"No."

"That's impressive. I lose my phone all the time. Thank goodness there's an app I use to find it."

"What kind of phone do you have?" asked Joe.

"An iPhone."

"Six or six plus?"

"Just a five," replied Michael.

"Maybe you should lose it for good. Then you can upgrade to a six S plus."

"That's OK. I'm fine with the five. I don't do that much with it other than make a few calls and look up movie times at the theater. So how do you manage to not lose your phone or iPad? You don't keep them with you all the time because I don't see them here now."

"They stay in my dresser drawer in my room. I only pull them out for short periods of time. You shouldn't use your phone, iPad, or computer for more than 13 minutes at a time."

"Why not?" asked Michael.

"Because that's how long it takes for them to trace your signal either online or through the phone lines and lock in on you."

"Who's tracing you?"

"The global government," answered Joe. "The ones who actually run everything. I call them the Globals."

"You mean like in the movie *The Adjustment Bureau*, where a group of people control the world by adjusting people's fates?"

"Come on, Michael," Joe responded condescendingly.

"That's a movie. I'm talking about real life."

Joe adjusted his seat on the sofa and leaned forward slightly.

"Haven't you seen how people are addicted to their phones and tablets?" Joe continued.

"Sure."

"They're constantly looking at videos or Facebook or Instagram or Twitter or Snapchat or texting each other. They walk down the sidewalk without seeing anyone else around them. They almost get run over by cars while crossing the street. The only things they care about are their machines. And that's because they're being controlled by the Globals. There's a hidden visual transmission embedded in everything you see on a phone or computer. And once they lock in on you, you become addicted to the technology. You may think you're just watching football highlights or a cat video, but what they're really doing is downloading instructions to you subconsciously. They tell you how to behave, what to eat, where to work, what to do with your money, even whom to fall in love with. It's quite ingenious, actually."

"Why would they do that?" asked the reverend.

"Because that's how governments control the people now in a 21st century world. They've always controlled us. You can't have an orderly, civilized society unless the people are being controlled somehow. Without it, humans will inevitably fall back into their basic, animalistic state. And then we have pure chaos, like back in the dark ages."

"How about before the Internet or cell phones? How did they control us then?"

"They used television. Before that it was radio and newspapers. And before that, it was religion."

"So religion is just a vehicle used to control people?" asked Michael.

"Not all religion. But sometime a long time ago, they took religion and twisted it around so they could use it to control the people. There was always real religion out there too, but it was very hard to tell the difference. It's kind of like with angels.

There are good ones, and there are bad ones. And sometimes it's tough to tell the difference."

"Have you seen an angel yourself?"

"Yes, many times. I see them helping people. Well, the good ones do anyway. But I've also seen the bad ones too. They try to hurt people."

"How do they do that?" asked Michael.

"The bad ones lurk around and try to confuse people, make them doubt themselves. It's very sad to see. They seem to mainly go after people who are weak and hurting."

"Do they bother you?"

"No, they stay away from me now. I told them I wasn't falling for their tricks, so then they left me alone. Every once in a while a good angel would check in on me, but not so much anymore. I guess they think I'm OK now."

"Do your sunglasses make you able to see these angels, both the good ones and bad ones? Is that why you don't hardly ever take them off?"

"No, these glasses protect me from the Globals. I try to stay off my phone and computer as much as possible and never use them for more than 13 minutes straight. But that's hard. These glasses were made before the Internet and protect my eyes from their hidden video transmissions. The newer sunglasses don't work. And forget about polarized glasses. Those are made especially to let in the hidden video signals."

"But you said the Globals were controlling everyone because that's what governments do and without that there would be chaos. Right?"

"Exactly," answered Joe.

"So then why do you care if those video messages get through to you? Why do you still wear the glasses?"

"Because I don't like to be controlled. I have free will, and no one can take that away from me."

"That's a very interesting point, especially since you're here at a place like St. John's," pointed out Michael. "Many people think this is like a prison where the guests can't leave. But that's not true. Anyone can leave whenever they want to. So why are you here?"

"I'm here because I choose to be."

Joe shifted back in his seat so his back was resting comfortably against the back cushion of the sofa. He was enjoying the conversation so far and wanted to keep talking as long as someone would listen.

"Let's get back to the glasses. OK, Joe?"

"Sure."

"You said you got them before the Internet started and that they block out the hidden video signals online. So why did you get them in the first place? Was it so you could watch TV and block those signals?"

"No. These glasses don't block the signals on the TV. No glasses do. That's why I don't watch TV anymore. I got my glasses because the bad angels wanted to take my eyes. They love blue eyes. And they were after mine. My glasses protect my blue eyes from the bad angels."

The reverend pondered what Joe had just discussed with him. With the exception of the secret government trying to control everyone and the bad angels wanting to take Joe's blue eyes, there were quite a few statements mixed in that Michael found insightful.

The timing of their session had expired, so Michael walked Joe back to his room and told him he looked forward to their next conversation. His watch read 3:04 p.m., so he still had some time before he had to be back at the church office. Reflecting back on what the Rector had discussed with him about getting help somewhere, he thought this would be a good time to stop by the office of St. John's Program Director, Dr. Ted Yost, to ask about any programs that might be available to help him. He was still reluctant to acknowledge that he might have an alcohol addiction, but he was open to talking about it if he could find the right venue.

The reverend lightly tapped on the open door of Dr. Yost's office before he was told to come on in and have a seat in one of the two chairs in front of the doctor's large wooden desk.

This office was larger than most of the others, denoting the occupant's importance within the center staff hierarchy. Besides the desk and chairs, there was also a separate seating area with a sofa and more chairs toward the back wall. The entire side wall opposite the door was a long glass window overlooking the river. An enormous oriental rug rested on top of the standard wall-to-wall, orange carpet. The walls were covered with stunning underwater photos of vibrant, multicolored fish and coral from diving trips to various Caribbean and Pacific islands. In the back corner behind his desk hung his diploma for his doctorate in psychiatry from Virginia Commonwealth University.

The doctor was in his late 40s and still had a full head of dark brown hair. His build was trim and fit, a product of many years of gym exercise and proper dieting, and he had slender facial features, including a pointy jaw and high cheekbones. A picture of his attractive wife in a gold frame was prominently positioned on the bookshelf behind his chair.

"There's our new chief fundraiser. How are you doing?" the doctor asked energetically.

"Not bad. How about you?"

"Can't complain. Everyone's talking about the donation from the Woodsons for the new wing. Great job on that by the way. The money will help us a great deal around here."

"Glad to hear it," the reverend replied quietly.

"So, other than dropping by to get a well-deserved attaboy, what brings you here?"

"Do you have a few minutes? I need to talk with you about a personal matter."

"Sure. I'm good until five o'clock. Until then, I'm all yours."

The doctor stood up from his desk chair, walked over to his office door, gently shut it, and returned to his seat.

"What's going on, Michael?" asked Ted, concerned about why the reverend was unusually serious.

"Can I assume that whatever we discuss in here is considered private and is covered by a doctor-patient confidentiality?"

"Of course. Everything stays in here."

"Ted, I need your help to find a treatment program for me."

"OK. What type of treatment?"

"I think I may need some help dealing with an alcohol problem. My drinking is starting to affect my life negatively, and I want to get a handle on things before they get out of control."

"Exactly how is your life being affected in a negative way? Give me some examples."

"First of all, I've got physical symptoms when I don't drink for a while. My left hand starts to shake, and the only thing that stops it is alcohol."

"How much are we talking about here? How many drinks a day on average?"

"Some days I can get by on two or three. Other days I have about six or seven."

The reverend lowered his head and grimaced in shame. The doctor noticed this body language and tried to reassure him.

"Listen, Michael. I'm not here to judge you. I'm here to help you. But I need you to be open and honest with me. You're holding back. Tell me everything."

The reverend took a deep breath and lifted his head back up so he could look the doctor in the eye. Opening up was difficult for him, but he knew he had to trust someone if he was going to get better. Ted was more than just a good friend. He was also one of the most respected psychiatrists on the east coast. If he couldn't open up to him, who else could he open up to?

"Alright, here it is. I'm going to lay it all out on the table. So brace yourself. Every day I have at least six drinks. And some days I have 10 to 12. I also use cocaine. That helps with the shakes in my left hand too. I'm so reliant on alcohol and cocaine, I don't know if I can get through a day without them. I hide the drinking by using mints or gum or even biting an onion at work to hide it on my breath. And I hate onions.

"If that's not enough, I'm also cheating on my wife. I'm having an affair with Betty Woodson, St. John's newest benefactor. Now you know why you're getting that new wing here.

"And for the cherry on the sundae, I've lost my faith. I used to feel so strong about God and Christianity and the Bible and Jesus' teachings. Not anymore. In my last sermon, I referred to a Bible passage as a story, probably because that's how I feel about them now. To me, they're stories that were written down sometimes hundreds of years after Jesus lived, if he even was really here at all. I mean, I still appreciate the meaning of the Gospels and the lessons they teach us. They're good, moral lessons. But the way the world is today, I don't see how anyone can believe in a benevolent God. There's so much pain, and suffering, and injustice in the world, not just today but throughout history. If you had the power to stop all that and make things better for everyone, wouldn't you do it?"

The doctor nodded his head.

"Of course you would," the reverend continued. "Anyone with a conscience would. But if there is a God up there, He's not paying attention to us right now. Innocent Christians are being murdered in the Middle East. Children are starving to death in Africa. And while all this is going on, most Americans only care about trashy reality TV shows and the latest music and fashion trends. It's like we're living in a futuristic version of ancient Rome. The decadence, self-importance, and lack of shame are astounding."

"Wow!" exclaimed the doctor. "That's a lot to take in at once."

"I warned you."

"OK, let's start with the symptoms first, the alcohol and the drugs. You need to get into a professional program right away. There's a great one specifically designed for clergy like you up in D.C. It's run by one of the leading experts in substance abuse and addiction in the country. I'll check and see when the next one starts. It'll probably be next month right after the holidays. Is that something you'd be willing to do?"

"If that's what it takes, then yes, I will."

"OK, great. Now in the meantime, you need to stop drinking and doing drugs. Would you like to stay here at St. John's for a while to help with that?"

"Hold on a second. Baby steps, doc. Baby steps."

"Michael, you've got some serious problems going on. Do you really think you can restrain yourself? You need help now."

"Alright. I'll cut back on my own until after the holidays. This is my busiest time of the year coming up, and I can't just leave the church for a personal sabbatical. I promise, right after New Year's, I'll be able to take the time I need to get right. Until then, I can hold it together."

"You're trusting me with all this right now, so I'll trust that you'll keep your word and get help next month. Deal?"

"Yes, definitely," confirmed the reverend.

"But if you can't control it and you need any help at all, will you promise to call me? Anytime at all? You're not alone in this."

"Sure. Thanks. I appreciate that."

"Before next month though, one thing you can do now is work with someone on the cause of these drug and alcohol and infidelity symptoms. I believe that cause is your lack of faith."

"So you think losing my faith caused me to drink and do cocaine and cheat? Not the other way around?"

"Exactly. But that's just my theory right now. We'd have to get into some things first to find out."

"When can we start?" asked the reverend.

"First I need to know if you're comfortable working with me on this. I know several other professionals you could speak with as well."

"No, if I'm going to do this, I want it to be with someone I already know and trust."

"Well, in that case, is next Wednesday OK? Same time?"

"Sounds good. I'll see you then."

They both stood up from their seats and shook hands goodbye, and the reverend walked toward the door to leave the office.

When his friend was halfway out the door, the doctor called out, "Take care of yourself."

"I will," Michael replied from a few steps down the outer hallway, no longer visible from inside the office.

Dr. Yost turned around from his desk, and his eyes searched the titles along the rows of his bookshelves. He found the two books he was looking for, pulled them out, and placed them on his desk. He opened the first book and scanned the table of contents. The title on the book's spine read *Addiction and Religion*. Just to the right of this book on his desk sat the New Testament. He had some reading to do before next Wednesday.

7 INTENTIONAL GROUNDING

A cold front with strong, blustery winds and rain showers had blown through Richmond late Wednesday night, so Thursday's temperatures were much closer to a normal December day in Virginia. Overcast grey skies and a damp, bone-chilling breeze were in stark contrast to the previous several days' beautiful weather.

Reverend Thomas sat at his desk preparing for his last religious history class of the semester at St. Philip's and beginning to draft the final exam questions. The dim lighting inside his church office fought in vain to brighten up the interior of the room against the gloomy, dark conditions outside the window. The strain on the reverend's eyes was taking its toll, so he took a break, removed his glasses, leaned back in his chair, and rubbed his eyes to help relieve them.

Once he put his glasses back on, he glanced down at his watch to check the time. It read 3:17 p.m. Earlier in the week he had told Betty Woodson he would drop by for a visit that afternoon. But after his meeting the day before with Dr. Yost and because of the dreary, cold weather outside, he didn't feel like going to see her. He didn't know if this was because of some newfound inner strength he was discovering that would allow him to resist her, or maybe it was because of the comments Richard Woodson had said to him the day before at the club about maybe seeing him sometime before the big party on Saturday. Either way, he decided to just stay at his office and not go to her house. Perhaps he was getting better on his own.

"Michael?" the voice of Nancy, the church secretary, called out over the intercom in the telephone on his desk.

"Yes, Nancy?"

"There's a call for you on line three. It's Mrs. Woodson."

"Thank you."

He stared at the phone for a few seconds and then hesitantly lifted the receiver up to his face.

"Hello," he greeted her.

"I'm sorry to call you on your office line, but I couldn't get through on your cell phone. It must be turned off."

"It is. I'm working."

"When are you coming over?"

"I can't today. I've got a lot to catch up on."

"What about tonight? Richard won't be back until tomorrow."

Michael once again felt sorry for her having to stay in that house all alone, but he couldn't let that dissuade him from sticking to his guns and not going over there.

"Betty, I can't tonight. It's the Tech/UVA game. I always watch it with the guys from school over at Buddy's. I can't miss this one."

"I have an idea. We still have plenty of time. Let's you and I take the helicopter up to Charlottesville and go to the game in person. We can watch it in the president's box. With all the money we've given them to get our kids in there, that won't be a problem at all."

"Listen. I appreciate your offer very much. It's extremely generous and tempting. But let's just wait until I see you this Saturday at your party. We'll have a great time then."

"I can't believe you'd rather spend time with your college drinking buddies instead of with me, but suit yourself. You'll just have to make it up to me at my party."

"OK, fine. I'll see you then. Bye."

The call ended without a goodbye from Betty. He could tell she wasn't happy, but he knew he needed to stay strong and not go over there. He buzzed Nancy on the intercom, told her to hold any more calls that might come in for him that afternoon, and then returned to his work.

Standing in front of the panoramic window in her bedroom and wearing a white silk robe that covered up expensive silk lingerie underneath, Betty Woodson hung up the call and tossed her cell phone gently on the bed. In her silk, high-heeled slippers, she carefully walked across the oriental carpets of her bedroom and continued along the hallway, down the winding spiral staircase, past the formal dining room, and into the huge gourmet kitchen. A middle-aged Hispanic woman wearing a white apron and a light-blue uniform underneath was chopping vegetables on the counter.

"Maria, there will just be one for dinner tonight, so don't worry about cooking the second steak," Betty told the woman.

"Yes, ma'am."

"Actually, Maria, go ahead and cook that second steak," a male voice called over from the living room next to the kitchen.

Betty spun around in surprise and quickly shuffled over to the living room. She rounded the corner to see her husband sitting on one of the sofas with a glass of cognac in his hand.

"Steak sounds really good tonight," he said with a wry smile.

"What are you doing here?" she shot back. "You said you were staying downtown tonight because of some board meeting."

"Plans change. Obviously you know that. Too bad your guest couldn't make it."

"Apparently your guest bailed out on you too."

"Touché," he replied as he stood up and walked over to the marble wet bar to refill his glass of cognac. Then he pulled out a wine glass and filled it from a previously opened bottle of

French burgundy. Betty carefully walked across the thick oriental carpeting to a wingchair next to the sofa where her husband had been sitting. After she sat down in the chair, she crossed her legs, and the split in her robe rode up to reveal her thighs. Richard walked over to put the glass of wine on a glass table next to her chair and sat back down on the sofa.

"You know, Betty, you've always been the one person who could keep up with me. That's one of the reasons I married you."

"What are the other reasons?" she said teasingly while rocking her upper leg and dangling her slipper on her foot.

"So far, we've been able to make our little arrangement work out quite well. You do your thing, and I do mine. We don't ask questions. And no one gets hurt."

"What's your point, Richard?"

"My point is, we had an agreement. And you crossed the line. You brought someone here, to my house."

"This is my house too. And why do you care what happens here? You're never around anyway."

"That doesn't matter. What does matter is you broke the rules. And I'm not going to tolerate that in my house."

Richard realized his voice was getting louder, so he took a moment to compose himself before he continued.

"We both have a lot riding on this. Discretion is very important here."

She fired back, "Oh, so you want to talk about discretion. OK, fine. Let's talk about it. Is it discreet when you parade your flock of floozies around with you at the club, where all our friends hang out? You didn't think I knew about that, did you, Richard?"

"I assume you're referring to Heather. She's a realtor. She's handling some real estate transactions for some of my clients. That's business."

"More like monkey business. Everyone knows what's really going on. You might want to be more discreet yourself next time."

"Fine. Point taken."

"You know, I finally realize what this is really all about. You haven't paid any attention to me in years. And now I'm finally spending time with someone I really care about, and it's getting to you."

"That's crazy."

"For the first time in a very long time, someone finds me attractive for who I really am. I'm finally happy again, and you don't like it one bit."

"If that's what you want to believe, fine, go right ahead."

Betty put the empty wine glass down on the table, stood up, and firmly stated, "Don't worry. I'll play along and keep everything quiet. We'll go to hotels and stay away from your precious house. But I expect you to do the same thing. Don't embarrass me in front of my friends like that ever again."

She walked with conviction out of the room and back upstairs to her bedroom. Richard watched her leave and thought to himself that maybe she was right about a few things. He hadn't felt much for her in a long time. But recently the women he was with just weren't interesting to talk to. Say what you want about her motives; Betty was sharp and intelligent. As time goes by and people get older, those attributes always remain attractive. Plus, the recent smile on her face and bounce in her step made her physically more attractive to him than she had been in years. He wondered if what he was feeling was real affection for her again or if it was just because this was the first time he felt he couldn't have her.

Buddy's had been a legendary local hangout in the Fan section of Richmond since the late '40s. Thursday nights were always busy, but this night would be extra crowded because of the annual Virginia Tech/UVA football game being broadcasted on ESPN. The normal occupancy for the bar was 110. This night they were expecting at least double that amount. The patrons who weren't early or lucky enough to get a seat in a booth or at the bar could stand in the covered patio area outside and watch the game on one of the three large-screen TVs.

As an insurance guy with a flexible schedule, Erik Majors was always the one who got to Buddy's early to save a booth for his college buddies. He had taken an Uber car and arrived around 4:00 in the afternoon, so he had a good head start on drinking by the time the other three friends arrived. Wearing street clothes comprised of blue jeans and a Virginia Tech sweatshirt instead of his work clothes, Michael made it there around 6:00 and ordered some chicken wings and a pitcher of beer for the table. Dr. Lee and John McDonald arrived just a few minutes later to fill out the four-person booth.

As you walked into Buddy's, a single, 50-foot long bar ran almost the entire depth of the left side of the restaurant. Lining the right side were 18 four-person booths and then a larger 8-person, round booth in the back, right corner. Beyond that were the restrooms and a narrow walkway that led to an exit door, which opened up to a 20-car, gravel parking lot behind the building. Multiple large-screen TVs, old sports memorabilia, and various traffic signs and license plates were hung all over the walls that were a faded yellow and covered in a slimy sheen of grease fumes and beer spray from years of rowdy partying.

With just a couple minutes left in the second quarter, Virginia Tech was leading 10 to 7 and driving down the field for another score.

"This happens every game," noted John. "They always play down to their opponent."

"They should be winning by more than two touchdowns by now," replied Erik.

"What was the spread on this?" asked Michael.

"I think it was Tech minus 17," answered Dan.

"They've had plenty of chances, but they keep turning the ball over," noticed Erik.

"That's coaching," said John.

"What do you mean?" disputed Erik. "The coach isn't out there fumbling the ball. The players are."

"Yeah, but good coaching means fewer turnovers," John affirmed.

Dan interjected, "Aw, come on, John. Beamer's gone. Let it go."

The quarterback for Virginia Tech was running for his life away from the rush of the UVA defense and threw a desperate pass that was intercepted by the Cavaliers. The half of the bar that was wearing blue and orange broke into a cheer. The other half wearing maroon and orange was stunned and upset.

"I can't let it go," admitted John. "And they can't keep playing like this."

The remaining minute of the first half expired without any further scoring, and then a mass of bar patrons went out the front door to either smoke cigarettes or make calls on their cell phones, while another mass of people headed for the restrooms in the back. Michael told his friends he was going to the bathroom. He squeezed his way through everyone waiting in line and eventually made it to the corridor that led outside to the back parking lot. Once outside, he scanned the lot and finally found the man he was looking for.

In the far back corner of the lot stood a short, skinny, early 30-something year old man wearing a burgundy Washington Redskins hat on backwards; a dark-blue, hooded sweatshirt; and blue jeans. He had a nervous, weaselly demeanor about him with his eyes darting back and forth as if on the lookout for someone.

Michael recognized and approached him first.

"Hey there, Mikey boy," the young man said once he saw the reverend clearly in the darkness. "Right on time."

He pulled a small notepad and ballpoint pen out of his back pocket and opened the pad up to the first blank page.

"How many this week?" he quickly asked the reverend. "Oh, yeah. A couple of spreads just changed a few minutes ago. The Patriots are minus nine point five, and the Redskins are plus four."

"I'm holding off this week, Tommy. None this time."

"None? What are you talking about? This is the first time in years you're not playing. What's going on? Are you working with someone else?"

"No, no, not at all. I've just decided to take a break for a while."

"OK, but you know that if you don't play, you're going to have to pay off your marker."

"I know," Michael said indignantly. "How much?"

Tommy flipped through his notepad and did some quick computations in his head.

"You haven't had a very good season this year. Let's see here. The total is 17,000. But of course you already knew that, didn't you?"

"I'll have to get it to you next week," responded Michael while ignoring the last comment.

"Are you sure you don't want to just place a few bets now? That way you wouldn't have to pay up for a little while longer?"

"No, Tommy. I'll get you the money next Thursday."

"Alright, but don't stand me up. Mr. Lupini wouldn't like that."

Tommy didn't say anything further. He didn't have to. Michael knew not to mess around with the Lupinis. He was going to pay off his debt and stay away from gambling for good this time.

As he slowly walked back to the rear entrance of the bar, he realized he only had one way to get the 17,000 dollars he owed the bookie. And for just a moment, he wondered which person, Mr. Lupini or Betty, would be worse to owe money to.

He looked down at his left hand and saw that it was trembling more intensely than ever before. He quickly veered to his right, ducked down behind a silver pickup truck parked along the edge of the lot, and pulled out the blue plastic tube from his front pants pocket. With his hand shaking so violently now, he couldn't pour out the white powder without spilling it all over the ground. So he took a long, deep breath and tried to calm himself. This helped steady his hand slightly, but it was still shaking. Squeezing his left hand tightly around the tube, he sprinkled the white powder as carefully as possible onto the back of his right hand into two inch-long parallel lines. He hastily snorted them up both nostrils, wiped his nose clean on the sleeve of his sweatshirt, and put the plastic tube back in his pants pocket with his now-steady left hand before going inside the bar to rejoin his friends.

8 CONSTANT CHANGE

Normally on a Friday, Reverend Thomas would be polishing up his sermon for the upcoming Sunday services. But even though he wouldn't be delivering a sermon this weekend or even teaching a class at Sunday school, he still needed to catch up on administrative church business, so he was spending this cold, sunny, windy day secluded in his office trying to get some work done. However, he found it difficult to make any headway when he was receiving phone calls every 10 minutes regarding one upcoming Christmas-related issue or another.

The Christmas season, combined with his other commitments to St. Philip's School and the St. John's Center, was the reverend's busiest time of the year. One of his most time-consuming jobs was to help direct and plan the church's Christmas pageant, an annual live procession of scenes from the Bible related to the birth of Jesus that took place each Christmas Eve. Every year, the children of the church would dress up in costume to represent various people from the first Christmas and act in scenes that moved on rolling flatbed trolleys down the middle aisle of the church during the service. Parents, grandparents, and all other related family members jostled for position so they could get clear photos of their children during this hallowed event.

Coordinating the pageant was a complex and important responsibility, and as the junior reverend on staff, it fell to Michael for the last few years. He had worked out most of the kinks in the process over time, but he was getting a late start this year, so he needed to make progress very soon to be sure all the children were organized and prepared properly and given enough time to know their roles and memorize their lines.

In the midst of all the phone calls to his office about which kid would be doing which role and what costumes had to be either repaired or replaced, he remembered he had to go down to the storage area in the basement below the chapel building to look over the trolleys and the sets to see what kind of work might have to be done to make them ready for the pageant. As he was getting up from his desk, he heard his cell phone ring in his coat pocket. After pulling out his phone and looking at the screen, he saw the familiar name and phone number of Betty Woodson.

He sat back down in his chair, knowing he would probably be on the phone for a while, and answered, "Hello. Don't you have a party to get ready for?"

"And that's exactly what I'm doing now," she replied.

"Well then, I'm honored you're taking time out of your busy schedule to talk to me."

"Hold on a second," she told him and then held the phone away from her mouth. "Put those poinsettias in the main living room," she commanded to workers in the background. "But the Christmas tree needs to go in there first. You can't arrange the poinsettias until after the tree is set up."

She held the phone back up to her mouth to continue her conversation with the reverend.

"I just don't understand these people. They work on this party every year, and they still don't know what they're doing."

"I'm sure you'll set them straight, Betty. You always do. So what can I do for you?"

"I just wanted to let you know it was a good thing you didn't come over yesterday afternoon like we had planned."

"Oh really? Why? Did one of your other boyfriends drop by unannounced?" he kidded her.

"Listen. I'm serious. Richard came home early. He never does that. And you can just imagine how surprised I was. Thank goodness you weren't here and we weren't, you know."

"That would not have been good."

Michael remembered what Richard had told him at the club a few days earlier about maybe seeing him before the party. In fact, it was this statement that gave the reverend pause about going over to see Betty on Thursday. Now he was worried that Richard may have known what was going on all along.

"Does he know about me?" the reverend asked nervously.

"Calm down, Michael. He does his thing, and I do mine. It's OK. I told you about this before."

"But does he know it's me?"

"I don't know. And even if he does, it doesn't matter."

"What do you mean it doesn't matter? Of course it matters. It's one thing to have an agreement with your wife and know she's out there with someone. But to know exactly who it is and have to interact with that person? That's a big problem."

"I didn't tell you this to get you all worked up and upset. It'll be OK. I just wanted to let you know what happened because we won't be able to meet at my house again. We'll have to go other places. But that'll be fun. We can mix it up. I've always loved the Jefferson Hotel. Oh, and you can carry me up the famous stairs in the lobby just like Rhett Butler did to Scarlett O'Hara in *Gone with the Wind*."

"Betty, I don't know. This is getting way out of control."

"I told you it's OK. Believe me, he has no grounds whatsoever to get upset about anything I do. I've put up with too much from him over the years."

"Let's talk about this later. There's a lot to think about here."

"What's wrong? Do you not like me anymore? Are you tired of me?"

The reverend realized he had to be very careful here. He knew he needed to ask her for the 17,000 dollars to pay off his debt to the bookie. But he also wanted to figure out a way to stop seeing her. This was going to be a lot more difficult than he planned, but he figured he had to play along and keep her happy until he got the money.

"Of course not," he reinforced to her. "You know how much you mean to me."

"Michael, this past year has been the happiest of my life. And it's all because of you. If something were to change between us, I'm not sure I could handle it."

"I'll tell you what. Let's talk more next week after your party. I'm sure I'll feel better about things by then. Everything will be fine. We'll figure it out."

He told her goodbye, ended the call, opened the door in his desk, pulled out the bottle of bourbon and the glass, poured himself a drink, and gulped it down in one swig. His life was becoming more and more of a mess, and he felt that whatever he did to try to make it better just seemed to make things worse. He wondered if he had dug himself into a hole that was too deep to ever get out of unscathed.

After a few minutes of stewing in his misery and futilely trying to come up with any solutions to his problems, he remembered he had to go down to the basement to check on the pageant trolleys and sets. He pulled out a tin of breath mints from his desk and popped a couple into his bourbon-stained mouth.

He went downstairs, exited the administrative building, and headed over to the chapel to get to the storage basement below. As he opened the door to the chapel, he noticed that, as usual, all the lights were on. But once he got inside, he saw the pews were empty. Usually on Fridays, especially in December, many individuals were sprinkled throughout the front pews for the sake of personal prayers and self-reflection. But on this particular day at this particular time, there weren't any at all.

He decided to go to the front right pew to a seat where he could see the brass cross on the altar and the giant stained-glass window above. He pulled the leather-covered and cushioned kneeler down to the floor and knelt with his hands resting on the railing on top of the three-foot-tall, engraved wood divider in front of his seat.

During his tenure at St. Andrew's, the reverend had occasionally dropped in to the chapel to pray by himself for sick parishioners and family members. But a couple years had passed since the previous time he had done that. His waning faith and busy schedule precluded it. At least that's what he told himself. But now he figured, why not? It couldn't hurt.

"Dear Lord," he prayed silently to himself. "I'm sorry it's been so long since I've prayed to You, I mean alone, just directly to You. I really don't have an excuse. Maybe I've felt, since I lead prayers in church, that those counted for me too. But of course I know that's not true. Please forgive me for not praying to You as often as I should.

"But I'm here now. I guess it's better late than never. Anyway, I'm not sure why my faith has been faltering. Maybe it's because of all the sins I've committed. Or maybe Ted was right, and I've committed these sins because my faith is weak. Whatever the reason, I do know that I need help. I can't fight these problems on my own. I'm not strong enough.

"Thank you for everything You've given me in this life. I know I don't deserve these blessings. But I want to earn them back. I want to earn back the love of my wonderful wife Beth. I want to earn back my faith. I want to earn back my life here in the church. And I want to earn back my own self-respect by staying away from drugs and alcohol and gambling and cheating.

"The trouble is, I've gotten myself into so many problems that I can't find any way out of them. It's like whatever I do, things get worse. I want to do the right thing, but everything's so turned around and upside down that I don't know what the right thing is anymore.

"I don't expect You to just suddenly fix everything for me. I know I have to work on that myself. But if You can just give me an idea of where or how to start, I would really appreciate it.

"I'll talk to You again soon. In the name of the Father and

the Son and the Holy Spirit. Amen."

Michael stood up slowly from the kneeler and stretched his creaky left knee to get the circulation going. The silence inside the chapel was eerily apparent. He turned around, looked toward the back of the church, and spotted an older man sitting in a pew alone, right near the doorway that led to the storage basement. He realized he had been so focused on his own prayer that he didn't hear the man enter the chapel.

As he approached closer, he saw the man was leaning forward while seated in the wooden pew with his hands folded in prayer on top of the back of the pew in front of him. His forehead rested on his hands, and his eyes were closed. A full head of wavy, thick, grey hair was visible from Michael's viewpoint above. Having heard the soft footsteps of the reverend on the polished brick floor, the older man raised up his head, sat back slowly, and then stood up to greet him.

The older man's eyes were a bright, brilliant hazel. The pale and leathery skin on his slender, drawn face showed years of wrinkles and exposure to the elements. He had on a navy blue, older-style, well-worn blazer with a solid-white, polyester, buttoned-down-collared shirt; dark grey pants; and black leather, wingtip, dress shoes. He wasn't wearing any jewelry at all — no rings and not even a watch.

Michael had never seen the man at St. Andrew's before, so he stopped and introduced himself.

"I'm sorry, sir," the reverend said when he saw the man stand up from his prayer. "I didn't mean to disturb you."

"Not a problem at all, Reverend. I was just finishing up."

"I'm Reverend Thomas. But please, call me Michael."

"I'm George," the man replied as he stuck his hand out to shake the reverend's.

The reverend returned the handshake and said, "I haven't seen you around here before. Are you new to St. Andrew's?"

"Not really. It's been awhile since I've been here in person, but years ago I used to come here all the time. The place still looks the same though."

"Very true. That's the way they like it. They don't want

things to change very much around here."

"Change can be scary for some people. But you know what they say? Change is the only constant in life."

"Yes, but I'm afraid the ancient teachings of Heraclitus aren't appreciated here in modern-day Richmond. So, you've come back to the church, and you're here praying alone on a Friday. Anything in particular on your mind? I'd be happy to hang out and talk with you for a while, if you like. But that's entirely up to you. No pressure."

"Thanks for the offer, Michael. I'm all right for now. But I saw you were praying alone yourself just a few minutes ago. I could say the same to you. Would you like to talk to me about anything? I'm a good listener."

The reverend was initially taken aback by the man's comments. This was the first time anyone, outside of the clergy or his wife or Dr. Yost, had offered to listen to him. He looked at the man's face and sensed a warm, sincere aura about him. For some reason he couldn't explain he felt comfortable talking to him and probably would've been able to have a lengthy, meaningful conversation with him. But he was still just meeting this man for the first time and wasn't quite ready to open up to a stranger about his problems, even though that's exactly what he had asked the older man to do with him.

"Thank you for the offer. But I have to get back to work and take care of a few things to get ready for the Christmas pageant. It's on Christmas Eve. I hope you'll be able to make it."

"I may be a little busy then, but I'll see what I can do," replied the man. "If I'm not here in person, I'll be here in spirit."

"OK, fair enough. Nice meeting you. Have a great day and a Merry Christmas if I don't see you again before then."

"Merry Christmas to you also, Michael. I hope you get what you were praying for."

The older man gave the reverend a gentle, sincere smile before walking down the center aisle, turning left at the cross aisle in the middle of the chapel, and going out through the side exit door. Michael continued on his way to the storage room so he could review the trolleys and sets for the pageant before it got too late in the day. As he descended down the staircase to the basement, he wondered if the older man would drop by again sometime when they both had more time to talk. He hoped he hadn't missed the opportunity completely.

9 PARTY FAVOR

Only one night of the year required Michael to wear a tuxedo, and this was that night. The Woodson Christmas party was a black-tie affair attended by every one of the city's most elite, including the Richmond 500, a group consisting of the 500 most influential and powerful people in town. Guests ranging from the governor to the mayor to judges to CEOs of major corporations wouldn't dare miss this party. The Woodsons kept track of who was invited, who attended, and who didn't show up. If you had the honor of being invited and didn't make it for whatever reason, you could forget receiving an invitation the following year.

Real winter weather had finally arrived in Richmond and had brought with it crystal-clear skies and crisp, cold temperatures. The frost-covered, blue Volvo station wagon slowly cruised through the dark night past the mansions and estates of Windsor Farms until it reached a stop at the end of the line of cars waiting to get into the driveway of Greenlock, the Woodsons' estate. Valet parking for the party had created a mini traffic jam on Lock Lane, but every carload of black-tie guests patiently waited its turn.

"What time did it start?" Beth Thomas asked her husband while she checked her hair in the mirror behind the sun visor with help from the headlights of an SUV directly behind them.

"Seven o'clock," he answered.

She glanced at the clock on the dashboard. It read 10:17. Then she remembered it was broken. Since she wasn't wearing a watch, she pulled her cell phone from her black leather clutch purse and looked at the screen. It was 7:44 p.m.

She remarked, "We had the same idea as everyone else. They all wanted to be fashionably late, but not too late. Oh well, serves us right, I guess."

The reverend's tuxedo showed only a modicum of wear from various parties and debutant balls over its 15-year life. However, his body shape had added a few pounds over that same time period, so the tuxedo fit more snugly than was comfortable. Since he only wore it sporadically, he didn't see the need to buy a new one yet, nor did he have the disposable income to do so. It would have to do for now, even if the jacket was a little tight in the stomach when he buttoned it. His solid black cummerbund and bowtie were only a couple years newer than the tux.

Beth borrowed her evening gown from a teacher friend at St. Philip's. It was a black, short-sleeve, mid-length dress with black sequins and a fairly conservative neckline. She wore a single strand of small white pearls around her neck, a gift from her parents when she finished college. Her matching, small white-pearl earrings and her simple diamond engagement ring and gold wedding band comprised the rest of her jewelry. She had splurged and spent a couple hours earlier in the afternoon at a salon to get her hair just right in a formal updo. A black wool coat with a grey faux-fur collar completed her ensemble for this special evening.

Michael looked over at his wife in the passenger seat and thought how beautiful she was. They rarely had the occasion to get all dressed up, and even though she wasn't wearing an expensive gown or jewelry, she still looked radiant. He felt bad he couldn't afford to give her all those things and that she had to piece together and borrow clothes for events like this. They would be the least wealthy people at the party. He could deal with that, but he didn't like that she had to.

Yet even more so, he felt guilty about what he had done to her and just hoped to make it through the party without Betty making a scene. The sooner he could end his affair with her, the better his chances were to move on and focus on his relationship with his wife. But tonight was not the time to do anything rash. He needed to remain friendly with her so he could borrow the money to pay back his gambling debt.

With still more than 10 cars waiting in line for valet parking ahead of the Volvo, Beth let out a sigh and said, "Too bad we can't just park on the street. I'd be happy to just pull over right here, even if I had to walk the rest of the way in these heels."

"We'll be there soon enough. Plus, every minute we wait here means one less minute at the party."

"How long do we have to stay?"

"Not too long. The rector told me this morning that Richard is going to make some sort of announcement related to the church, so we need to be there for that. But I can't imagine it'll be longer than a couple hours."

"I hope I'm getting points for this. You owe me at least one chick flick in return."

"OK, OK. Fair enough. I'll make it up to you."

"You better," she said playfully with a sweet smile.

After five more minutes of waiting, finally they reached the valet. Michael and Beth got out of the car, and the couple walked across the cobblestone driveway to the red front door. Christmas decorations were draped everywhere on the exterior of the house and the adjoining garage. Huge gold wreaths were hung on each of the six garage doors, with an even larger and more ornate one gracing the front door of the main house. Multiple decorated trees lined the driveway, and strands of white lights were strewn over virtually every tree and bush in the front yard. A single white, electric candle had been placed in each of the 38 windows facing the driveway.

Beth had been to Greenlock once a year every year for this party since she and Michael first arrived in Richmond more than 10 years earlier, but each time she saw the size and grandeur of the house up close and in person, it still shocked her.

"It's hard to believe places like this actually exist in real life," she said under her breath to her husband as they approached the line of people waiting to get in the front door. "Just imagine how many people you could feed or give health care to for the kind of money it took to build this."

"But the Woodsons do give a lot of money to charity to help people."

"They should. They've got a ton to begin with."

In the entry foyer stood a greeting line consisting of both Richard and Betty Woodson and a few other close friends and family members who were co-hosts of the party, including Richard's parents. Of course Betty was the first person to greet the Thomases right as they stepped inside the house. She wore a tight, form-fitting designer dress that was gold, strapless, and low cut. Beth didn't keep up with the latest fashion designers, but she could tell this dress was from a very expensive Italian design house, as also were Betty's shoes. Her jewelry was composed of an overwhelmingly bright array of diamonds, with the lone exception being an immense, round, brilliant-blue sapphire in the center of her diamond necklace.

"Oh Beth, it's so wonderful to see you again," Betty exclaimed loudly upon seeing her guest in the entry hall, right before she gave her a big, tight hug. "Thank you so much for coming."

"Thank you for inviting us, Mrs. Woodson," Beth replied.

"Please, call me Betty. Mrs. Woodson is my mother-in-law."

"OK, thank you, Betty. I just love how pretty your home looks. It's gorgeous. And so are you. Your dress is amazing."

"You're so sweet, honey. I can see why Michael loves you so."

Betty then turned to the reverend; gave him a gentler, more innocuous hug; and said, "Oh Michael, you look so dashing in your tuxedo. It's nice to see you without your preacher clothes on for a change."

"It's nice to see you too, Betty," he replied with a smirk. "You look great, as always."

Betty looked the reverend square in the eye with a huge, happy smile. He saw a joyous twinkle in her eye and tried to smile sincerely back at her. Beth and Michael then moved down the line to be greeted by Richard Woodson in his black tuxedo and silk, gold-patterned bow tie and vest.

"Merry Christmas, Mrs. Thomas," Richard greeted her. "No wait, it's Becky, right?"

"Beth," she replied, amused at his mistake. "But you can call me Becky if you like. I won't mind."

"Beth, Beth, Beth. That's right. I'll get it one of these days. Anyway, thanks so much for coming over. It's a pleasure to see you again."

Richard then turned toward and firmly shook the hand of the reverend before Beth had a chance to reply.

"Reverend, don't you clean up nice? The last time I saw you, you were in golf clothes."

"Yes, Richard, that was a good day. Thanks for having us here tonight. I'm sure it will be another great event."

"It definitely will. Stick around for a while. I've got an announcement later I'm sure you'll want to hear. In the meantime, don't have too much fun."

Richard punctuated his final comment with a tight, smug grin. The reverend hesitated for a moment and then continued down the reception line. While he exchanged pleasantries with the rest of the greeters, he kept reflecting back to Richard's last remark.

Michael wondered to himself, "He couldn't be so bold as to expose his wife's affair in public, could he? Not even Richard would dare do that, would he? Maybe he just meant not to drink a lot. I'm probably reading way too much into this. Get a hold of yourself. In just a couple hours, it'll all be over. Until then, just stay cool."

He looked down at his left hand and saw it was beginning to tremble, so he hid it in his left pants pocket. He had intentionally left his blue plastic tube of cocaine back home so that he wouldn't be tempted to use it at the party, but he needed something to take the edge off. He and Beth left the entrance hall, gave her coat to the coat check attendant, and entered the enormous main living room. He spotted two bartenders at a bar in the far corner that only had a couple people waiting to order.

"Nice place. I love a living room you can land a plane in," she joked to her husband.

"Good one. From the film *Arthur*, right?"

Beth nodded her head yes.

"What would you like to drink?" he asked his wife.

"A glass of chardonnay would be nice."

"Be right back," he said, leaving her alone in the middle of the room.

The main living room of Greenlock was the focal point of the party. Much of the room's regular furniture had been removed to create space for the hundreds of partygoers expected to arrive. In the corner of the room stood a 30-foot-tall Virginia fir Christmas tree, highly decorated with gold-plated ornaments, thousands of tiny white lights, and a three-dimensional crystal star on top. A concert piano had been set up midway along one of the walls with a man and woman duo playing Christmas songs. A foursome of Victorian-style holiday singers surrounded the piano to provide lyrical accompaniment to the music.

Strolling throughout the party revelers were various musicians and entertainers such as a violinist, a harmonica player, a female magician, and a juggler dressed in a jester's costume. In the center of the main living room, an 8-foot-tall silver fountain sprayed a cascading waterfall of champagne into crystal flutes arranged in a ring around the base. In an adjoining sitting room, a 12-piece mini orchestra played traditional Christmas music across from a North Pole setting that housed Santa Claus in his big, red chair and three helper elves. And through the glass doors overlooking the backyard could be seen a full-sized nativity scene that was probably larger than the original setting in Bethlehem, complete with live animals and real human actors, except for an extremely lifelike animatronic doll that played little baby Jesus.

Waiting patiently for her husband and her wine to arrive, Beth noticed two older women passing behind her and conversing in a loud, shrill tone. They stopped temporarily just a few feet away from her and continued their discussion. Beth didn't intend to eavesdrop, but their voices were so high-pitched and piercing that she couldn't help but hear every word.

"So when did you give her the gift?" the first woman asked.

"Over a month ago," the second woman responded.

"And you still haven't heard anything from her?"

"No, nothing at all."

"I just don't understand this younger generation. They don't seem to know anything about etiquette."

"I'm not looking for some special kind of recognition. I was happy to give her the gift. But you'd think that if you spent a thousand dollars on someone, they would at least send you a thank-you note."

"Nowadays they're more likely to send you an email. Or even a text, heaven forbid."

"I'd rather get nothing than one of those damn emails. Doesn't anyone know how to write a note by hand anymore? It's just common courtesy."

Beth had heard enough and left to find her husband. About halfway to the bar, Michael was talking to a couple while holding his bourbon and water and her glass of chardonnay. She walked right up to them to try to save her husband.

"Beth, this is Mr. and Mrs. Taylor," the reverend said, introducing the couple to his wife. "And this is Beth, my better half. The Taylors here are longtime members at St. Andrew's," Michael told his wife as both of the Taylors shook Beth's hand. "We were just talking about their son, Sean, who is a student at St. Philip's and is taking my religious history class."

"Oh, he just loves your class, Reverend," said Mrs. Taylor. "He tells us how interesting you make the material for everyone."

"That's certainly nice to hear," the reverend replied. "Some of that history can get a little dry, especially for high school boys. I try to make it both educational and somewhat entertaining at the same time."

Mr. Taylor added, "From what I hear, you do a great job of it. By the way, Sean's getting his applications ready for colleges now. He really wants to go to UVA. Would you mind giving him a recommendation for his application?"

"I'm not sure a recommendation from a Virginia Tech Hokie would do a lot of good at UVA," the reverend answered, leading to laughter from both of the Taylors. "But I'd be happy to help Sean out with a recommendation. He's a good kid."

Michael and Beth finished their conversation with the Taylors and moved along to the adjacent dining room. An arrangement of gourmet food was spread out across the 32-foot-long dining room table, including platters of beluga caviar, lobster tails, lamb chops, roasted turkey, Beef Wellington, Caesar salad, Dover Sole, and fresh asparagus. They each filled a small plate and took their food to a group of round tables set up in another sitting room just off the main living room. One of the tables had two open seats next to each other, with the remaining eight seats filled by couples who, based on their conversations and the free-flowing laughter, apparently already knew each other.

The Thomases sat down and began to enjoy their extravagant dinner. Food this expensive was a special treat for them. With their busy schedules and tight finances, they usually ate simple meals like spaghetti, chicken, and meatloaf. They savored every bite of the lamb, tenderloin, and lobster because they knew it would be a long time before they had any again.

Two couples sitting behind the reverend were engaged in a detailed discussion about Florida. They talked only amongst themselves and hadn't noticed Michael and Beth joining them at the table.

"I think next year we'll be able to establish residence in Florida," said the first man sitting next to the reverend. "That should save us a ton in taxes."

"Just don't forget about the insurance rates down there," warned the second man sitting across the table. "Everybody knows they don't have state income tax. But what they don't tell you is how high the insurance and the property taxes are. The insurance on my boat is three times as much as it was in Virginia Beach. And the property taxes are twice as high."

"Sure, but I've run the numbers," countered the first man. "If you make at least seven figures, then you come out ahead, even with the boat and the club membership and the Ferrari."

Beth leaned in closely to her husband and whispered, "Rich people problems."

They both laughed together at their private joke. Moments like these reminded Michael of why he fell in love with Beth in the first place. Her razor-sharp wit made light of any situation. She never complained about not having the money and lifestyle of the other guests at the party. He had always been the one who wanted more for them.

The two couples behind Beth were arranged so that the two women sat side-by-side and the two men sat next to each other a little farther around the table. The two women, sitting directly on the other side of Beth, were engulfed in their own discussion about a couple they both knew.

"I don't know who they think they're fooling anymore," said the first woman. "Their entire marriage has been a fake."

"I heard she stays at home crying alone while he's out at all hours with his gay friends," the second woman replied.

"That is so sad."

"I know. Can you imagine how their kids feel? At least they're grown now and out of the house."

"Why did he marry her in the first place? Don't you think he knew he was gay, even back then?"

"Times were different. I guess he thought he needed to marry a woman. She was his, what do they call that now, his beard?"

When Beth heard the last comment, she started to choke on her sip of wine. She couldn't believe what the woman had just said. She put her right hand on top of her chest and caught her breath. Michael leaned in closely to check if she was all right. They began to laugh together.

After they finished eating their dinner, they left the group of round tables and strolled through the multitude of rooms on the first floor of the mansion to take in the entire scope of the massive event. Multiple living rooms, sitting rooms, formal studies, and dens all played host to hundreds of revelers enjoying the most lavish Christmas party of the year.

The reverend and his wife stopped to chat with various guests as they toured the house, including several sets of parents who asked Michael to give their children college recommendations, a couple involved in the church's Christmas pageant who wanted to talk about the schedule, and James and Sarah Howard who told them how excited their son Billy was to be going on the church trip to Israel in April.

Several times throughout the evening, Michael would notice Betty holding court with various groups of guests. She was always the one talking, and everyone within earshot was eager to be in her audience. She was the belle of the ball, and she loved every second of her onlookers' admiration.

He glanced at his watch and realized time was going by very quickly. He needed to speak with Betty privately at some point during the evening to ask for the money for his gambling debt. He had exhausted every other option for getting the 17,000 dollars without success. He didn't have any equity in his house, he couldn't cash out his 401K, and he didn't have any investments or stocks he could sell to raise the funds. He had even thought about asking Erik Majors, the most successful of his friends, for the money. But Erik previously told his friends how he had to take out an equity line on his house to pay for some unexpected hospital bills for his mother. There was no way he could ask Erik for help after that. Even with all the strings that would be attached to it, Betty Woodson was the only way for him to get the money, and he wanted to get it that night so he wouldn't have to come back to that house ever again.

In the back of the kitchen up against the windows overlooking the back yard and swimming pool were several sofas and chairs arranged into a U-shaped sitting area. This spot offered a secluded place to escape the congestion of the party, as well as watch the precise movements of the synchronized kitchen staff. Michael and Beth entered the kitchen to see how large it was and check out the operation of the staff during an event like this, and the familiar voice of John McDonald called out from the sitting area.

"Hey, it's Michael and Beth! Come join the party!" John yelled over the clanging of pots and pans in the kitchen.

The reverend and his wife both looked over in the direction of the voice and saw John McDonald, Erik Majors, and Dr. Dan Lee sitting on the sofas with their wives. Michael and Beth carefully weaved their way through the kitchen workers to meet up with their friends. Mrs. McDonald was a medium-height brunette with a black, long-sleeve gown. Mrs. Majors was a tall, thin blond dressed in a white, short, formal dress with gold accents that complimented her athletic figure. Mrs. Lee was Korean, just like her husband, and had black, shoulder-length hair and a dark-blue sequined dress. John and Ben wore black tuxedos with dark-patterned ties and vests, while Erik matched his wife by wearing a white dinner jacket with a gold-accented tie and vest. All three seated men stood up when the reverend and his wife approached the sitting area.

"You guys have the right idea," Michael told the group as he and his wife sat down in two empty spaces on one of the sofas and the three other men sat back down in their spots.

"All parties end up in the kitchen eventually," said Beth.

"This party is out of control," said Mrs. McDonald. "We couldn't take any more people bumping into and pushing us. This place was the only safe haven we could find."

"And I'm about ready to smack the next one of those minstrel singers I see," said Erik.

"Calm down there, buddy. How many of those have you had?" asked Dan, pointing at Erik's empty drinking glass.

"Not nearly enough," Erik responded.

Erik motioned to one of the kitchen staff, a young female worker in a white commercial catering uniform. She rushed right over.

"Would you be so kind as to go to the nearest bar and get me a bourbon and water with just a couple cubes of ice?" Erik persuaded her while handing her his empty glass. "Thank you so much."

She grabbed the glass and rushed out of the kitchen and toward the main living room.

Mrs. Lee said, "So Beth, we've been talking about doing a girls' trip this spring. The guys have their special little guys' weekend in the summer, so we need to have some fun too. When is your spring break this year?"

Beth responded, "It's the first week in April, but we've got a church trip to Israel that Michael and I are chaperoning. Maybe we could do something in May?"

Mrs. Majors interjected, "Just not in early May. We're going to the derby, and then Erik's got some bourbon tour of Kentucky he's dragging me to."

"Why are you going all the way to Kentucky for bourbon?" asked John. "We've got plenty of it right here in Richmond."

They all raised their drinks in the air, clinked their glasses, and laughed heartily in unison.

"So, Israel," commented Mrs. Lee. "I've always wanted to go there and see the religious sites."

"I'd invite you to join us," replied Beth. "But it will be a group of lower and middle schoolers. Probably not what you had in mind."

Mrs. Lee smiled and shook her head no.

Beth continued, "But it'll still be fun. We're going all over, to Jerusalem, Bethlehem, Nazareth, Galilee."

Michael added, "Neither of us has ever been over there. It will be nice to see all those places in person that I've studied and read and talked about."

"Why are you going all the way to Israel for Jesus when we've got him right here?" Erik joked while pointing out the kitchen window toward the huge nativity scene in the yard.

They all laughed again together at the sheer ridiculousness of their surroundings.

Michael anxiously glanced down at his watch again and realized how much more time had gone by since the last time he checked. He was just about to excuse himself from his friends and wife to go find Betty when he heard a familiar voice call out from across the kitchen.

"Lawdy, lawdy, lawdy!" Betty Woodson exclaimed to the group sitting on the sofas in her kitchen.

She carefully pranced over to them, trying not to fall in her high heels after having a few too many cosmopolitans and glasses of champagne over the course of the evening. The four men stood up from their seats to greet the hostess.

"Well, isn't this a rowdy-looking crew?" she facetiously commented in a tipsy slur. "Why are you all in here? The party's out there."

"We were just taking a break from all the festivities," responded the reverend.

Betty continued, "I guess what they say is true. All parties end up in the kitchen eventually."

Everyone on the sofas turned toward Beth and gave her an approving smile of acknowledgement.

"Thank you so much for inviting us all to your beautiful home," Mrs. Lee said. "It's such a wonderful way to enjoy the Christmas season together."

"Why, thank you, darling. I'm so glad you all could come."

Betty then raised her hands to just below each armpit and wrestled the top of her formal strapless dress upward a couple inches.

"These dresses are made for show, not comfort. Right, girls?" she commented.

The group didn't know how to respond, so they just sat there dumbfounded and nodded in agreement.

The reverend broke the awkwardness and asked Betty, "Do you have a minute? I need to talk to you about Richard's announcement tonight."

Noticing the serious and tense look on his face, Betty

replied, "Of course, Reverend."

"Pardon me, everyone," he said as he excused himself from the group.

"Just stay here with them," Michael leaned over and whispered directly to his wife, resting his hand on her shoulder, trying to keep her at ease. "I'll be right back."

Erik and John sat back down in their seats, but Dan looked at Michael with an expression that silently said, "Do you know what you're doing?"

The reverend looked back at Dan with a smirk that implied, "It's OK. I'm not that stupid. Trust me."

Betty and Michael made it about three steps outside the kitchen and into a side hallway before she turned around and asked, "What is it you really want to talk to me about? I know it's not about Richard and his big announcement."

Michael looked around to make sure no one was nearby to hear their conversation and answered, "Is there somewhere private we can go?"

"Oh, Michael, as much as I'm flattered, isn't that a little bold, especially with all these people in the house?"

"I'm serious, Betty. It's important."

She was slightly sobered by his change in temperament and said, "What is all this about? Just tell me, and I'll do whatever I can to help."

The reverend paused for a moment and confirmed again that no one was around to hear them.

"I hate to do this. And believe me, I wouldn't if I didn't absolutely have to."

"Spit it out, Michael."

"I need to borrow some money."

"OK, that's not a problem. If there's one thing I have plenty of, it's money. Let's go upstairs to my bedroom."

"I'm not playing around here. I'm not going up there to…"

Before he could go any further, Betty cut him off and interjected, "Calm down. My checkbook is upstairs in my bedroom. If you want the money, that's where it is."

"Sorry. Fine. Let's go then."

They headed down the hallway off the kitchen away from the party and toward a back set of stairs that led to the second floor. They climbed the stairs together, walked down a short hallway, made a left turn down a longer main hallway, passed a few closed doors, and finally reached Betty's bedroom, which they entered, closing the door behind them.

"Hold on a second," she told him, tipsily making her way toward her enormous walk-in closet. "I've just got to change this damn strapless bra. It's pinching the hell out of me."

He walked over to the panoramic window and looked out at the dark horizon in the distance. There were many more points of light shining now compared to the last time he had been there a few days earlier.

She went into her closet and called out to him from around the corner, "I'm glad you felt you could come to me for help. That's means a lot to me. So what is this all about?"

"I owe someone a lot of money. Well, it's a lot to me, but it's probably not much at all to you."

"Michael, if you're going to ask someone for help, you shouldn't insult them. I'm not some ditzy bimbo who doesn't know the value of money. You forget, I didn't grow up with all this. Richard did."

"You're right. You're right. I'm sorry."

Betty finished changing her bra, came out of the closet, walked over to her desk by the window, opened the center drawer, pulled out her Louis Vuitton-covered checkbook, sat down in the chair, and opened a pen sitting on top of the desk. He noticed that the top of her dress wasn't zipped up all the way in the back.

"How much do you need?" she asked as she began to fill in the name, date, and signature lines on the check.

"Seventeen thousand," he replied while his face flushed red with embarrassment and self-hatred.

His left hand started to tremble again, so he put it inside his front pants pocket so she wouldn't see.

"Why do you owe someone this much money? Is it the coke?"

He didn't want to tell her the real reason, but he felt like he had to tell her if he was going to get the money.

"It's for a bookie. I've been betting on football games, and obviously I've been losing."

She finished writing the check, folded it in half, put the checkbook away, closed the drawer, and clumsily stood up out of the chair. She held the check out to give it to the reverend but then pulled it away right as he was getting ready to grab it.

"If I give you this money, are you going to stop gambling for good?" she asked.

"Yes. Actually, I've already quit. That's why he's demanding the money I owe him now."

"OK, one last question. Will you promise you won't try to repay me this money? I want you to move on from your gambling problem without worrying about having to pay me back. Is that a deal?"

"Betty, I'm not asking for a handout. I'm going to pay you back. I promise."

"I know that's what you intended to do. And I believe you would have paid me back eventually. But I don't want you to. Listen. The interest alone on this account has probably added up to more than 17,000 dollars just in the time since we left the kitchen. I don't want you worrying for months or even years about how you're going to save enough money to pay me back. That's how I feel about it, and that's all there is to it. So, do you want the money or not?"

She held the check closely to her chest, waiting for his answer. He knew he wouldn't be able to change her mind, so he agreed to her demands.

"Alright, Betty. You win. Thank you for this. I won't ever forget it."

She handed him the folded check and gave him a tight hug just under his arms with her head gently buried into his chest. He hugged her above her shoulders and around her neck, still holding the check tightly in his right hand. After a few seconds, he let go of her and pulled away to end the hug. A couple more seconds later, she finally unwrapped her arms from around his chest. Invigorated and ready for more festivities, she spun around and stumbled toward the bedroom door to rejoin the party.

After having followed her for a few steps across her palatial bedroom, he unfolded the check to make sure everything was filled in correctly. Immediately his eyes were drawn to the box next to the dollar sign where the numerical amount was written. It read, "50,000." Next he looked at the line where the amount was written out in words, and it read, "Fifty thousand and 00/100 dollars."

He exclaimed, "Wait a second. Betty, this is for fifty thousand dollars. Not seventeen thousand."

"Oh, is it really?" she replied mischievously.

"This is too much. I can't accept it. Come back over here and write another check."

"Don't worry about it, Michael. I'm sure you can put the rest of it to good use somehow. Just don't gamble with it. Remember? You promised."

"Yes, but…"

"Jeez, you worry too much. Just chill out. Relax. The check's already made out, and I don't feel like walking all the way back over to that desk in these heels to write another one. So you can either take it or leave it. It's up to you."

He reluctantly folded the check, slid it into the inside pocket of his tuxedo jacket, and followed her out of the bedroom. After following her halfway down the hallway, he noticed again that the zipper on the back of her dress was down a few inches.

"Hold on a second," he said while grabbing her shoulder to stop her. "You can't go down there like this."

He pulled the zipper all the way up and carefully hooked the fastener at the top of the zipper.

"Thank you, dear. Once it's off, this dress is just impossible to get back on properly."

"There you go. You're all zipped up and ready for more. You look as good as new."

"I'm glad we took that little break. Now I'm ready to crush

the rest of this party."

They continued down the hallway, turned right at the end, and took the back staircase down to the first floor. In the center of the main hallway on the second floor, only a few feet away from where Michael had just zipped up Betty's dress, a previously closed door opened slowly to reveal a man standing in the room just inside the doorway. It was Richard Woodson.

Richard had gone back to his bedroom to get his notes for his big announcement. But when he was getting ready to leave his bedroom to go back to his party, he heard two familiar voices out in the hallway, so he held off until they were gone to come out. While he waited behind the closed bedroom door, he clearly heard every word of his wife's chat in the hallway with the reverend, including the buzz of the zipper on her dress while it was being closed.

"That defiant little whore!" he thought to himself. "I knew she couldn't keep her promise. And here she goes having sex with that damn preacher in my own house during my Christmas party. Well, if she wants to play that game, I can play it too. Only I'm much better at it."

10 ONE JOURNEY ENDS

Betty and Michael entered the kitchen from the back hallway, he thanked her again for helping him out, and she left to go see the rest of her guests, beginning in the main living room. He saw his wife on the opposite side of the kitchen and started walking toward her when he was intercepted by the rector.

"There you are, Michael" the rector remarked. "I've been looking all over for you."

"Well, here I am. What's going on?"

"I need you to join me and the rest of the clergy who are here tonight for a few minutes. Mr. Woodson is getting ready to make a big announcement to everyone, and it's very important to all of us at St. Andrew's. We're going to have to say a few words afterward, so we need to make a plan first."

"Sure. Let's go then."

The two priests left the kitchen, weaved their way through multitudes of drunken guests, and headed toward a small, secluded sitting room at the other end of the first floor.

Beth was still engaged in conversation with her friends on the sofas in the sitting area, unaware her husband had come back to the kitchen or that the rector had commandeered him. In mid-sentence, she felt a gentle tap on her shoulder that stopped her from continuing the discussion with Mrs. Lee about their favorite restaurants in the Fan section of Richmond.

"Mrs. Thomas, I'm so sorry to interrupt," said Manuel, one of the head staff members at Greenlock. "Mr. Woodson has asked if you would please join him for just a few minutes. He says it's very important."

Beth looked over at her friends with an expression of surprise and indecision. She hesitated for a moment until Manuel motioned for her to follow him.

"Please, Mrs. Thomas. He's this way."

She stood up from her seat on the sofa, grabbed her clutch purse off the table, and half-jokingly said to her friends, "I'm not sure what this is all about, but if I'm not back in five minutes, call the authorities."

Erik fired back, "Don't worry, Beth. He won't do anything here. Too many witnesses."

The rest of the group laughed at his comment, leading Erik to let out a loud belly laugh himself.

Beth turned around and followed Manuel out of the kitchen and down a private side hallway leading to the back, eastern corner of the first floor, secluded from any wandering guests or noise from the party. They came to a closed door at the end of the hall, on which Manuel gently knocked three times.

A voice from inside, recognizable to Beth as belonging to Richard Woodson, replied, "Come in."

Manuel opened the door; Beth tentatively walked inside a large, wood-paneled, private office; and the door closed behind her with Manuel staying outside in the hallway. Richard was standing in front of a dark-green marble wet bar, pouring himself a glass of port from a square, crystal decanter.

"Would you like a glass of tawny port, Mrs. Thomas?" he offered.

"No thank you. I'll wait until communion tomorrow."

"Very funny," he said with a chuckle. "Please, have a seat," he continued, gesturing to two low-backed, quilted red leather chairs in front of an enormous wooden, intricately carved desk.

She sat down in one of the chairs, and Richard walked around to the other side of the desk and sat down in a tall-backed desk chair that was made of the same quilted red leather. She visually scanned the entire room. Dark-brown mahogany paneling lined all four walls from floor to ceiling. Green, red, and blue plaid carpet covered every square inch of flooring. Wooden beams crisscrossed the plaster ceiling to form a latticework of brown and white. A wide, panoramic window that would have offered a beautiful, expansive view of the river in the daytime was now shrouded mostly in black with just tiny flickers of light in the distance. The fireplace was stoked with a gently rolling fire made from real burning and popping wood, not natural gas. A massive, mounted elk head hung on the wall just behind and above Richard's chair. Beth winced at how real and creepy the dead animal looked, especially its black, glass eyes.

"So, Mr. Woodson, does this have anything to do with the big announcement you're going to make tonight?"

"Please, call me Richard. And in a way, yes it does."

He leaned forward in his chair, set his glass of port down on a crystal coaster, and rested his arms on top of the desk. She instinctively leaned back slightly in her chair to be farther away from him.

"It seems you and I have a mutual concern," he continued. "Once I knew for sure the facts of the situation, I felt the decent thing to do was to let you know what is going on."

"What in the world are you talking about?"

"There's no easy way to say this, so I'll just be blunt. My wife and your husband are having an affair."

Beth sat in stunned silence.

"I suspected Betty was being unfaithful to me for quite some time now. So a few months ago I hired a private investigator to follow her. And he confirmed what I had feared all along."

Finally shaking herself out of a dazed stupor, she jumped up out of the chair and shot back at him, "I don't know what kind of sick, twisted trick you're trying to pull here, but I'm not going to listen to any more of this. I know my husband, and he would never do anything like that."

She spun around defiantly and stormed away toward the door.

"I have proof," he said as he pulled an iPad out of the desk drawer.

She stopped dead in her tracks.

As much as she didn't want to believe him, she had a sickening feeling deep down in the pit of her stomach that maybe there was a slight chance what he was saying was true. Beth had noticed some odd and peculiar behavior from Michael recently. He would act nervous whenever both she and Betty were around at the same time. Occasionally when she did the laundry, she smelled a lot more cologne than normal on some of his shirts, almost like he was trying to cover up another scent. And he seemed to be unusually distant from her emotionally, not kissing her as often or being as intimate with her as before. But more concerning than anything else, Beth had a gut feeling that something was wrong with Michael, and she hadn't been able to put her finger on exactly what it was.

"What kind of proof?" she asked sharply with her back still facing him.

"Come over, and I'll show you."

The last thing she wanted to see was a photo of her husband in bed with another woman. But as hard as she tried to fight it, she couldn't help but give in to the temptation of knowing the truth. So she turned around and reluctantly dragged herself back to the chair she had been sitting in.

Richard held the iPad up so she could see the screen clearly and tapped one of the icons. A window opened and began playing a video file. Beth leaned forward against the desk and watched a green Jaguar convertible coming into frame with Michael driving and Betty as the passenger. The car slowly pulled up to the front door of Greenlock and stopped. After a few seconds, Michael leaned over and hugged and kissed Betty passionately. The video then cut to a zoom closeup of Betty walking in the front door of the house with Michael patting and squeezing her rear end.

"That's enough!" she cried out, turning her head away in disgust.

"Nice car, right? Betty was very generous to buy that for your husband."

Richard put the iPad facedown on the desk and said, "I'll spare you the details, but I also have proof that my wife and your husband have been intimate together here in this very house. In fact, do you know where your husband was about 15 minutes ago?"

"He said he had to speak with your wife about your announcement."

"That's interesting. Because she has no idea what I'm announcing tonight. I hate to tell you this, but I was just upstairs, and I heard them coming out of her bedroom together. You can figure out the rest."

Beth's eyes began to fill with tears.

She pulled out a tissue from her clutch purse, dabbed her eyes, and uttered to him between sobs, "I don't want to hear any more about this."

"Fine. I understand. It's very upsetting news. I'm sure you're in shock now. But I've had a little while to take it all in and digest it. And I've come up with a solution to this problem that I'm sure you'll agree will help both of us."

She turned back around, looked at him through teary eyes, and asked nervously, "What are you planning to do?"

"Tonight I'm announcing a large donation from the Woodson Foundation to St. Andrew's. Some of the money will be used to establish a scholarship program for worthy children in the church. We're also going to build a whole new administrative building. It'll be much larger and nicer than what's there now. They'll even have space for more Sunday school classes, choir and music rooms, and day care and preschool. St. Andrew's will become one of the best churches in the entire state. No expense will be spared."

Beth could read between the lines and knew exactly what

this meant for her husband.

Richard continued, "But since this will be such an important project for both St. Andrew's and my foundation, I plan on getting more personally involved with the ongoing operations and management of the church."

"Is Michael going to be fired?" Beth asked bluntly.

"That's entirely up to him. If he does the right things to uphold the Christian values of the church, then he has a long, bright future ahead of him. Who knows? He may even become the next rector. But we can't have a priest representing us who conducts in illicit and immoral acts."

Beth sat up straight in her chair, pulled herself together, and put the used tissue away in her purse.

"Your wife isn't exactly an innocent bystander in all this. I've heard the stories. This isn't the first time she's cheated on you."

"That's true. She hasn't been particularly discreet with her past dalliances. And we may not have the perfect relationship. I have my fun, and she has hers. Until now, we've made it work. But this time, it's different. I believe she cares for your husband very deeply. I think she may actually love him. And I can't have that."

The reverend's wife pushed herself up from the chair defiantly, collected herself in an effort to get ready to leave, and told him, "Listen clearly. I'll handle my husband and my marriage. You do whatever you think you need to do. But don't you dare mess with my life or my husband's career."

"Of course not. I'm merely buying insurance that he'll do the right thing."

"Don't ever speak to me about this again."

Beth resolutely spun around and marched out of the private office, down the hallway, and into a small guest bathroom just outside the kitchen. Her reflection in the mirror showed streaky mascara and smudged makeup. She grabbed some tissues from a silver box on a glass shelf and tried to clean herself up as best as possible.

Then she took a deep breath, looked in the mirror, and told

herself, "You can handle this. You've been through tough times before. God will give you the strength you need."

Just as she opened the door to leave the bathroom, she heard a booming voice echoing throughout the entire house. A deep male voice on the internal speaker system was directing all the guests to convene in the main living room for a special announcement by their host, Richard Woodson. She saw Mrs. Lee farther up the hallway and fought her way through the jostling crowd to reach her.

"Can you give me a ride home?" Beth asked her friend. "I don't feel very well."

"We didn't drive. Dan and I rode here with the Majors. Don't worry though. Erik needs to stay to hear Mr. Woodson's announcement. But right after that, we'll leave."

Mrs. Lee paused for a second and then asked, "Where's Michael? Can't you get him to take you home now?"

"No. It's a long story. Don't worry about it. It's fine. We can go then."

The two women were carried along in a wave of people until they rounded the corner into the main living room. Hundreds of guests were packed into the room, all of them facing toward a group of five people standing in front of the giant Christmas tree. Richard Woodson stood on the far left, and to his right were Betty Woodson, the rector, and then finally Michael. After the two piano players and the four Victorian singers and the various traveling musicians and all the guests finally settled down to a soft murmur, Richard Woodson began speaking into a microphone that sent his voice booming throughout the house via the internal speaker system.

"Hello everyone. Betty and I would like to thank you all again for coming to our home to celebrate the most wonderful time of the year, Christmas."

The crowded guests altogether let out a polite cheer of "Merry Christmas!"

The host continued, "We're also glad you could be here with us so we can tell you about something very special that's going to happen for our friends at St. Andrew's. Ever since I was a young boy, I've been lucky enough to call St. Andrew's my home church. I think they also do great things for our community, including offering important programs for the homeless, for people who need help feeding their families, and for those who have lost their way in life."

By moving his eyes only and keeping his head still, Michael covertly glanced over at the rector standing directly next to him and noticed a subtle yet perceptible smile start to form on his boss' face. If the rector was happy, Michael assumed this was going to be a very positive announcement.

The reverend then looked over at Betty's face. Her expression was blank and empty with just a small, polite smile emanating from her mouth. Michael knew her well enough to realize she had no idea what her husband was getting ready to say.

"So in the spirit of giving," Richard proclaimed, "the Woodson Foundation is proud to announce our gift to St. Andrew's in the sum of twenty million dollars to help the church build a new administrative building and to also create the Woodson scholarship program for deserving students."

The guests all clapped loudly in unison and cheered the host for such a charitable and generous act. Mrs. Woodson clapped politely with a stunned expression at first followed by a forced smile of pride. The rector's smile grew even larger.

"Thank you all very much," Richard told the crowd while trying to hush their cheers. "I've only got a little bit more to say, so please let me finish up so we can get back to enjoying the party.

"While I haven't spent as much time lately in church as I should have, I do look forward to working closely with the good rector here and his staff and clergy over the coming months and for many years to follow. Together, we're all going to make St. Andrew's the best church in the Commonwealth of Virginia."

Once again, the crowd erupted into cheers and whistles of approval. With a dumbfounded expression of shock and concern, the reverend looked over at Betty. She stared back at him with wide eyes and a frozen expression that looked as if every facial muscle had been injected with Botox. They both knew what this meant for each of them, and they couldn't have been more surprised if they had been sucker-punched in the gut by Santa Claus himself.

After coming out of her temporary state of shock, Betty turned to her husband and under her breath sharply asked, "What the hell are you doing?"

Richard smirked and replied to her out of the side of his mouth, "I'm just trying to make the world a better place, dear."

Michael turned back around toward the crowd to see if he could find his wife. After a few seconds of scanning hundreds of guests, he finally spotted her in the back of the room. Beth was looking directly at him. The moment their eyes met, the defensive wall she had tried to build up since her conversation with Richard came tumbling down, and her emotions poured out. She burst into tears and immediately ran out of the room and toward the front door.

The reverend instantly began to push his way through throngs of partiers toward a nearby doorway. Once he made it out of the living room, he darted down the hallway until he slid to a stop in the entry foyer. He desperately looked in every direction. Beth was nowhere to be found. Thinking she must have already made it outside, he opened the front door and saw her rushing away from the house.

"Beth!" he shouted out to her. "Wait!"

She ignored his calls and kept walking as quickly as she could over the uneven cobblestones toward the parking valet stand on the other side of the courtyard.

"I need my car, please!" she barked out at the valet attendant in between sniffles and sobs.

"Do you have your ticket, ma'am?" the attendant responded, uncomfortable and unprepared to deal with a crying woman.

"No, I don't have my damn ticket! It's the blue Volvo wagon. And I need it now!"

The attendant opened a hanging metal box and quickly scoured the vertical rows of high-tech, luxury car fobs until he found the plain metal Volvo key. He grabbed the key off the rack and took off sprinting down the driveway toward the darkness. Slowing down and stopping from a careful jog across the cobblestones, Michael arrived next to his wife and put his hand on her shoulder to turn her around to face him.

"Beth, what's wrong? Why did you leave the party like that? Are you feeling sick?"

"Leave me alone!" she barked back as she pulled her shoulder out of his grasp and turned her back to him.

Realizing how upset she really was, he put both his hands in the air in a gesture of surrender and said, "Alright, alright, I get it. You're obviously mad about something."

She rifled through her purse looking for another tissue. He pulled his handkerchief out of his back pocket and handed it over her shoulder to her. She snatched it from him and began to dab her eyes and nose with it.

"Come on, Beth. Can't we discuss this?"

"Not here. Not now."

She realized she wasn't in the proper state of mind to be driving, so she accepted the fact and told him, "Just take me home."

They both waited in silence for what seemed like an eternity until the familiar boxy shape of their car appeared out of the darkness. Michael opened the passenger door for his wife, closed it after she got in, walked around to the driver's side, tipped the unfortunate valet, received a look of condolence from the attendant, settled in behind the wheel, and sped away. It was several minutes and over two miles down Cary Street before Michael had the nerve to say anything.

"Honey, I really have no idea what's going on here. If we could just talk about it, I'm sure we can work things out, whatever it is."

A few more blocks went by until Beth responded. Her sniffles and tears had now subsided to a point where she could speak clearly and directly.

"Michael, I know we've been through a lot in the time we've been married. It certainly hasn't been easy. But I need you to be perfectly honest with me."

"Alright."

"Tonight at the party, when you said you went to speak with Betty about the announcement her husband was going to make, is that what you really did?"

"Where is this coming from?"

"Just answer the question? Did you talk to her about the announcement?"

Michael hesitated for a moment but quickly realized he had to be totally honest with her. Considering the frame of mind she was in, he felt his marriage depended on it.

"No, I didn't. I talked to her about borrowing some money."

"Money? What for?"

"I owe someone some money, and Betty was my only option."

"Why didn't you come to me about this?"

"Because I was ashamed. And we don't have enough."

"How much are we talking about?"

"Seventeen thousand."

"Seventeen thousand?" she repeated, stunned and shocked. "What have you done, Michael?"

"Over the past couple years, I've been betting on football, and obviously I've been losing. So last week I finally decided I wasn't going to bet anymore. I'm done. I mean it. I'm out. But when I told that to the guy who takes the bets, he called in my marker. That means I have to pay him all the money I owe by next week. And the only way I thought I could get that kind of money right away was from Betty."

"Did she give it to you?"

"Uh-huh."

"OK, alright. We'll deal with the gambling and the money stuff later. But right now there's something else I need to know. Please tell me the truth here. Did you have sex with Betty tonight up in her room when you asked her for that money?"

"Of course not!" he asserted strongly. "Are you kidding me? Why would you think such a thing?"

"That damn Richard Woodson. I knew I shouldn't have believed a word he said."

"What do you mean? What did he tell you?"

"When you were upstairs with her, he told me you two had sex together."

"I can't believe that guy! What is wrong with him? Beth, I swear to you, Richard is lying. What he told you was a straight-up lie."

The blue Volvo made a right turn off Cary Street at the country club and continued down a two-lane road called Three Chopt Road. Coming up on the right in a few blocks was St. Andrew's, which they would pass on their way home.

"But Michael, there's more. He suspected Betty was cheating on him, so he hired a private investigator to follow her around. He showed me a video of you two kissing."

Beth's strong façade weakened, and her eyes started to tear up again. Michael could here the sadness in her sniffles and sobs but couldn't bear to look at her. And just then, he remembered the dark grey Volkswagen Passat he thought had been following him. It all made sense now. He hadn't been imagining things. Someone was watching him after all.

He tried to figure out when the video could have been taken, and suddenly he flashed back to when he kissed Betty while sitting in the Jaguar convertible in her driveway. He knew this was going to be a very serious and crucial discussion, and he didn't want to have it while he was driving.

"Look, Beth. Betty's marriage has been on the rocks for years. Her husband cheats on her all the time, and everyone knows it. She just looks for attention to help fill the void in her life. It's really complicated. Let's please just talk about this when we get home. OK?"

"I believe you didn't sleep with her tonight in her bedroom during the party. But have you slept with her before? I mean, ever before?"

"Oh come on, Beth! That's ridiculous. I don't want to talk about this anymore until we get home."

"Answer the damn question, Michael!"

The reverend thought to himself and considered his options. He could lie and buy more time. He could tell her the truth now. Or he could try to stall her a little longer until they got home. He instinctively decided to try to hold her off so they could finish the conversation at home.

He replied, "Kissing her was a big mistake. Obviously, I admit that. And I promise you it won't ever happen again."

Michael turned to look at her to finish his thought and said, "Beth, I love you. And that won't ever change. No matter what I…"

At that moment, he froze. He couldn't look her in the face and keep talking around the truth. He didn't know what else to say.

She saw the expression of guilt and shame on his face, and the truth hit her like a freight train. She turned away from him in disgust, gazed out the passenger window toward the sky, and found herself looking directly at the steeple of the chapel of St. Andrew's.

She started to cry again and mumbled softly, "God, please help us."

The reverend wanted to reach over and hug her and tell her everything was going to work out. But he couldn't. Instead, all he could do was watch her shoulders shake from the convulsions of her crying.

He turned back to check the road ahead and was immediately blinded by two headlights heading directly at him.

"No!" he yelled out in desperation.

"Michael!" his wife screamed in panic.

Time slowed down for him, and the next couple seconds seemed to elapse in slow motion. The two lights were directly in front of him in his lane, so he didn't have enough time or room to swerve his car left into possible oncoming traffic or right into trees and a ditch. Just as the other car was about to hit the Volvo head-on, Michael dove to his right and laid himself out in front of his wife. Then everything went dark.

Beth awoke to the loud scraping sound of her passenger door being forcefully pried open by a fireman. The crystalline pings of bits of shattered glass hitting the pavement sounded like a hailstorm pelting a concrete bridge. Her fuzzy vision could barely make out the red flashing lights of the fire trucks and ambulances parked all around the crushed Volvo.

She could feel her legs fine, but her thighs were being squeezed against her seat by the bottom of the dashboard. She wasn't able to lift them up or turn her body and get out of the car.

"Ma'am, you've been in an accident," the fireman yelled to her above the noise of the rescue vehicles. "We're going to get you out now. So just sit still, and we'll handle the rest. Everything's going to be OK."

Shaking from the shock of the collision, she slowly and carefully turned her sore neck to look around the area of the front two seats of the mangled car. She saw the twisted remains of the dashboard with two deployed airbags deflated and hanging limp, a completely shattered windshield, and the crumpled metal hood now shaped like an accordion that hid the other car from her point-of-view. A tiny pool of partially coagulated blood had collected in her lap, but she didn't feel the pain of any cuts on her bruised body. That's when she realized her husband wasn't there.

"Where's my husband?" she shouted out to the fireman.

"He's on his way to the hospital. He's stable, but that's all I know right now about his condition. Please, try to relax, and we'll get you out of here."

She sat completely still in the remains of the Volvo, waiting for the rescuers to free her. The overwhelming emotion of both the evening and the accident flooded over her as if someone had dumped a bucket of cold, murky, gloomy water on her head. Tears poured from her eyes and down her cheeks, and she began to wail.

11 ANOTHER JOURNEY BEGINS

Cool, moist wild grass brushed gently across his face and gently roused Michael from his sleep. He awoke slowly at first, taking a little time for him to focus on the dimly lit weeds and blades of grass directly in front of his eyes. Then suddenly remembering he was just in an accident, he abruptly pushed himself up with his arms so that he was sitting upright on the ground.

"Beth!" he shouted out to the darkness just beyond his immediate range of sight. "Beth! Are you there?"

There was no response. He jumped all the way up on his feet and called out for his wife a couple more times.

"Beth! Beth! Can you hear me?"

Still nothing.

With a little time having passed since he had woken up, his eyes started to adjust to the darkness. He could make out the faint, dark shapes of trees and bushes about fifty yards away. He turned around and saw the jagged outline of a rocky ridgeline rising up toward the sky and beginning no more than thirty yards directly ahead of him. Following the rough terrain of the hill with his eyes skyward, his gaze eventually reached the faintly backlit glow behind a large, puffy, dark cloud. Moments later, the trailing edge of the cloud passed by and revealed a full, bright, glowing Moon.

He made sure to look closely at the clearly lit surface of the Moon to confirm that it was, in fact, the Earth's Moon. He recognized the Sea of Tranquility, the Sea of Serenity, and even the Copernicus crater. So he knew he hadn't been kidnapped by aliens and taken away to a distant planet. But what he didn't know was where he actually was.

The sharpness of the Moon and its geography shocked him. He hadn't seen it this clearly in years. He reached up to check his glasses to see if they were different somehow, but they weren't on his face.

"How can I see so well without my glasses?" he wondered.

Next, he looked down to see if his glasses had fallen on the ground, but before he had the chance to search the grass for his glasses, he realized he didn't have on his tuxedo. Instead, much to his surprise, he was wearing a coarse, cotton, long-sleeved robe, light brown in color, with a simple, narrow, brown-leather belt tied in a knot and cinched around his waist. He untied the belt, opened up the robe, and underneath saw a tan, linen, short-sleeved, seamless tunic that covered him all the way to just above his feet.

On his feet were brown sandals made of thin leather with a sole that seemed extremely flimsy compared to the flip-flops he used to wear on vacation to the beach. Because he didn't know if anyone else was around, instead of lifting up the tunic to see what he was wearing as underwear, he took his hands and felt his sides through the cloth. By the feel of it, he guessed he was wearing some type of cotton undergarment that was wrapped around his waist and between his legs. It was comfortable and didn't bind him, so he left it alone.

After closing his robe and tying the belt tightly around his waist, he touched his arms, shoulders, chest, legs, and face to check if anything hurt. He felt completely normal. Actually, he felt better than normal. He was full of energy, he didn't feel any aches or pains, his eyesight was sharp, and his bad left knee from an old sports injury didn't hurt at all.

"How is this possible?" he thought to himself. "The last

thing I remember is seeing the headlights of a car coming right at me. There's no way I didn't hit it. It was too close to miss. So how could I have been in a head-on car accident and then wake up fine like nothing happened at all? And where in the world am I, anyway?"

It didn't take him long to come up with a theory for his situation.

"Oh my God!" he continued thinking to himself. "I must have been killed in that accident. I must be dead!"

The largest goose bumps he'd ever felt shot up his arms, neck, and face. His legs instantly lost their strength, sending him tumbling to the grass-covered ground.

"But I don't understand," he thought. "This doesn't feel like heaven, or at least not what I thought it would feel like. There was no bright light leading me here. Oh no! I hope it is heaven and not the other place!"

He sat up and looked all around at his surroundings, now able to see more because of the bright moonlight. The ridgeline in front of him and the trees and bushes behind him were all much clearer. He was also able to make out a narrow, ten-foot-wide pathway just a few feet away between himself and the base of the rocky hill. The path was just a small dirt road that looked like it had been created from years of traffic wearing away the grass.

His legs gathered their strength back, and he stood back up and took a few steps out of the long grass and over to the dirt path. Looking to his right, he saw the path rising upward as it wrapped around the hill and out of view. Turning to his left, the path appeared to go downhill slightly and straight, with the side of the rocky hill to the right and fields of wild grass and bushes off the left side of the path. For some reason he sensed but couldn't explain, going to the left felt like the better way to go, so he started following the path in that direction, hoping the answers to his questions lie somewhere ahead.

The twin doors of the elevator opened slowly, and Beth Thomas was rolled out in a wheelchair by a nurse onto the fourth floor of St. Mary's hospital. She sat silently in the chair as she was pushed down the hallway, past the nurses' station, and into the Intensive Care Unit. Once they reached room 414, the nurse walked around the chair and knocked softly on the closed door. Mrs. Thomas began to tremble slightly, nervous at what she might see inside the room.

The hospital room door was opened slowly from the inside by another nurse. After being rolled in and parked on the right side of the lone hospital bed in the room, Beth leaned over in her chair and, with both hands, held the hand of her husband, who was lying unconscious in the bed.

"Michael! Michael!" she pleaded as tears welled up in her eyes. "Please wake up! Wake up, Michael! Come back to me, please!"

A nurse inside the room gently placed a box of tissues on the tray table directly in front of Mrs. Thomas, who pulled one from the box and dabbed her eyes and nose. After her eyes were wiped dry and could see clearly, she looked over at her husband and saw three IV lines going into his right hand and arm. His left leg and left arm were both in casts, and his left shoulder was bandaged. His face was bruised black and blue with a few spots of red on his cheeks. An elastic bandage was wrapped around his forehead, and two pieces of white tape sealed his eyelids shut.

The windows to her right let in some of the winter sun's low-angled rays, which reflected off the metallic sculpture of Jesus Christ in the one-foot-tall crucifix hanging on the wall behind Michael. An EKG monitor beeped repeatedly and showed an electronic graph for his heart rhythm. The readout indicated a pulse of 54 beats per minute.

"Mrs. Thomas?" a deep, male voice inquired as it startled her from behind. "I'm Dr. Thurman."

Not being experienced in how to operate a wheelchair, she awkwardly spun around to face him and replied, "Hello."

Extremely thin and dynamic, Dr. Thurman had a receding hairline with twin patches of thinning, light brown hair desperately clinging to the sides of his head just above his ears.

Narrow, tortoise-shell-framed glasses surrounded his friendly green eyes and rested on a tall, thin, pointed nose.

"How are you feeling today?" he asked.

"I feel fine. And I really don't know why I need to stay in this wheelchair."

"Well, you were in a serious car accident, and you did lose consciousness. It's only for a little while longer, just as a precaution."

"But what about my husband? How is he?"

"Unfortunately, he suffered several injuries. His leg and arm were broken. His shoulder was dislocated. And his rotator cuff was torn. We operated on all those, and they should heal properly in time. I understand from the rescue squad that he was found next to you on the passenger's side of the car."

"It's a little hazy to me still, but I think I remember Michael diving over in front of me at the last second before we were hit."

"That's probably why you were spared of any serious injuries. He may have saved your life."

With tears flowing down her cheeks, she grabbed another tissue to wipe her eyes and nose and asked, "Why is he still unconscious? What are you not telling me?"

Dr. Thurman replied, "Since he was lying across you in the car when the accident occurred, he hit the front of his head on the bottom of the dashboard, probably underneath where the airbag was when it inflated. This blunt force to his head caused a frontal skull fracture and a hematoma, which is a blood clot in the brain. When the brain experiences trauma of this scale, usually it swells in size, thereby creating pressure inside the skull. It's called cerebral edema. And some of the time, edema can lead to the brain shutting itself down temporarily and going into a coma so it can repair itself. This is what has happened to your husband."

"A coma? Oh no! When is he going to wake up?" she asked nervously.

"That's still too early to know for sure. We've run some more tests, so when I get the results back from the lab, I'll be able to give you a prognosis. But most of the time, we can't accurately predict how long something like this will last. Everyone's different. In the meantime, I recommend you remain strong and speak to your husband. I've read a lot of research indicating that people in a coma can sometimes sense and even hear what is going on around them, at least to some minor degree. Any positive influence around your husband can only help him."

Beth wheeled herself back around to face her husband, leaned over, and put her cheek against Michael's hand. She began to pray for a miracle.

"Ow!" Michael exclaimed as he winced in pain from stepping on a sharp stone in the dirt path. His sandals offered hardly any protection from the rocky terrain. He veered over toward the left edge of the path, hoping there would be fewer rocks and more grass and softer conditions. Looking up at the sky directly ahead, the full moon was just to the right and hung in the air above the ridgeline of the steep hill. Even though he had never been in a place like this previously, something about the setting looked familiar. He was experiencing déjà vu, but he couldn't remember where he had seen these surroundings before.

Even with a completely full moon illuminating the sky, he could still clearly see more stars than he had ever seen in his life. When he was in college, he had gone skiing with some friends in the mountains of West Virginia and saw an entire sky full of stars because of the lack of nearby light pollution and the low humidity in the crisp, winter air. But this night's sky was even more packed with stars, reminiscent of deep-space backgrounds in science fiction films showing thousands of points of light.

All the regular constellations were visible. Ursa Major. Ursa Minor. Orion. Even the North Star. But they all seemed to be a little lower in the sky than normal.

As he walked farther down the path, he began to smell the pungent aroma of wildflowers. This smell reminded him of when he had visited his uncle in Phoenix as a kid. The desert flowers were unusual to him then, and the dry air allowed his nasal passages to open up and take in all the wonderfully new and beautiful scents of Arizona. With the rocky hill to his right and the smell of wildflowers all around, he figured he must be in some sort of desert environment.

"Considering the positions of the constellations and the North Star, I must be farther south than Virginia. Maybe I'm in the desert in Arizona, or even Mexico. But look at Orion. That's not where it was the other night. It must be later in the year. I think it's spring now. Somehow, I've gone farther south and forward in time a few months. But how is this possible?"

He decided to keep moving down the path. A slight chill permeated the dry night air, yet with a robe on, he felt warm and comfortable. He could move easily with such unrestrictive clothing, but his sandals continued to feel thin and flimsy. They weren't much better than walking barefoot.

Another odd aspect of this strange environment was how calm and quiet everything seemed to be. No loud exhausts from cars or trucks. No airplanes or helicopters in the air. No people talking or music playing. Not even the sound of wind blowing. The only sounds he heard were the sharp chirps of crickets and other insects hidden in the still, tall grass.

After he walked for what seemed like a mile or so, a grove of 40-foot-tall, bushy trees with thick, gnarled trunks appeared off the left side of the path. This group of trees continued down a gentle slope for a few hundred yards. As he drew closer, he could make out the faint glow of dozens of lights sprinkled throughout the trees, all about head height off the ground. A waist-high row of rough, prickly, untrimmed bushes ran parallel to the path, separating the trees from those traveling along the dirt road.

He had to continue walking down the road a few hundred yards past where the trees first started before he found an access pathway through the bushes and into the grove. He cautiously paused for a moment at the opening of the grove and then decided to see what was inside.

The trees were lined up in rows just like when he had gone apple picking with Beth a few years earlier in Maine. But these trees certainly weren't apple trees. He stepped closer to one of the low-hanging branches and saw small, light-green, oval spheres hanging from stems between the leaves. He plucked one of the spheres, smelled it, and rolled it between his fingers. He took a bite and instantly recognized its bitter flavor. These were olive trees, and he was standing in the middle of a large olive garden.

"I've been to Olive Garden many times for dinner," he joked to himself. "But this is the first time I've been to a real olive garden."

One of the glowing lights he had seen earlier from a distance could now be seen more clearly through layers of branches and leaves a few trees over, so he turned right on a side path to go parallel to the main dirt road and walked toward the light. Once he got within 50 yards of it, he could see that the light was coming from a dimly burning torch on top of a seven-foot-tall wooden pole. He kept going until he was standing right next to the torch. He was surprised to see that it didn't look like one of the cheap, metal tiki torches he had in his backyard. Instead, this one was made of wood with some material he couldn't identify wrapped like a serpent around the top that burned and fed the weakening flame. Just like his clothing, this torch was ancient in design and construction. In fact, nothing within eyesight or that he had seen since he had woken up was from the modern world.

Continuing his journey down the garden path, he passed several more torches, which helped illuminate the way. After ten more minutes of walking, he could see a grouping of five torches up ahead and to the left of the path. Once he got closer, he noticed several people lying motionless in the short grass.

There were eight bodies, all dressed in the same type of clothes as Michael, resting on the ground of an oval-shaped plot of land surrounded around the perimeter by olive trees. This secluded, inner garden was 40 yards wide and 70 yards long. The eight people were all huddled together near the front entrance of the inner garden next to the pathway Michael was walking on.

Michael approached the eight people carefully and quietly because he wasn't sure who they were or if they might try to hurt him. Once he entered the inner garden and was within 10 yards of them, he could tell they were all men. They all wore the same style of robe, just in different colors, and some even had stripes. He didn't see any guns or swords anywhere around, but he couldn't tell if they had weapons like knives or pistols hidden under their robes. Being careful not to startle them and unsure if they were armed, he quietly stepped through the short, uneven, patchy grass and tentatively approached the one nearest to him.

The man was lying on his side and faced toward Michael, so he could see his medium-length brown hair and a narrow brown beard that ended a couple inches past his chin. His robe was brown with two tan horizontal stripes running around the midsection. His eyes were closed, but he didn't appear to be dead. Then Michael heard the soft, faint sound of air vibrating out of his mouth. He was asleep, and he was snoring.

Michael put his hand on the man's shoulder and delicately shook him, hoping to wake him up. After a few seconds of being disturbed, the man grumbled some indistinguishable words and rolled over on the ground so he was facing away from Michael. None of the other seven men moved at all or even seemed to notice Michael's presence.

Since all these men were fast asleep, their snoring permeating the still quiet of the nighttime air, Michael didn't want to press his luck and make them angry, so he turned and walked down the length of the inner garden toward the back. He thought maybe there was another path at the other end that might lead him to some other people or anything that might help explain where he was.

He had guessed correctly because there was another pathway out of this inner garden. But right next to its entrance were three more men lying on the ground dressed in similar robes. Their snoring, particularly that coming from a man with bushy, black hair and a thick and long black beard, was even louder than the other men Michael had first encountered. Not one of them seemed even halfway awake, so he walked right by and followed the pathway for 30 yards through dense and dark foliage until it ended and opened up into a clearing of another inner garden hidden amongst the olive trees.

This new, second hidden garden was circular and about a third the size of the first one where all the men were sleeping. Olive trees lined the edges of the front half of the garden like a semicircle, but the back half was completely open and devoid of trees and appeared as though it ended at the edge of a cliff, similar to the effect of an infinity swimming pool.

Quickly growing frustrated, tired, and impatient, Michael walked toward the back of the garden to see if there was a way down past the infinity edge of the patches of dirt and grass. As soon as he passed the last olive tree on his right, a wide panoramic view opened up ahead, and a strange and surprising image was now clearly visible. Directly in front of him about 500 yards down the slope, across a deep ravine, and perched on top of a hill stood an ancient city surrounded by 60-foot-tall, stone walls.

The glowing lights of torches ran along the tops of the walls and elevated towers that anchored the corners. The city inside the walls was made up of hundreds of small buildings that extended off into the darkness. But one structure he could see rising above all the others was an enormous, white, rectangular plateau with walls that seemed to be higher in elevation than even the top of the exterior city walls and contained a large, square-shaped building standing in its center.

Michael couldn't believe what he was seeing with his own eyes. He rubbed them with his hands and looked back across the expanse again. The city was still there.

"If that's heaven," he wondered, "it's not at all what I imagined. But then again, thank goodness, it doesn't look like hell either. So maybe it's someplace else. It could be Purgatory. I've never personally believed it existed. But hey, you never know. I guess I have to find a way down this cliff so I can get over to it."

He walked along the edge of the grass and searched for a path or even some steps down the rocky cliff below, but no safe route down the hill could be found. He finally resolved himself to the fact that he would have to turn around, go back through the inner gardens, find the main dirt road past the entrance to the olive grove, and try to make his way over to the city.

But just as he was walking back across the circular hidden garden to find the pathway he had used to arrive there, he heard a soft whispering coming from a dark area to his left that was shaded from the bright moonlight by the olive trees. He cautiously approached the darkness. Once he crossed over the edge of the shadow of the moonlight, his eyes adjusted, and just ahead he could see the back of a man who was kneeling on the ground with his back to Michael.

The man wore a light tan robe, and since his knees were on the ground, the bottom of his worn, old sandals were visible from behind. His elbows rested on a wide, flat, grey rock that extended 20 feet to both his left and right. The top, flat surface of the rock sat two feet above the ankle-high grass on the ground.

Michael could hear the man talking in a hushed, somber tone but couldn't make out his words. However, after years of being a reverend, it was easy for him to tell that the man was praying. Hesitant to interrupt the man's prayers, he waited a minute or so. Yet the man wasn't stopping. After a few more minutes, the man finally paused, and Michael took this opportunity to approach him.

"Excuse me, sir," Michael politely interrupted while standing directly behind him.

The man didn't react at all.

"Sir? Do you have a second?" Michael asked, this time standing right next to him.

The man still didn't move or say anything in response. His eyes were closed, and his hands were clenched together on top of the rock in prayer. Michael reached out and gently put his hand on the man's shoulder. The man slowly opened his eyes, turned his head to face Michael, and calmly stood up.

He had piercing, deep, loving hazel eyes above a trimmed, brown beard. His nose was tall and thin yet substantial on the sides. Medium-length, brown, curly locks of hair rolled back on each side of his face, and the hair on top of his head was mussed as if someone had combed it with their hands. Thick, bushy, brown eyebrows were perfectly proportional to the size of his face, beard, and hair. And the visible skin on his cheeks and forehead was clear, flawless, and medium tan in tone, but not quite as dark as that of the first man Michael had seen in the other inner garden.

"Hello," the man replied with a somber yet welcoming look on his face. "I always have time for a friend."

"How do you know I'm a friend?" Michael asked. "You don't even know who I am."

The man managed a very slight smile by barely raising the edges of his mouth and answered, "You're right. I don't know you. But that doesn't mean you're not a friend."

Michael lifted up both his hands with his palms facing the sky and asked, "Where am I? Is this heaven?"

The man appeared perplexed at first, but then his expression changed to one of understanding as he replied, "No, this isn't heaven."

"It's not hell, is it?" the reverend nervously asked.

"No, not that either."

"Well, if it's not heaven, and it's not hell, are we at least someplace on Earth?"

"You ask strange questions for someone who seems to be rational in thought. Of course this is Earth."

"But where on Earth?" Michael asked, growing frustrated and impatient.

"You're in Jerusalem. Well, just outside it, to be exact. You can see the city clearly if you walk over there to the edge of the cliff."

The reverend's eyes grew large, and giant goose bumps

appeared again on his arms and face. He had to sit down on the rock to regain his composure. The man sat down next to him and compassionately put his arms around Michael's shoulders.

"Are you feeling sick?" the man asked.

"No, I'm alright. I just need to catch my breath."

"Was it a long journey for you to get here?"

"Yes, but it's not that. I'm not tired from walking here. I just didn't expect to be here, to be in Jerusalem, of all places."

"Where did you expect to be?"

"Listen. I know you won't believe me, and that's fine. I wouldn't believe me if I were you either. But here's the truth. So take it for what it's worth. I'm not from here. My home is thousands of miles away in the United States. And I was just there until about an hour ago when I suddenly woke up lying in the grass only a couple miles up the road."

"You say your home is in the United States. Where is that?"

Michael looked incredulously at the man and responded, "Where is the United States? Are you serious?"

The man nodded his head yes.

Michael explained, "It's a country on the other side of the Atlantic Ocean, just north of Mexico and south of Canada."

The man looked confused and asked, "What is the Atlantic Ocean? And what is this Canada you speak of?"

"Is this some kind of joke? Are you pulling my leg here? Because it's not funny. I don't appreciate being made fun of."

"I'm not ridiculing you. I just don't understand some of the words you say. These places you describe are foreign to me."

Michael stood up from his seat on the rock, walked over to where he could see the city on the hill, and asked, "So, that's Jerusalem, right?"

"Yes."

The reverend tried to focus on the city harder with his eyes and make out more detail with the available moonlight. Then it occurred to him that he had been asking the wrong questions.

"What is the date today?" he asked the man.

"As of sundown, it is now the thirteenth day of Nisan."

"Wait a second. Nisan? That's the Hebrew name for the first month of the religious year. It's roughly the equivalent of April on the Gregorian calendar."

Michael turned around to face the man and asked, "What year is it?"

"Three thousand, seven hundred, eighty-nine."

"No, no, no! That can't be right. How could I be so far in the future? Nothing around here is even close to modern. Was there an apocalypse or something, like in *Planet of the Apes*? Did all the technology get wiped out, and they started over?"

The man sat silently while Michael tried to figure things out.

The reverend continued, "Hold on. Hold on. You said it was the thirteenth of Nisan, which is a Hebrew month. So going by the Hebrew calendar, thirty-seven eighty-nine would be, let's see?"

Michael pointed at imaginary numbers in the air while he performed the calculations in his head.

"29 A.D.!" the reverend yelled out. "Are you telling me it's 29 A.D.?"

"No, it's three thousand, seven hundred, eighty-nine."

"What is going on here? How in the world could I be sent back in time almost two thousand years and end up thousands of miles away from Richmond? This has to be some kind of dream."

Michael leaned down to the ground and picked a few tall blades of wild grass.

"But everything feels so real," he continued. "And it doesn't feel like heaven either. Wait. Maybe I'm in Purgatory and have to pass some tests or something to move on to heaven. Maybe the Catholics were right after all."

Of all the theories he could come up with regarding his situation, this explanation made the most sense to Michael, so he felt obliged to follow it.

"Well, it looks like I may be here for a while, so let me introduce myself. My name is Michael Thomas."

The reverend extended his arm so he could shake the man's

hand. The man stood up, walked over to the reverend, ignored his outstretched arm, and hugged Michael tightly.

"Shalom aleikhem," the man greeted him.

Michael recognized the Hebrew phrase and responded properly, "Aleikhem shalom."

The man released Michael from the hug and said, "My name is Jesus."

Michael jumped back several steps, shocked from what he had just heard, and almost fell to the ground. But after regaining his balance and thinking rationally about it for a moment, he sarcastically responded, "Oh, sure You are. That's just perfect. So You're Jesus, and somehow I'm magically here in Jerusalem in 29 A.D." He looked up into the sky and yelled, "What kind of game is this? Why is this happening to me?"

Michael took a few moments to calm down, stepped back closer to Jesus, and asked, "So Jesus, You're from Nazareth, right?"

Jesus replied, "Yes, Nazareth is my home."

"And You were born in Bethlehem, right?"

Jesus nodded and answered, "Correct."

"So if this is really happening to me, and I'm not saying I believe it's true, but if it is, then how am I able to speak with You in English? In Your time, that language hasn't even been developed yet, but somehow You can speak it fluently."

"What is this language you call English?"

"English is what we're speaking right now, to each other."

"You seem somewhat confused, Michael. We're speaking Aramaic, not this English you speak of."

Michael smirked and replied, "Well, I can't argue with that. If You say you're hearing Aramaic, and I'm hearing English, then I guess there's no way to refute it. Score one for You, Jesus."

"I didn't realize we were playing a game."

"I don't know what all of this is, but it's definitely not a game to me. It doesn't look like I'm going to get back home anytime soon, unless a helicopter magically appears or I'm suddenly transported back home. So I guess I'll have to play along and see what happens. If I am dead and this is some kind of test, then I hope I can pass it."

"Is that why you think you're here, to pass a test?" Jesus asked.

"I have no idea how or why I ended up in this place. Since You're Jesus, You probably know. Why don't You tell me?"

"My Father sent you here for a reason. That reason is still to be seen, but I'm sure we can both figure it out together."

Jesus knew that Michael was under serious stress and wanted to help him, so he began by asking him a few questions.

"Michael, earlier you said you were at your home very far away and then you suddenly woke up here in Jerusalem. What is the last thing you remember before you woke up?"

"My wife and I had just left a party, and we were driving in our car when another car ran head-on into us. The last thing I remember was the other car's headlights right as it was about to hit us. I don't remember the accident itself or anything else after seeing the lights right in front of me."

Michael saw Jesus' puzzled reaction and then realized He didn't understand half of what the reverend had just told him.

"OK, sorry. Let me back up first. There's more to what's going on here than just my being from another place very far away. I'm also from a different time period than this. Very, very different, in fact. The last moments I remember were almost two thousand years from now. Actually, nineteen hundred and eighty-seven years in the future, to be exact."

Michael waited to see Jesus' reaction to his last statement. Jesus simply looked at Michael calmly and waited for him to continue.

"You don't seem surprised or shocked by what I just told You," the reverend observed. "I said I'm from two thousand years in the future. Do You understand that?"

"Yes, you're from a different place and a different time. I follow."

"Why is that not unbelievable to You?"

"Are you telling Me the truth?" Jesus asked.

"Yes."

"Then it is believable. Our Father can do anything and forever has done that which is seemingly impossible to men."

Michael furrowed his brow in confusion.

"Do you not believe in our Father's almighty power?" asked Jesus.

"Of course I do. But You have to admit, something like this is very unusual, especially since I'm the one actually experiencing it."

"Let's go back to what happened right before you got here."

"OK, sure. My wife and I had just left a social gathering. We were traveling in a vehicle very similar to what You would call a chariot or a wagon. In my time, the technology is much more advanced than what You have here. We have these things called cars, which we can ride in to go from place to place. We don't use horses or wagons anymore, except for fun. But anyway, my wife and I were riding in our car, and we got into an accident with another car. And that's the last thing I remember."

"Tell me about your wife. What is her name?"

"Her name is Beth. Actually it's Elizabeth, but she prefers Beth. And she's the best thing that ever happened to me. I still can't believe she married me. Oh no, I hope she's all right. If I'm dead or something, I can only imagine what happened to her."

"You obviously love her very much."

"Definitely. But starting last year, or at least my last year, I really messed things up. I started an affair with another woman, another married woman in fact."

"If you love your wife so much, which I believe you do, then why would you sin against her like this?"

"I don't have a legitimate excuse. I was weak, and I was tempted. Maybe if I were a better man or had a stronger will, I could have resisted her. But I wasn't able to. And right before the accident, Beth had just found out about my sin with the other woman."

The reverend's eyes lit up at the realization of the timing of his accident.

"That's right!" Michael continued. "The accident happened exactly at the same time my wife found out for sure that I had sinned against her. Do You think that has something to do with why I'm here?"

"Perhaps. What else was going on in your life before this accident?"

Michael was embarrassed to tell Jesus about his life choices in the recent months and years, but he felt he needed to open up if he wanted to find out why he was there. Also, there was something about this man or apparition or spirit or ghost or whatever He really was that made Michael feel comfortable talking to Him.

"My life has been a complete disaster recently. I've committed many sins against my family, my friends, and myself. In addition to cheating on my wife, I've been drinking way too much alcohol. I'm addicted to using cocaine, which is a very powerful, illegal, and immoral drug. I've been gambling excessively and lost more money than I can afford to repay. So I borrowed money from the wealthy woman I sinned with to repay my gambling debt. I've done all these terrible things, and I've got no one else to blame but myself."

"Your sins can be forgiven. All you need is faith in our Father and Me. Do you have that faith?"

"I used to, when I was younger. But as I got older and saw all kinds of bad things happening to good people, it became harder and harder for me to keep believing. You see, my world is a much different place than this one. Science and technology have explained most of the mysteries of life and the universe. And we don't get miracles like the ones I've read about happening here. That reminds me. Did You really turn water into wine, walk on water at the Sea of Galilee, raise Lazarus from the dead, and heal lepers?"

"You know about those? So My disciples do pass along My teachings as I've instructed them to do."

"Oh, You have no idea," Michael replied sarcastically.

"Back to your question. What you're really asking is did I perform those acts or were they just stories My disciples and I tell people so they'll believe I'm the Son of God? The answer depends entirely on your current point-of-view. Let's take the negative side first. If you don't believe those miracles actually happened, then just because I tell you they did happen won't convince you unless you have proof or were there to see them with your own eyes. And if I tell you they didn't happen, then that just confirms what you already thought to be true."

"What about if I did believe in Your miracles?"

"If you have faith and believe what you have either been told or read and I tell you these acts did take place, then again, I am simply confirming what you already believed. But if I tell you they did not happen at all, then as disappointing as it may be, it would be easy for you to believe Me and change your mind to realize that miracles don't exist."

"Please, just tell me the truth, and let me decide for myself," Michael implored, trying to cut through everything and find out what really happened.

"I did not perform those acts. Our Father did, and He did them through Me. Everything I have or have done is because of God. He healed the blind and the sick. He multiplied the fishes and loaves of bread. He allowed Me to walk on the water. And whether you believe that or not, the same can be said about you and what you've accomplished."

"So what was the point of all that stuff You said about it depends on your point-of-view? What did that really mean?"

"To say it simply, it is much easier to change someone's mind if they believe than if they don't believe."

"So You mean if I believe in God or You or Santa Claus, then it's easier to make me not believe than it would be to make me believe in them if I didn't already?"

"Exactly. Although, I don't know this Santa Claus person you mentioned. But regardless, that's why faith is so hard to get and so precious to hold onto."

"Unless there's evidence that disproves what I believe in, right?"

"The meaning of faith is to believe in something you can neither prove nor disprove. So no evidence or lack of evidence should be able to change your faith. That comes from inside you. It's what you feel right here."

Jesus took His hand and placed it gently on Michael's chest. A feeling of warmth emanated out of His hand and into the reverend, as if a warm shower had just been pointed at him and the soothing water flowed all over and through his body. This wonderful jolt of warmth and comfort momentarily took away the strength of Michael's knees, forcing him to slowly drop down to the ground. Jesus helped him by steadying his shoulders as the reverend sat down and folded his legs underneath him. Jesus sat down directly alongside him in the cool, dew-covered grass.

12 DESTINY OR FREE WILL

"Mrs. Thomas, the test results have come back," Dr. Thurman announced when he entered room 414 at St. Mary's Hospital with a clipboard, the patient's file, and a manila envelope in his hands.

A nurse was just finishing up giving the patient a warm sponge bath on his chest, careful to avoid the EKG sensors still sticking to his skin all over his upper torso. Beth sat in a wheelchair next to the bed and held her husband's hand, hoping he could in fact feel her presence or maybe even hear her talking to him, something she did constantly in the hours she had been sitting there even if he hadn't shown any signs of awareness at all.

"Your husband's injuries to his arm and leg seem to be doing well," the doctor continued. "But there's no change on his cerebral edema. The pressure is holding steady, so the good news is it's not getting worse. But it's not getting better either. The hematoma is in a tricky location of the brain, so we can't operate on it. All we can do for now is continue the medication and wait for his body to heal itself."

"Have you had any other cases like this one, doctor?"

He knew what she was really asking, and he answered, "Every case is unique. There are no set rules or recovery times.

Your husband seems like a strong person, and that's what will help him fight this and get better. Just you being here will help him, probably more than anything further we can do at this point. So stay strong and hold on to your faith in him."

Beth nodded in acknowledgement of her intention to do whatever she could to help bring her husband back. The doctor turned some pages of the file then ran his finger down a row of numbers until he found the section he was looking for.

"The blood tests also came back from when he was first admitted. Let's see. Here it is. His blood alcohol level was point zero two, so no worries there. He was well under the limit for drunk or even impaired driving."

"Michael didn't have much to drink at the party. It's not exactly proper behavior for a priest to get sloppy drunk at a Christmas party."

The doctor chuckled at that comment and the ridiculous imaginary scenario of his patient dancing on tables while wearing a lampshade at a formal party. But his expression grew somber as his finger slid down to other numbers on the chart.

"They also did a tox screen, which is standard procedure in accidents like this. Your husband had some traces of cocaine in his system."

"What do you mean, traces of cocaine?" Beth fired back with a tone of denial. "That has to be a mistake. They must've mixed up Michael's results with the other driver's."

"No, they double-checked it. But a trace doesn't mean he was high or impaired at the time of the accident. It means that at some time within the past few days he ingested the drug. It was probably twenty-four to forty-eight hours before the accident."

The doctor could see that Beth was completely taken off guard by this revelation and had no idea her husband had been using drugs, so he was careful to be gentle with his next comment.

"Ma'am, nothing serious will probably happen to your husband legally, but the police will want to talk to him, when he's conscious."

Beth turned to her husband, tears welled up in her eyes and trickled slowly down her cheeks, and she mumbled between sobs, "Michael, what kind of pain have you been going through that would lead you to drugs? Why couldn't you turn to me about this? After all we've been through, I thought we were a team. I thought we could handle anything, as long as we did it together."

The doctor waited a few moments before he handed her the manila envelope he was holding under his clipboard and said, "Here are your husband's personal items."

She took the envelope, rested it on the blanket on her lap while she deliberately tore open the sealed edge with her index finger, and poured the contents onto the blanket, careful not to let anything fall on the floor. Mixed among her husband's family-crest ring, wallet, and keys, she noticed a folded piece of paper. She opened it and realized it was a check made out to her husband from Betty Woodson for fifty thousand dollars. Her fingers tightened around the paper and crumpled the edges as she pressed it firmly against her face. Her tears caused some of the handwritten lines of ink to smudge.

"Are you feeling ill?" Jesus asked with one of his hands resting on the reverend's shoulder.

"No, I'm not sick. I'll be OK. I just feel this overwhelming sense of shame, like I've disappointed You severely with my lack of faith."

"Michael, I am not here to force anyone to have faith in Me or God or to judge those who don't. That choice is entirely up to you and every human being on Earth. God has given all of us the gift of free will. We can believe in whatever we choose. But you definitely shouldn't believe in anything, or anyone, for fear of disappointing someone. Free will is yours entirely to do with as you choose."

"Sure, I've read and studied all about free will. It's the most heated topic I hear about from people when they discuss the idea of destiny. But it's very difficult to explain to someone that both free will and destiny can exist harmoniously together.

Do You think they do? Can people have both free will and a destiny?"

"Yes, but I would phrase it a little differently. I believe people have free will and destinies."

"How can people have multiple destinies?" the reverend asked. "Don't we all end up eventually at a single destination in our lives? There's only one reality that we each arrive at, sooner or later, right?"

"I would have to disagree with you on that. People have multiple destinations they can go to. Sure, they will end up at only one of those future destinations, but they could have gone to any of the possible places their life might have taken them."

"I'm confused," Michael commented as he covered his face with both hands in frustration.

"Let Me give you an example. Let's say a young man is born into a family of fishermen. As he grows up, he is trained very well in the techniques and art of catching fish. He is told repeatedly his destiny is to become the best fisherman in Judea, and maybe even the entire world. But that destiny is not carved in stone. He can choose to follow that path, work hard, and put in the time to learn the craft as best he can. Then he may very well end up at that destination in his life.

"But he could also just as easily decide that he doesn't want to catch fish for the rest of his life. He may enjoy the idea of becoming a carpenter, or an architect, or even a tax collector. And if he chooses one of those paths, it will lead him to another destination in his life. And along each possible path are other smaller side paths that can lead to totally different destinations, or these side paths may just create a temporary detour that still leads to the original destination. The point is that we all have our own lives to live, and our lives are based on the choices we make. We can choose to work hard or not hard at all. We can choose to honor God or not at all. And we can choose to follow our heart or not at all."

"But doesn't God know where our destiny ultimately lies? And if so, do we really have free will at all?"

"Of course our Father knows which paths we will take and

where they will lead us. Time does not limit Him. He knows everything that has happened and will happen. But just because He knows what will happen doesn't mean we didn't have the free will to choose that path. He does not force us to make particular decisions or go certain directions in life. We choose for ourselves. He just knows where we're going before we do. And do you know why He lets us choose our own path, even though the choices we make aren't always the best ones?"

"Because He loves us?"

"Exactly. You're very smart, especially for someone from the future. So you understand that God gave us free will because He loves us. You cannot love someone if you control them."

"Yes, that's true in theory. But what if He knows the decisions you're going to make are the wrong ones and will end up hurting you and the ones you love in the end? Wouldn't that be a good reason for a little helpful intervention from above? If He loves us so much, wouldn't He want to save us, even from ourselves?"

"Are you speaking from personal experience?" Jesus asked Michael, sensing doubt about God from His new friend.

"Maybe. But I don't want to talk about that. I just don't understand how God can let people ruin their lives and not help them."

"But He does help them. If someone is going down a bad path, God will give them a sign or put someone in their life to help them along. And if they pay attention and follow their heart, they'll know which way to go. But because our Father loves them, that person has the freedom to make their own choices. God wants to help us, but He will not force anyone to be good. It pains Him terribly to see His people commit sins and choose poorly. But that pain is one of the reasons he sent Me here."

"So You really are who You say You are? You're the Messiah sent here for our salvation?"

"Just as you asked earlier about the miracles, what you believe is up to you. But I can tell you this — I am the Son of

God, the Messiah."

Michael jumped up on his feet quickly and stood facing away from Jesus and looking up to the stars. He thrust his arms downward toward his sides in anger and frustration, still confused about where he was and why he was there.

"How am I supposed to handle this?!" he yelled into the sky. "This cannot be happening! Of all the people who have lived in the last two thousand years, am I really supposed to believe that You sent me back here to talk with the real Jesus? Seriously?! What kind of test is this?"

Michael took a few deep breaths to calm down, turned back toward Jesus, who was now standing, and said, "I'm really sorry about all this. You seem like a very nice person, whoever or whatever You are. But this is all way too much for me to deal with. I apologize for interrupting You when I first arrived. You were obviously deep in prayer, and I shouldn't have bothered You. Why don't You go back over to that rock where You were and pick up where You left off? I'll rest over here for a while and then make my way into town at first light."

"Michael, you're certainly not bothering me. I enjoy speaking with you. Let's take a break from all this deep talk and just chat for a bit. Come on, follow Me. There's a great view of the city over here."

Jesus put His hand on Michael's shoulder, which calmed him down immediately, and led him over to the infinity edge of the garden. They both sat down with their feet hanging over the edge. Michael looked down and saw a fifty-foot drop to jagged rocks and boulders directly below them. His fear of heights kicked in momentarily, but then he looked over and saw how calm and comfortable Jesus was, which enabled him to relax and focus on the beautiful view of ancient Jerusalem.

Jesus broke the silence and asked, "What is it like to live in your time? Do you enjoy it?"

"If you're the Son of God, don't you already know what happens in the future?" Michael asked with sincerity, not understanding how Jesus couldn't already know the answer to his own question.

"Without getting too deep into matters, no, I don't know yet what the future brings. I haven't risen yet to be with My Father. Once I ascend from death, then I will be with Him in Heaven, and all will become known to Me."

"But if this is really 29 A.D., and You are really Jesus, should I tell You about the future? Won't that mess things up?"

"You're only telling Me, and I've already chosen my path."

"In that case, I guess it's alright. Well then, where should I start? Life in the future. First of all, the year I am from is called two thousand and sixteen, not five thousand seven hundred seventy-six."

"Why is that?"

"Because of You. Our years are numbered starting at the year of Your birth."

Michael looked at Jesus to see His reaction to this information, but Jesus didn't seem to react either positively or negatively. He simply sat there listening as if someone were telling Him a story.

"But there were some miscalculations along the way," Michael continued, "So they were a few years off. That reminds me, when exactly were You born?"

"The third day of Nisan, in the year three thousand seven hundred and fifty-six."

"Was that the year before Herod died?"

"Yes, one year before his death. You know your history well."

"Then that means in our calendar You were born on April 4, 5 B.C."

"I suppose that is correct. You say these years like 29 A.D. and 5 B.C. Tell me, what do *A.D.* and *B.C.* mean?"

"Again, they're about You. *A.D.* is short for *anno Domini* in Latin, which means *year of the Lord*. So 29 A.D. is 29 years after You were born. However, as I said before, the numbers are about five years off because the calendar used in the future isn't created until hundreds of years from now. They make some mistakes in their calculations, but we figure that out later.

I always believed You were born in 5 B.C., so it's nice to know I was right."

"What does *B.C.* mean? Is that Latin also?"

"No, it stands for *before Christ* in my language. We use the word *Christ*, which is from the Greek and Latin words meaning *the anointed one*, to refer to You as the Messiah."

"So are you telling Me that everyone in the future believes that I am the Messiah, the Son of God?"

"No, not everyone. But a whole lot of them do, including most of the people in my country. In my time, there are about seven billion people in the entire world. And 2.2 billion of us call ourselves Christians. Just in my country alone, 80 out of every 100 people are Christians. Christianity is the largest religion in the entire world. To us, you are Jesus Christ."

"Thank you for telling Me this. I have taught My Apostles so that they will spread the word of God. Apparently, they will do it well."

"Yes, they will, or they did, however you want to look at it. It's still confusing to me how this time thing is working here. Regardless, You can be very proud of them. They each accomplish amazing things and spend their lives passing on Your teachings. But unfortunately that comes at a great cost to almost all of them. John is the only one who lives to an old age and dies a natural death. All the others are killed for their faith."

"I am very sorry they have to go through such pain and suffering. But Our Father has selected them to do so, and I can think of no greater glory than to do His bidding."

"Wait a second," Michael interjected after coming to a realization. "The men sleeping in the front sections of this garden. Are they Your Apostles?"

"Yes."

"The man with the large black beard and thick black hair. Is that Peter?"

"Yes, that is he."

"And the one with the brown robe with two tan stripes. He has a smaller beard and brown hair. Who is that?"

"His name is Andrew. He is Peter's younger brother."

"Both of them are crucified, but each in different ways. Peter is nailed to the cross upside down. And Andrew is tied to an X-shaped cross. Out of respect to You, they both didn't want to be killed the same way as…"

Michael stopped himself mid-sentence because he realized he was being insensitive to the warm, gentle man sitting next to him. He had come to appreciate the kindness of this person or spirit or apparition he was seeing as Jesus, and he didn't want anything bad to happen to Him. Jesus understood why the stranger suddenly stopped talking and tried to reassure him.

"I know what must happen to Me. It's no secret. I've been preparing for it My entire life here on Earth. You do not need to feel pity for Me. After all, I'm doing this for you and everyone else."

"I know. I know. It's just that, there must be some other way. Your teachings are so powerful, and You lived Your life in a perfect way. Surely those are enough to carry forth and become Christianity? You don't really have to be crucified, do You? Wait. I have an idea. Since this is supposed to be 29 A.D., let's leave Jerusalem right now and go to Rome. We can see the eternal city in person. The Forum, Circus Maximus, the baths, the palace of Tiberius. We could see them all. Of course, the Colosseum isn't built yet, but that's OK. Listen, all we'd have to do is just walk out the back entrance of the garden and leave town. They would never find You. Have you ever been to Rome anyway?"

Jesus just smiled at Michael, appreciating the newfound concern this man had for His well-being.

The reverend realized Jesus wasn't going to avoid His destiny and said, "It was worth a try."

"Thank you for caring about me. But we all have responsibilities we must carry out."

"You mean, we all have our cross to bear?"

"Interesting choice of words. You could put it that way. But running away from the pain of our obligations doesn't work. It will catch up to us, sooner or later. It seems like that is what has happened to you. Do you want to talk more about it?"

"Not really, but it doesn't look like I'm going anywhere anytime soon, so I might as well."

Michael shifted his seating position on the ground slightly to take the pressure off his left leg, which had been beginning to go to sleep. He was careful, though, not to lean forward and risk falling down into the ravine.

"But You are right," Michael continued. "I have been trying to run away from the pain. I tried to numb the pain with alcohol and drugs. I tried to avoid the pain by being unfaithful to my wife. And I tried to distract myself from the pain by gambling with money I didn't have, thinking that if I won and had more money, then I could buy expensive things and make it up to Beth."

"Michael, don't be too hard on yourself. Those are all very common ways to try to deal with problems. Unfortunately, they never work. The only way that does work is through God. Only He can forgive your sins. And only He can help you get back on your proper path."

"I know You're right. I've always known it. But I don't have the strength to do what's right."

"It's true, you do not have the strength on your own. But with God, you do. If you trust in your faith in God, He will help you. But it all begins with faith."

"That's exactly the problem. I don't have the faith that I used to. And I don't know how to get it back. Blindly accepting God back into my life is as scary to me as falling off this cliff and believing somehow I won't hit the ground and die."

Jesus could sense that Michael was getting agitated again, so He felt it was best to talk him off the ledge by changing the subject.

"I think we're getting too serious again," Jesus said. "So let's talk about something less intense."

"Good idea."

"Tell me more about your world. How is it different from

My time here?"

"I guess the biggest differences are the advancements in technology. I already told you about the cars we have. But we also have many other machines that make everyday life much easier to deal with. Our homes are full of machines that allow us to store and cook food easily, stay warm in the winter and cool in the summer, and have light shining whenever we want, day or night. We have pipes inside our homes that bring in and take out water so we can take baths and get rid of our bodily wastes without having to go outside. And we have controlled electricity, just like in a lightning bolt, so that it runs on metal wires and powers the machines.

"But the most significant machine of all is something we call a computer. It's like a simple form of an artificial brain that does a lot of basic operations for humans. It can do millions of mathematical calculations in only one second, which means it can run other complicated machines for us, ones that we couldn't control using just our own brain. Many people have computers in their homes, and there are smaller ones they carry around with them every day. We use them to talk to each other over great distances. We can read books on them. We can access all the known information from anywhere in seconds. And we can share new ideas and learn about what's going on right now all over the world."

"All this technology sounds impressive, but what have you accomplished with it?"

"We've been able to eradicate many deadly and destructive diseases like polio, smallpox, the plague, and yellow fever, many of which people have experienced here but didn't know what they were. Leprosy only exists in very rare instances in remote locations. The average life expectancy is 80 years compared to 35 years or so in Your time. There are much fewer cases of starvation worldwide. People are in better shape physically with fewer health problems.

"We have machines that fly in the air and move quickly across the seas, allowing us to travel easily around the world and see and meet different cultures."

Michael then turned around and pointed at the full Moon shining behind them.

"We even built machines called rockets that carried men up to the Moon and returned them safely to Earth. With the help of a technology called television, millions and millions of us were able to watch these men land on the Moon and walk and explore its surface. That was one of the greatest accomplishments we've ever achieved."

Jesus remarked, "Those sound like great achievements. But they are all related to technology and science. What about God? How has His glory been honored? What advancements have you made in your relationship with our Father?"

"Well, that's the problem. I already told You how far and wide Christianity has spread around the world. Throughout the centuries, technology definitely helped more people in more places learn about God and You. But more recently, science has been able to explore almost every boundary and mystery that was previously unknown. We now know how the smallest particles in the universe work and how they come together to form life. We know how the stars and galaxies and planets were created, how old the universe is, and how large it is. We know how the human body works, and we can repair most of its problems. We can travel many times faster than the speed of sound, and we can send satellites to Mars, Jupiter, and even Pluto, which is a planet that hasn't even been discovered yet in Your time. We can even see and talk to people on the other side of the world as if they're sitting right next to us, just like You and I are doing right now.

"But with all this technology and knowledge comes the potential for skepticism that everything we know was created and is cared for by an all-knowing, all-powerful being. Many are beginning to doubt the existence of God, and the more we learn about how the universe works, the more doubt creeps into people's minds. Technology has made it very easy for this doubt to spread quickly. Just as You said to me earlier, it's much easier to change someone's mind if they believe than if they don't believe."

"Can't they understand that God created everything? And just because they have a better knowledge of how everything works, can't they still know that God is behind it all?"

"You're exactly right. That is what many people call Divine Design, the idea that God created everything to work in ways that science finds logical and understandable. I personally believe that's how He created the universe to function. I think religion and science can live together in harmony without having to prove or disprove each other."

Jesus asked, "So if people are beginning to doubt that God exists, what do they believe in?"

"Not much of anything, really. They try to fill the void in their lives, the one where God should be, with trivial things like buying expensive items, if they have money, or immersing themselves in superficial relationships on something we call the Internet. The Internet has provided us many opportunities to make the world a better place to live. For example, it's easier for people in need to get help. And we can use the Internet to communicate with each other all over the world. But many of these connections between individuals are shallow and incomplete. Instead of developing deep, meaningful relationships with each other in person and with God, many are using machines to communicate in a cursory or even a damaging way. This allows them to remain isolated and seemingly shielded, but also empty and incomplete.

"It doesn't sound like humanity has really made that much progress in two thousand years. In fact, it's extremely disappointing."

"In many ways, You're right. We haven't progressed nearly as far as we should have. One of my favorite scientists wrote something interesting in one of his books that has always stayed with me. He wrote that human beings are capable of such beautiful dreams and such horrible nightmares. We feel so lost, so cut off, so alone. Only, we're not."

"He's right. We're not alone. We have God. All you have to do is let Him in, and you'll never be alone again."

"You're pretty smart for a mirage, or a spirit, or a figment of my imagination," the reverend commented.

Jesus simply smiled in return and then remembered He needed to check on his friends who were sleeping in the other areas of the garden.

"Stay here," Jesus told Michael as He carefully stood up from sitting along the cliff's edge. "I need to go check on My friends, the ones you passed back there. But I'll be right back."

Jesus walked toward the pathway that was the only entrance into this section of the garden. But after only a few steps, He stopped and turned back around to face Michael's direction.

"This has been a very pleasant and interesting conversation, Michael. I look forward to talking with you more."

That simple comment made Michael feel happy and content. He looked across the ravine at the ancient city of Jerusalem, which was completely quiet and asleep in what was probably the middle of the night. But Michael didn't feel tired at all. Instead, he was wide awake and ready for more discussion with his new friend.

After about ten minutes, Jesus returned to find Michael still sitting on the edge of the cliff. Jesus sat down in his previous spot beside him, which was now a dry island surrounded by damp grass.

"They were all still sleeping," Jesus told him. "They're so exhausted, they couldn't even stay awake for an hour."

"Hold on a second!" Michael exclaimed, realizing where he was. "This garden we're in. Is this Gethsemane?"

"Yes, that is its name. Why do you ask?"

Michael's eyes grew large again, and he answered Jesus' question with another question.

"Did You just have a large Passover dinner, or should I say supper, with all 12 of Your Apostles at a friend's house, in an upper room, on Mount Zion?"

"Yes. How did you know?"

"That's the Last Supper! That's the last meal You have with Your…"

Michael stopped himself again out of respect, but Jesus gave him a look of acknowledgement and told him, "Go on.

Don't worry. You won't offend Me."

After a moment of hesitation, Michael continued, "We call it the Last Supper. It's where You instructed Your disciples to break bread and drink wine in remembrance of You. We still practice this ritual during worship. We call it the Holy Communion because sharing in Your body and blood is our way of communing with ourselves and with You. It's an integral part of all Christian rites."

"I am well pleased this is passed along to future generations."

"And You were right about Peter denying You three times. That does happen, unfortunately. But he spends the rest of his life honoring You and passing on Your teachings. So he kind of makes up for it, I guess."

"Peter is a great man. He has already been forgiven."

"But Judas, on the other hand, isn't so great. Just as You foretold, he will betray You with a kiss, right here in this very garden. If I'm still here then, I don't know if I can watch that."

"Don't be hard on Judas," Jesus said compassionately.

"How can you say that? He is responsible for You being turned over to the Romans and put to death."

"Judas is like a brother to Me. I regret that he has to be the one to betray Me. But someone must. He is the only one of them strong enough to carry this burden."

"Unfortunately, history doesn't see him so sympathetically. His name is synonymous with betrayal. And many believe the real reason he turns You over is to coerce You into beginning a revolutionary uprising against the Romans here in Jerusalem. He tries to force Your hand."

"He knows Me better than that. You cannot change the world for the better through violence."

"Or to put it another way, if you live by the sword, you die by the sword. Right?"

Jesus simply nodded His head and smiled at the way Michael phrased His philosophy so simply and effectively.

The reverend continued, "Whatever his motive may be, Judas does end up regretting his betrayal. He hangs himself later tonight after he hands You over."

"May God forgive him for what he is about to do," Jesus said sadly as He looked back toward the pathway that entered the garden. "I'm sorry it had to be you, Judas."

Michael was surprised to see this show of emotion from Jesus toward Judas of all people. Maybe there was more to one of history's most vilified people than what was written down in the Bible. But then he remembered another question he wanted to ask about the Last Supper.

"Jesus, I'm curious about something at Your dinner earlier tonight."

"What?"

"This may sound a little unusual, but please, bear with me."

Jesus' face bore an expression of curiosity as He nodded yes in reply.

"The cup You drank wine with at dinner. Do You know what happened to it?"

"My cup? Why do you ask?"

"Well, that cup is something we call the Holy Grail. Thousands of people over the centuries have tried to find it. They believe it has supernatural powers to cure the sick and provide everlasting life."

"Do you believe that's true?"

"No, not really. It makes for interesting stories, but I think the real power is through You, not some cup You drank from."

"Be careful, Michael. Your faith is starting to show," Jesus said with a smile and a soft chuckle. "But as for the cup, I don't know what happened to it. There were actually a lot of cups we all drank from and passed around and shared, so I couldn't tell you which one was which. They all looked the same to Me, just like any ordinary cups. Many of the cups and plates were broken throughout the evening too. So this grail, as you call it, is probably just a bunch of broken pieces of pottery in the trash."

"Oh well, I had to ask."

Michael gazed out toward the city of Jerusalem directly

ahead and marveled at the gleaming white walls of the Holy Temple brightly lit by torches evenly spaced along its surrounding protective walls. Something about its simple, elegant design denoted an impression of grace and purity.

The reverend commented, "The Temple over there certainly is beautiful. It's quite a sight in person."

"It's a shame what they've done to it," Jesus replied strongly in a rare expression of anger. "All the money changers and merchants are a scourge on our Father's house."

"Well, again You were right when You predicted it would be destroyed again. I think You used the phrase 'there shall not be left here one stone upon another that shall not be thrown down.' In about 40 years, the Jews of Judea are able to successfully execute a full-blown revolt against the Romans and drive them out of Jerusalem. But You know better than I how the Romans are. They don't play around. They surround the city walls with four legions and eventually stomp out the rebellion. As punishment, they destroy the Temple.

"All that's left of it in my time are sections of the outer retaining walls and the steps to the entrance of the courtyard. The wall over on the far side, the western side, is what we call the Wailing Wall. A large portion of that survives in the future and becomes the holiest site in all of Judaism. Jews from all over the world go there and pray and write prayers on pieces of paper and stuff them into the cracks in the wall between the giant stones as a way to reach out to God."

"You seem to know a lot about the history of Jerusalem, Rome, and even Me. And this is all thousands of years before your time. Why is that?"

"I am a teacher. I teach religious history to 17- and 18-year-olds in school. In fact, the school is called St. Philip's. It's named after Philip, one of Your Apostles sleeping out there in the garden. Plus, remember when I said how many people are Christians all around the world? Well, I don't want to overdo it with praise or anything, and I know this isn't important to You, particularly considering what You're about to do. But over the next two millennia, You are the most famous person who ever lived. So, You're kind of a big deal, especially in a religious history class."

"I never tried or wanted to be famous," Jesus said, beginning to get agitated and upset. "It's the glory of God that should be known throughout the world."

"For many people, You and God are linked together. They can't imagine One without the Other."

"God is the One. I am only here to glorify Him. That is why we are all here, to glorify God."

"Yes, but because You do such a perfect job of glorifying Him, history focuses on You and Your teachings as well. I know You don't want any of this, but unfortunately it comes with the territory of being the Son of God."

Jesus calmed Himself down by closing His eyes and meditating for a few moments. Michael knew to just give Him some time to relax and let Him process what He had just been told about the future.

After what seemed like an eternity, Jesus finally broke the silence and said, "So, you're a teacher of religious history. I assume that includes Christianity, as you call it. Then you must know about My teachings. Do you have any questions about them?"

"I know a fair amount. I've studied them since I was a young boy. But there are some things not in the Scriptures that I'm curious about. For example, from when You were 12 years old until You were about 30, we don't know anything about what You did or where You were. Those 18 years are completely missing from history. One day You're a 12-year-old teaching in the Temple, and then the next thing we know is when you arrive to be baptized by John in the Jordan River near Jericho. What happened during those 18 years?"

"When I was very young, King Herod was told that a new king was coming to take his kingdom. So in a sinful fit of rage, he had all of the young boys in Bethlehem killed."

"I know about this. We call it the slaughter of the innocents. Mary and Joseph took You to Egypt, where You stayed until Herod died about a year later. Right?"

"Yes. But later when I was 12 years old, I learned in a dream that I had to leave Palestine again. Herod's son Antipas had just become ruler of Galilee and Perea, and a soothsayer told him that the man who was to take his father's kingdom was still alive. So he picked up the search for Me again. It wasn't even safe to stay in Judea, so we left the region and traveled to Egypt and India and Greece, where I continued My studies of God and His Holy Scriptures."

"I wonder why that part of Your life is missing from the teachings."

"I suppose because it never seemed relevant to tell anyone."

"Hmm, I guess that makes sense. So while You studied and traveled, did You ever go to Rome?"

"No. That would have been too dangerous for us. But I did get to see many fascinating places and meet many interesting people along the way. After 18 years of traveling and learning about the world, an angel told Me in a dream that it was time to come back to Palestine and start My ministry. That's when I went to my cousin John to be baptized, and I was blessed with the Holy Spirit."

"I was baptized when I was 2 years old. I don't remember it at all, but I do know they sprinkled Holy water on my forehead as they said a prayer for me. I had always wanted to come here to visit Israel and get baptized again in the Jordan River, just as You did. But this isn't the way I expected to come here."

"God sent you here for a reason, so remain patient," Jesus said, trying to reassure the reverend. "It will reveal itself in due time."

"You sound like my wife. She has more faith in God than anyone I know."

"She must be a wonderful woman."

"She is. Oh, I hope she's all right. If I'm really dead or in a coma, then she must be devastated. I wish I could let her know I'm OK."

"From what you've told Me about her, she already knows."

Michael was able to force a half smile on his face, but he

was still upset over the last hurtful words he and Beth had spoken before the accident. He regretted that those would be the final ones they would ever speak to each other.

"Speaking of wives," Michael remarked after another question for Jesus popped into his head, "What is the deal with Mary Magdalene? Are You and she a couple?"

"That's a rather interesting question. Where did that idea come from?"

"That's just one of many theories about You that people have devised over the centuries. Some think You married Mary Magdalene and had children together before You were… Anyway, they believe Your bloodline carried on through Your children."

"Mary is a wonderful woman and one of My favorite disciples. I do love her, but not in that way. I love her as a brother loves a sister. No more. No less."

"I always thought that was a crazy theory, but it made for a fun movie."

A puzzled look came over Jesus' face, and Michael realized He didn't know what a movie was. There was so much more he could tell Jesus about the future, but this didn't seem like the right time to keep talking about it.

"Look, Jesus, I'm really enjoying this unbelievable opportunity to sit here and talk with You. It truly is the chance of a lifetime. But if this is the night after the Last Supper and we're sitting here in Gethsemane, then You have something to do that is much more important than just answering my silly questions."

"Michael, God sent you here for a reason. I know you don't believe this is real, but that is not what's important. What is important is finding out why God wants you here with Me, right now."

Jesus put His arm around Michael's shoulders and gave him a reassuring hug that helped the reverend feel calmer. They both sat together in silence, as if waiting for a sign from above to help them know what to do next. But the sign they did receive wasn't from above.

"You're right, Jesus," a voice from the darkness called out. "There is a reason Michael is here. But it's not the one either of you think it is."

Startled and confused, Michael jumped up to his feet and helped Jesus up and away from the edge of the cliff. They cautiously approached the black, shadowy area near the olive trees from where the mysterious voice originated. Before they could take more than a few steps, a figure in a black, hooded robe slowly but confidently emerged out of the murky darkness and into the bright moonlight. Jesus immediately recognized him, but Michael didn't.

"Who are you?" the reverend asked boldly while trying to hide his anxiety.

The dark figure responded with a deep, evil laugh and said, "You know me by many names."

His voice reverberated through the air on a frequency that penetrated Michael's ears like the piercing feedback of an electric guitar set at an extremely high volume. The hissing sound of his S's seemed to reach right inside Michael's skull and scratch his brain. The reverend desperately covered his ears with his hands in a futile effort to stop the pain, bending over at the waist and clenching his jaw in agony.

The enigmatic figure continued, "But I prefer to be called by my given name — Lucifer."

13 AN UNINVITED GUEST

Seeing how destructive the noise was to Michael, Jesus commanded, "Stop hurting him now!"

The painful reverberations stopped, after which Lucifer smugly declared, "I always forget how weak and frail these puny humans can be."

Michael took a few moments to regain his balance and shake off the effects of Lucifer's voice. When he was able to stand back up straight, he turned directly toward Lucifer to get a good look at his face, since that was the only part of him that wasn't concealed by the black robe. At first, the shadow of the hood hid Lucifer's face from sight, but then he turned his head slightly, and the moonlight illuminated his evil visage.

The Devil's face contained two glaring red orbs for eyes that didn't blink at all, continuously burning like lasers locked on a target. Michael felt as though they would bore two holes into his soul if he stared at them too long. His cheeks, forehead, nose, mouth, and chin all formed a single flashing screen of constantly changing faces with no two being the same. It was like looking at a TV with a thousand faces appearing and disappearing, one right after the other, every minute.

"Go away, Devil!" Jesus ordered. "You could not tempt me

in the desert. And you won't do so here either."

"Ah, but this is much different," Lucifer responded eagerly. "Back in the desert, You didn't yet know what impact Your life, and death, would have on the world. And because even I have to play by certain rules, I wasn't able to tell You. But now that God has sent Michael here and he told You what the future holds for Your followers, all bets are off. Or as the lawyers in Michael's time say, 'The door to this line of questioning has been opened.'"

Lucifer turned his back to Jesus and Michael and moved a few yards toward the front section of the garden that looked out upon Jerusalem, but with the long, black robe covering his legs and feet entirely, he appeared to glide along the ground. The way he pronounced his S's didn't physically hurt Michael anymore, but the hissing sound agitated the reverend in a way reminiscent of a girl he once knew back in sixth grade. She hadn't been particularly nice to Michael as a kid, and now he had an idea why.

Jesus countered, "He's already told Me about the future."

"He's only told You some of it," Lucifer explained with his back still facing the other two. "He conveniently left out the good stuff."

Michael interjected, "I only told Him a few things. Nothing significant."

"That's not true," Lucifer rebutted as he spun around sharply. "You said plenty, but you only told Him one side. He needs to hear both sides, especially before He allows Himself to be tortured mercilessly and have nails driven into His hands and feet so that He can hang on a cross for hours, slowly and painfully suffocating to death while He is mocked and ridiculed by His own people."

"That's enough!" Michael shouted before realizing he was yelling at the Devil.

"Jesus, You know I'm right," Lucifer calmly stated. "It's only fair You hear both the good and the bad. Which is which depends on your point of view, of course."

Jesus sighed in reluctant agreement and answered, "It won't

change anything, but fine, I'll listen to both you and Michael."

"What are you saying?" Michael exclaimed. "You can't seriously be willing to listen to him. He's the Devil. How can you believe him?"

"I believe the truth," Jesus replied. "Yes, he is the Devil, the great deceiver. But he cannot lie to Me, or anyone of faith for that matter, and get away with it. He knows that. I know that. And like he said, it's only fair to hear both sides."

Jesus put His arm around Michael's shoulder and disclosed, "I think it's becoming more apparent why our Father has sent you here."

"Let's get started then," Lucifer anxiously insisted as he nimbly lowered himself to the ground like a robot fluidly folding its legs underneath its body.

Jesus and Michael both sat down the traditional human way into a comfortable cross-legged position. They were arranged like the three points of an equilateral triangle, with Lucifer's back facing toward the edge of the cliff at the end of the garden that looked out upon the ancient city. With the Moon shining over Michael's left shoulder, the moonlight illuminated Lucifer's face and made it clearly visible whenever he turned to look in Michael's direction.

"What a beautiful night for a nice, pleasant chat among friends," Lucifer began. "I think I'll kick things off. So Jesus, aside from the obvious pain and humiliation You'll face by being crucified, have You considered the effect it will have on all Your friends and family and the rest of Your followers?"

Jesus responded, "Michael's already told Me what happens to My Apostles. They know their paths will not be easy and are prepared to face the consequences of representing Me and the Lord God Almighty."

"Yes, but think about how much it will hurt Your mother Mary and Mary Magdalene," Lucifer shot back.

"Jesus comes back after He rises from the dead," Michael interjects. "His mother and Mary and all His Apostles, except for Judas of course, see Him several times before He ascends to Heaven. They all acknowledge that He is, in fact, the Son of

God, even 'doubting' Thomas."

"Your followers, however, aren't so lucky," noted Lucifer. "Those who believe in You over the next few centuries and aren't fortunate enough to see You in person are continuously tormented, vilified, and hunted down by those in power. Kings, generals, chiefs, even emperors — they all persecute and execute Christians to protect their power. Ah, but the Romans. Yes, they are the worst of all. For hundreds of years, Christians are tortured and forced to die like common slaves in amphitheaters. They're stoned to death. They're eaten by vicious, wild beasts such as lions and tigers. They're burned alive at the stake. They're forced to fight experienced, ruthless gladiators with no way to defend themselves. All this happens in front of the mocking jeers of the massive audiences, and it's only because of their blind faith in You."

Michael turned toward Jesus and responded, "Jesus, while it's true these martyrs are tragically killed because of their faith, they also are fortunate to be able to represent something so important that they are willing to die for it. Their names and actions go down in history. For the first time ever, people believe that, because of their faith in You, their sins will be forgiven by God and they will be able to join Him and You in heaven. For them and all Christians, death is no longer the end.

"And as brutal and ruthless as the Romans are now, in about three hundred years, a Roman emperor converts to Christianity. I know it's hard to believe, but an actual Roman emperor named Constantine becomes a Christian and helps spread Your teachings all over the known world."

Lucifer anxiously interjected, "Good old Constantine. I suppose you're going to tell us that old, tired story of how he sees a light in the sky in the shape of a cross and some Greek words that say *in this sign, conquer* right before the Battle of the Milvian Bridge. So he puts the Greek symbol for Christ on his army's shields, they win the battle, and Constantine becomes emperor."

Michael affirmed, "That does happen. What's your point?"

"Watch your tone, Michael!" Lucifer demanded. "Show a

little respect, especially if you wish to keep that sharp tongue of yours."

"Lucifer, I didn't realize you were so sensitive," Jesus commented. "I thought you were tougher than that."

The Devil silently glared at Jesus with his red eyes as though he wanted to burn a hole right through His head.

"Don't threaten My friend Michael," Jesus warned, "or else this conversation is over."

A few seconds later, Lucifer continued, "Yes, it does happen. But there's more to the story. Constantine doesn't credit God or You with helping him win. He erects the Arch of Constantine to celebrate his victory, but there aren't any Christian symbols or references to Christianity anywhere on it. This sudden so-called conversion to Christianity seems a little suspicious, don't you think? He knows there are many closet Christians in his army, and what better way to motivate them than to acknowledge their religious beliefs. And do you really think God helps him win the battle and become emperor simply because he puts a cross on some shields? That's not the God I know."

Michael countered, "Regardless of his motives before the battle, Constantine does become a devout Christian. He sends his mother Helena here to Palestine to discover important sites so he can build churches to commemorate where You were born, died, and ascended to heaven. These are the holiest places in all of Christianity. Helena even brings back pieces of Your cross, the True Cross, to Rome so everyone there can see and experience these important relics in person."

"Do you actually believe those shards of wood are really from Jesus' cross?" Lucifer sarcastically asked. "It's just like that cup you asked about earlier or the countless supposed religious relics scattered all over the world. There's enough old junk out there to account for dozens of crosses, hundreds of cups, and over 50 spears. Oh, I'm sorry, Jesus. You'll find out about the spear later, I'm afraid. That is, if You still plan on going through with this senseless suicidal act."

Surprised at Lucifer's comment about the cup, Michael

asked, "How did you know I asked about the cup? How long have you been listening in on us?"

Lucifer answered, "Oh, come on, Michael. Who do you think you're dealing with here? Remember when you were 12 and stole candy from the 7-Eleven? Or that time you used a fake ID to buy beer? And let's not forget your special friend Betty Woodson."

Michael conceded, "Alright. I get your point. Anyway, back to Constantine. You can't deny that he does convert to Christianity and significantly helps organize and build the Christian church."

Lucifer responded, "Sure he does, but not for the reasons you think. After his so-called conversion, he doesn't change the official religion of Rome to Christianity. That doesn't happen until more than 40 years after he dies. And he doesn't get baptized until just days before he dies, which is 25 years after he claims he converted. No, there are other, more practical reasons why he suddenly becomes a Christian. I already mentioned about how most of his soldiers at the Battle of the Milvian Bridge are secretly Christians. That becomes more and more the case with the general population in Rome. Constantine knows that the old polytheistic religion is dying out. Even ancient minds eventually find it hard to believe that Apollo drives the sun in a chariot across the sky or Zeus throws lightning bolts. He has to switch religions publicly if he wants to maintain control of Rome and his empire."

Michael fired back, "But Roman emperors try for centuries to destroy Christianity, and they can never do it. The reason so many Romans become Christians is because they truly believe in the goodness of Jesus Christ. And you can't discount Constantine's reasons for converting either. But also, what about the Council of Nicea? Constantine is instrumental in this first major gathering of religious leaders that helps legitimize and unify the church."

Lucifer replied, "I just love how Christians always look at the Council of Nicea as if it's the birthplace of the modern church. But that's simply not true at all. Constantine is tired of all the unrest and debates regarding Christianity, so he calls a group of bishops together to sort out some issues about conflicting Christian beliefs. But the most infamous part of this council is when they decide what books are worthy enough to become part of the New Testament. Then they burn the ones that aren't so that only their version of the truth can be passed on."

"Nice try, Lucifer," Michael refuted. "But that last part isn't true at all. There's no evidence whatsoever that the Nicene Council tries to edit or censor the New Testament. The books that make it into the Bible aren't selected by Constantine or those bishops in Nicea."

"You're smarter than I gave you credit for," Lucifer admitted.

The constantly flashing and changing images on Lucifer's face had become dizzying to Michael, so he refrained from looking directly at them as best he could so he wouldn't get nauseated. However, when the Devil actually paid him a compliment, Michael glanced over at Lucifer's face and saw the image of his third-grade teacher pausing there for a full second, seemingly smirking at and mocking him for what felt like minutes. Mrs. Carter was the only teacher Michael ever truly disliked, and now he realized why.

"So maybe I exaggerated somewhat about how the New Testament is put together," Lucifer continued after his little face game. "But that is the speculation about the Council of Nicea. Many people think a bunch of pompous, political bishops get together and decide what the New Testament should and shouldn't include, and then they destroy the rest. People believe it happens, and that's what's really important after all."

Michael countered, "The truth about Nicea is there for anyone to discover. It's not a secret anymore. But what really matters is that the New Testament is written and becomes the most important book in the world."

"What is the New Testament?" Jesus asked.

Michael explained, "The New Testament is what we call the

part of the Bible that tells us about You and how You're the Son of God, our Savior. What You currently think of as the Hebrew Bible is what we call the Old Testament. Together, the Old and New Testaments form our modern Bible. The main part of the New Testament is made up of four books we call gospels that are narrations of Your life, Your teachings, Your death, and Your resurrection. In fact, two of those gospels are written by John and Matthew, two of Your Apostles who are sleeping right out there somewhere as we speak. To put it simply, the New Testament shows us that You are the Messiah. It's the basis of all Christianity."

"And it's a complete fraud," Lucifer declared.

"What are you talking about?!" Michael fired back loudly.

The Devil answered calmly, "The four gospels are written at least 40 to 50 years from now. I don't care how smart or dedicated someone is, no man's memory is that good. And if you look only at the two that are written by people who are actually here now and may have seen some of these events happen in person, John and Matthew, then you'll see many variations between them. Which one is right? Are any of them really right?"

"The gospels may be officially finalized four or five decades from now," Michael responded. "That much is true. But John and Matthew don't wait that long to start writing down Jesus' words and teachings. As they live through this amazing time in history, they take notes and write down Jesus' teachings along the way. You're trying to make it sound like they wait years to write down everything from memory after they get older. That's simply not true."

"But what about John's version being different than Matthew's and the other two?" Lucifer countered.

"They're not that much different at all, really," Michael stated. "John writes about Jesus' ministry by focusing on His time going to and from here, Jerusalem. And the other three focus more on His time in Galilee. But John's account is great at augmenting the other three. His does not preclude the others. He simply adds his understanding and reflections from after the crucifixion to provide context and expand the narrative.

"Lucifer, you can try to twist the truth all you want, but that won't change the fact that the New Testament, brilliant in its simplicity, tells us all we need to know about Jesus."

"Fine," the Devil barked. "See it however you like. Let's move on to something a little more controversial, shall we? Let's talk about the Crusades."

Jesus piped up and inquired of Michael, "What are the Crusades?"

Michael exhaled a sigh of frustration and answered with regret, "They're a series of Christian military campaigns…"

"Invasions," interrupted Lucifer. "They're invasions, not campaigns."

Michael turned toward Lucifer and rebutted, "Some would say the Turkish militants are the original invaders and the crusaders are just taking back the land that had previously been taken away by the Turks."

"Anyway," Michael continued as he turned back to Jesus, "The Crusades are a series of military operations authorized by what we call the Catholic Church. But before I can describe the Crusades, first I need to give You some background information. In about six hundred years from now, a new religion called Islam emerges. Followers of Islam are called Muslims, and they believe in God and prophets such as Abraham and Moses and even You. But they see You strictly as a prophet, not the Messiah. So as You can see, there are some fundamental differences between Christianity and Islam. The problem is, a lot of the important religious sites and locations for Christianity, Judaism, and Islam are all in the same area. Many are right here in Jerusalem.

"So about a thousand years from now, Muslims forcibly take over most of the Mediterranean coast, including Jerusalem and the rest of Palestine."

"These Muslims are able to defeat the Romans here?" asked Jesus.

"No, the Romans as You know them are long gone by

then. In about three hundred years from now, the Roman Empire is divided in two and becomes the Eastern Roman Empire and the Western Roman Empire. A hundred years later, Rome is invaded and conquered by barbarians, which leads to the end of the Western Roman Empire. The Eastern Roman Empire still exists in a thousand years, but it's nothing at all like the military power Rome is now.

"So the Eastern Roman Emperor Alexios the First asks the leader of the Catholic Church, Pope Urban the Second, for help in fending off the Turkish Muslims. Since Islam is at odds with Christianity and the Catholic Church wants to maintain control of the religious sites of Christendom, the Pope calls for Catholics around the world to join together and crusade against the Turkish Muslims who have seized control of most of the lands around the eastern part of the Mediterranean.

"Over the course of two hundred years, several hundred thousand Christians fight in nine crusades again the Turkish Muslims. The Christians win some battles, but the Muslims come right back and regain the territories that had been lost. So in the end, the Crusades are simply a futile effort to drive out the Muslims from Christian sites, while thousands of Christians, Jews, and Muslims are killed in the process."

Jesus asked, "Are you saying that the church built on My ministry of peace, this Catholic Church, has soldiers and wages war against another religion so it can control land?"

"Unfortunately yes," Michael sadly admitted. "It is definitely not a high point in our history."

"Tell me more about the Catholic Church," Jesus requested.

"It's the oldest and largest Christian church in the world. They claim to be the direct descendants of Your 12 Apostles, and they're led by a bishop called the Pope, who claims to be the successor to St. Peter."

"You said 'they,'" Jesus noticed. "Are you not a Catholic, Michael?"

"No, I am part of another branch of Christianity called the Episcopal Church. I am an Episcopalian."

"And tell Him why there are so many branches of Christianity, Michael," Lucifer ribbed.

Michael inhaled deeply, trying not to get riled up, and said, "The Catholic Church starts out as the dominant Christian church in the world. But after centuries of disagreements and some questionable behavior by its Pope and other leaders, several other Christian sects are created, and they separate away from the Catholic Church to form their own denominations."

"Questionable behavior?" Lucifer snickered. "That's quite the understatement. Is that how you would describe the Crusades? Or the Inquisition?"

Michael ignored Lucifer's verbal jab and, still facing Jesus, continued, "While it's true some very bad things are done in the name of Christianity throughout history, the church also carries out a tremendous amount of good works for those in need."

Jesus asked, "What is the Inquisition?"

Michael clenched his jaw tightly in frustration at Lucifer but continued in answering Jesus' question, "After the Crusades end, the Catholic Church investigates Christians suspected of heresy. If a person does not follow the strict doctrine of the Catholic Church, then they are considered a heretic."

"And what happens to these heretics, Michael?" the Devil asked sarcastically.

Michael hesitated a few seconds before answering, "They are tortured, and some are even executed."

Lucifer immediately continues after Michael, "And You would not believe how creative these Christians are with their tortures. Thousands of innocent, good people are burned alive, painfully strangled to death, and stretched out until their limbs are torn from their bodies. They're treated almost as bad as the unlucky souls who end up in hell. The Inquisitors carry out quite a few other, more devious forms of torture, but You get the idea."

Jesus sunk to the ground in despair and slammed His fist against the cool, damp grass. Droplets of dew flew up into the air and covered His robe and face like a shaken soda can being opened.

"How can My disciples, the leaders of My ministry of tolerance and peace, treat their fellow man this way?" Jesus yelled to the ground.

Lucifer looked at Jesus, turned to see Michael's reaction of sadness and sympathy, and then looked straight ahead into the distance. He didn't need to say anything more to make his point.

After waiting awhile for Jesus to vent His anger, Michael tried to add some words of solace.

"Jesus, despite these bad mistakes along the way, the Christian church is an overwhelmingly positive influence on humanity over the next two thousand years. You set the perfect example of how to be a compassionate, loving person, and people throughout the centuries try to emulate You. They take Your message to heart about treating others as they would like to be treated, and life is much better for us because of it.

"Because of You, millions of Christians are baptized. They pray to God and You every day. They go to church regularly and participate in religious activities that bring people together. They go to Christian schools so they can get educated and have a chance to be productive members of society. They volunteer their time and money to the church and other Christian charities to help the sick, people in poverty, and those without food. They get married in churches so they can begin their lives together as Christians. They have their funerals in churches so they can end their earthly lives as Christians.

"Yes, some bad men do abuse their power within the church and cause pain and suffering to the innocent. Sadly, this has happened throughout all of history and for many different reasons other than religion. It seems to be a dark side of human nature. But after You, in many countries and across many eras, the church is the only power strong enough to protect ordinary people from the potential abuse of corrupt governments. Kings, monarchs, emperors, and presidents can no longer go unchecked without any opposition and rule over their people with total immunity. The church is a government's moral compass and, by balancing against corrupt and power-hungry people who may try to overstep their authority, helps protect the people from being abused.

"As You know, democracy first started in Greece and then later existed in Rome for hundreds of years until it became an empire. But after the Roman Empire falls, democracy is able to reemerge in large part because of Your teachings. Because of Christianity, people finally realize they're just as important as their leaders. And they create governments that are run by the people and for the people.

"I'm lucky enough to live in the best country that has ever existed. No civilization has ever been as free, as fair, as prosperous, as moral, as compassionate, as charitable, as tolerant, or as forgiving as the United States of America. We make incredible advancements in science and technology and exploration. And we defend other countries and their citizens who are oppressed by their enemies. But the main reason we're lucky enough to be able to live in a democratic nation of freedom and fair laws is because it was built on Judao-Christian principles. The founders of my country were Christians, and they helped build a free and fair society based on Your teachings.

"So You see, despite the evil carried out by crazed demagogues who infiltrate the church over time, what You've done here already and what You're about to do matter a great deal to a great many people."

Lucifer slowly clapped his bony, pale, claw-like hands, dramatically pausing between each clap for effect. They sounded like two corrugated sheets of steel smashing together, letting out piercing, metallic echoes that passed like waves directly through Michael's head.

"Michael, what an inspiring and moving speech," Lucifer facetiously remarked. "It almost makes me want to cry while I sing the national anthem. That is, if I didn't know better. But let's forget all about America's failures for a minute. I want to go back to something we were talking about earlier — the

Christian church. I'm sure Jesus would love to hear about all the impressive cathedrals and chapels and monuments that are dedicated to Him."

"He's not vain like that," Michael fired back.

"Maybe not," replied Lucifer. "But isn't it interesting how much money and time the church puts into its buildings and works of art instead of using those resources to help people. Seems a little vain, to use your wording, don't you think?

"Take St. Peter's Basilica, for instance. You once told Peter he would be the rock on which Your church is built. Well, they sure do build quite an immense church and name it after him. And it's in Rome, of all places. Oh, Jesus, You should see it. Over five million square feet of marble, stone, and gold with enormous arches and columns and statues of all Your Apostles and You. It's much more impressive than any of the palaces the Roman emperors build. Quite a vulgar display of wealth, not particularly in keeping with Your teachings I would say.

"And that's just one of many churches and monuments dedicated to You. There's even a 125-foot-tall statue of You on top of a huge mountain."

Lucifer laughed an evil hiss of delight.

"Even though you mock these churches and statues," Michael retorted sharply, "they are important symbols for Christians everywhere."

Michael turned toward Jesus and continued, "When I was nine years old, my parents took me to Rome, and I got to see St. Peter's Basilica and all the amazingly beautiful works of art inside that were inspired by You. Millions of people go to sites like this to feel Your presence and see Your influence on history. They don't belong to individual people or private organizations. The world gets to enjoy these incredible monuments and share in Your glory. To both Christians and non-Christians, these places are inspirational."

Lucifer countered, "Sure, by measly human standards they may be extraordinary architectural and artistic accomplishments. But what's really interesting is how the church gets all that money to build them. Jesus, I'm sure You'll be glad to know that the Catholic Church grows to be so powerful that it becomes corrupted by its own success. Instead of receiving forgiveness from sins by having faith in Jesus and asking God for redemption, the rich are able to buy forgiveness from the Catholic Church. When you corner the market on sins, that can be a very lucrative business."

Michael countered, "Jesus, this is definitely not a good moment in history for the church. But a monk becomes inspired by when You threw the moneychangers out of the Holy Temple in Jerusalem — his name is Martin Luther — and he stands up to the Catholic Church and challenges its practice of allowing people to pay to have their sins forgiven. His defiance against the Catholic Church helps spark the beginning of the Reformation, which leads to other denominations being created within Christianity, as we talked about earlier. Christianity splits into multiple sects, and Your teachings are followed by innumerably more people who aren't previously exposed to them."

"Alright, as much as I would love to continue the Christian bashing," Lucifer said, "And believe me, Jesus, there's plenty more to bash. Just ask Michael about televangelists if You have some spare time. But I'd be remiss if I didn't point out the impact Your potential, rash, suicidal charade has on Your own people, the Jews.

"If You somehow insist on going through with this needless crucifixion, it's not the Romans who get blamed for it. While Roman authorities are the ones who actually sentence You to death and carry out the execution, it's the Jewish religious leadership that gets blamed in the end. To all Christians throughout history, the Jews are the people who killed Jesus. And millions of Jews are persecuted, tormented, and killed because of it."

"That's completely untrue," interjected Michael.

"Oh really," Lucifer replied arrogantly. "Which part?"

Michael answered, "The last part about all Christians blaming the Jews for the death of Jesus. We know why and how He is killed. And we don't all blame the Jews for that."

"Then how do you explain the Holocaust?" asked Lucifer.

"You know very well that's not why the Holocaust happens," Michael said resolutely. "I'm sure you are there and do your best to help it along. As the song goes, you rode a tank, held a general's rank, when the blitzkrieg raged."

Lucifer responded, "Of course I'm there. I wouldn't miss it for anything."

"What is the Holocaust?" Jesus innocently asked.

Michael answered quickly because he didn't want to give Lucifer the chance to start telling any more lies.

"During the century before my time, there are two world wars that involve countries all over the globe, including America, the country I live in. In the second of these wars, our main enemy, Germany, commits one of the most horrific acts in history. They round up and execute six million Jews who are living in Germany and the countries that Germany conquers. But they don't kill them because they believe the Jews are responsible for Your death."

"Of course they do," rebutted Lucifer. "They're Christians. And they even march behind the symbol of a cross."

"It's not a Christian cross," Michael fired back. "It's a twisted cross, an ancient symbol first discovered over ten thousand years ago that is used by a twisted society. They may claim to be Christians, but they aren't, and they certainly don't act like it. Millions of Christians, along with Jews, atheists, and members of many other religions from countries all over the world, all band together to fight against an unimaginable evil and win."

"So then why do they hate the Jews so much?" Lucifer questioned the reverend. "It can only be because the Jews kill Jesus."

Michael turned to face Jesus and answered Lucifer's question not to the Devil, but to Jesus instead.

"That's not why the Jews are killed in Germany. The real reason doesn't make any more sense, but here it is. Remember when I mentioned there were two world wars?"

Jesus nodded a silent yes.

Michael continued, "At the end of the first world war, the old leaders of Germany make a bad peace settlement that causes their country to suffer economically for almost 20 years. Most Germans don't have jobs, and food becomes scarce and very expensive. They're looking for hope, any hope that can help them survive. A new group of psychotic, immoral political leaders take advantage of the desperate times and falsely blame the Jews in Germany for the bad settlement that is signed at the end of the first world war, thereby helping them take control of Germany. The Jews become scapegoats for all the suffering in Germany over those previous two decades. Unfortunately, most of the non-Jewish Germans believe these lies and go along with the horrific treatment of the Jews."

Michael turned back to the Devil and continued, "So as you already know, Lucifer, the real reason Germany kills so many Jews has nothing to do with Jesus' death. But the reason millions of Christians risk their own lives to fight against Germany and defeat them has everything to do with Jesus' death."

Lucifer glared at Michael again, upset that he had underestimated the reverend's knowledge and tenacity. But just then, another sinister idea entered his evil, vile mind.

"Michael, the arguments you present are extremely logical and cogent. I applaud you. Well done, especially considering they're coming from a Christian priest."

Michael felt a rush of blood race to his face as he felt flushed, embarrassed, and angry all at the same time.

"You son of a ..." Michael yelled at Lucifer before stopping himself.

The reverend reluctantly turned to see Jesus' expression of surprise and disappointment.

After a few moments of painful silence, Jesus finally spoke, saying, "Michael, you're a leader in My church, a disciple of My teachings, and you couldn't tell me the truth? You led Me to believe you're a history teacher in a school. Why would you hide your true self from Me?"

Dozens of possible answers to Jesus' questions flew around

inside Michael's brain. Just as his recent, wayward life had depended on him saying the right lie at the right time to survive, he tried to quickly determine which lie would work in this situation.

But suddenly it hit him like a bolt of lightning — he realized he didn't need to lie. It was as if a cloud of confusion and uncertainty had been pushed out of his head, and now he could see clearly for the first time in a very long while. Whether or not this was really Jesus or just some elaborate test to see if he deserved to go to heaven or hell or wherever else might exist, he now knew there was no reason for him to lie anymore.

"Jesus, I am extremely sorry I didn't tell You the truth about me earlier. I wish I had been honest with You from the start. But the reason I wasn't honest is because I'm ashamed. I'm ashamed of myself for how I've acted in my life as one of Your disciples. Somewhere along the way, I lost my faith in God and in You. When I was younger, I had a very strong faith. I could feel both You and God inside me. I never doubted it for a second. But something I can't quite understand happened to me. And I lost my faith. And I lost my self-respect. And I lost my reputation. And I lost the trust of my wife. And apparently, I lost my life."

"You know very well why you lost your faith," Lucifer asserted. "It's the same reason you started drinking too much. It's why you did drugs. It's why you gambled with money you didn't have. It's why you cheated on your wife. And it's why you lied to everyone you care about to try to cover it all up."

"Why?" Michael hesitantly asked.

"Your lust for riches," answered Lucifer.

These words from the Devil pierced Michael's soul like a scorching-hot spear from hell. He knew Lucifer had seen past all the excuses and lies and, ironically, was able to pull out the truth.

Lucifer resumed, "All your problems boil down to this one sin — your lustful craving for money. You want so bad to be rich and powerful, just like Richard Woodson."

The flickering faces of Lucifer stopped momentarily on that of Richard Woodson. Then after a couple seconds, they continued to change and flash on and on.

"Of course, you weren't always this way," Lucifer kept going. "You grew up in a solid, middle-class family. You never wanted for food or clothes. It was a special treat to go out for pizza or drive to the beach for a vacation. All your friends' families were like yours, so you didn't know anything different.

"But when you got older, you were exposed to more of life's finer things. In college, you gravitated toward people with money. You got to go to their vacation homes in Florida and their ski houses in Colorado. They drove BMWs and Range Rovers. You had a rusted-out Jeep.

"You had to work during college, while they didn't have to worry about anything except which fraternity or sorority they were getting in. And then for seminary school, you were able to get a scholarship and go to Yale. And guess what Yale has, besides a top-notch seminary program?"

Michael nodded his head, already knowing the answer.

"A lot of rich people," Lucifer said, answering his own question. "Whom you were quick to pal around with. Remember your girlfriend at Yale? Carol?"

Michael nodded yes silently again.

Lucifer continued, "Her family was loaded. Maybe not as rich as the Woodsons, but they were very well off. You could have married her and never had to work a serious job for the rest of your life. Think of all the golf and skiing and exotic sports cars you could have had. But I give you some credit. You resisted that temptation and kept true to yourself."

"Why didn't you marry her?" Jesus asked. "Did you love her?"

"I wanted to love her," replied Michael. "She was beautiful and nice to me, and like Lucifer said, her family was very wealthy. But she wanted me to give up on becoming a priest. That didn't fit her idea of a fairytale life. I guess I finally realized I didn't really love her and she didn't really love me."

Lucifer remarked, "Like I said, you dodged that bullet. But

afterward, bitterness began to grow inside you. You realized you couldn't follow your dream of becoming a priest and also earn enough money to buy the things and possessions you had quickly grown very fond of and comfortable with. Moving to Atlanta for your first job out of school didn't help very much either.

"Jesus, Atlanta in the future makes Gomorrah look like Bethlehem. Anyway, I digress. But talk about new money and a city full of temptation, Michael. You couldn't have picked many better places than Atlanta, where you kept dating girls from wealthy families and enjoying all the luxuries that come with it.

"That is, until you met Beth. She was different than your usual girlfriends. She didn't come from money. And you didn't want to fall in love with her. You wanted to find a wealthy girl who didn't mind being a preacher's wife. But unfortunately for me, there's no denying true love. However, it wasn't 'and they lived happily ever after.'

"Michael, you had it all. You had a beautiful, loving wife who supported you unconditionally. You had a growing career with a natural talent for helping and teaching people. You had people in your church and community who loved you and looked forward to your becoming the next rector. But all that wasn't enough for you. You just couldn't resist the inner part of yourself that wanted the money, the cars, the houses, the fancy restaurants, and the jewelry that everyone else around you seemed to get so easily."

A dozen more faces of people Michael recognized from his congregation, the community, and the city, including his student Paul who supplied the cocaine, momentarily appeared on Lucifer's face screen.

"It's true," Michael admitted to Jesus with a nervous quiver in his lips. "As hard as I tried to deny it, I wanted those things. Everyone I know, all my friends and most of the people in my church and community, they all have so much. After years and years of being exposed to all that money and what it can do for you, I couldn't take it anymore. I wanted to get my own."

"You felt like God was an anchor," Lucifer pointed out. "Holding you back from your desires. You needed to break free from those bonds and live the life you deserved. And it was this inner conflict that drove you to alcohol and drugs. Since you weren't getting the money, you thought drinking and cocaine were the only things that could ease the pain and stop the madness. Oh how wrong you were. They may numb the pain temporarily, but when that wears off, the pain comes back even stronger. Thank goodness for drugs and alcohol. Or should I say, thank God? They make it so much easier for me."

Lucifer hissed his evil laugh, content to point out the reverend's vain attempts at fixing his soul, before continuing, "And when you realized they couldn't help you, you tried a different approach to getting what you wanted. You turned to gambling. First it was only lottery tickets. If you could just win the Powerball jackpot, that would solve all your problems. Of course, that didn't happen, so then you moved into the big leagues, literally. Football seemed so easy to figure out at first, but soon you came to understand how hard it is to win at gambling on sports. It's no surprise you got in the hole so quickly. With your pathetic gambling record, I would love to see what you would do in Vegas. Oh my!"

Michael lashed out at Lucifer and yelled, "So that's how you do it?! You put people in bad situations and then turn luck against them so they always lose and never get out of it?!"

"Now Michael, you know better than that. I don't control luck. I don't control people. All I do is tempt them. The rest is entirely up to them. They have the choice to either resist or give in.

"Jesus, in the future there's this quaint little folk tale about how people sell their soul to me. The story goes that they either sign a formal, legal contract or just simply promise me their soul if I give them success or fame or power or whatever they wish for. My favorite version of this story is the crossroads demon. It makes for great reading and storytelling, but it doesn't work like that at all. Does it, Michael?"

The reverend, staring down at the ground in shame, shook

his head no.

"No, what really happens is much more straightforward," continued the Devil. "Michael, imagine a driven, intelligent, ambitious man who works in a big company. As he's climbing the corporate ladder, he gives in to temptation and does some questionable things along the way to help further his career. Things like taking credit for someone else's idea, verbally and mentally abusing people he works with, lying to his boss and blaming others to cover his mistakes, spreading false rumors about a more qualified coworker to get them fired, and having an affair with his boss to get a promotion. Each sin he commits breaks off a little piece of his soul, until one day, maybe even when he becomes CEO, he doesn't have a soul left at all.

"There are no contracts or promises or crossroads demons. This is how it really works. There are many paths that lead to success in life. And the weak ones always try to take the shortest, easiest path. When they do, piece-by-piece their soft, weak, fragile soul gets destroyed. And I get to pick up all the pieces and keep them for myself.

"This is what happened to you, Michael. You gave into temptation and tried to take the short, easy path to success. Actually, you tried to take the shortest, easiest path to success of all. You slept with it. You cheated on your loving, faithful wife Beth and slept with Betty Woodson."

Michael looked at the Devil's face to see if Betty's image was going to appear there, but it didn't.

"When you met Betty Woodson, that was your opportunity to have it all. You could finally be with someone with money who actually liked that you were a priest. I don't have enough time or energy to get into her issues, but let's just say she owes me a lot. Not as much as her husband does, though.

"I just love rich people. They're so easy to tempt, and so easy to manipulate by threatening to take away their wealth. What was it You once said, Jesus? Oh yeah, I remember now. It's easier for a camel to go through the eye of a needle than for a rich man to enter the kingdom of God. In the future in

Michael's time, the world is a much richer place, money-wise I mean. With all their technology and abundance of food and energy, they don't need God. And they don't see the miracles all around them. So more and more people turn their backs on God and on You. Instead, they worship money and power and the ability to accumulate more of both. God may be able to offer them forever, but all they want is now.

"Yet even the coldest, meanest, most ruthless people have some kind of moral compass inside them they have to battle with. Since you, Michael, are much more moral than most, your internal battle was much harder to fight than most. There were casualties — your health, your reputation, your marriage. But ultimately in that battle inside you between God and money, God lost. And while you didn't lose your entire soul to me, you lost something just as important. You lost your faith.

"It would be somewhat understandable if you and your wife suffered some terrible tragedy like the senseless loss of a child or coming down with an untreatable disease. Many people turn away from God when those things happen. But you lost your faith simply because you couldn't get the material objects you craved. You weren't rich. You weren't powerful. Yet you had everything a man could ever want, and you threw it all away. How pathetic."

Lucifer hissed his snickering laugh, proud of himself for calling out the reverend's weakness and besting him finally. Michael slowly looked up from his sullen gaze at the ground and reluctantly turned to face Jesus. Having seen Jesus' eyes full of compassion and sadness for him, which only added to his guilt, Michael's protective wall of denial crumbled away, and all the emotions he had been hiding and holding back for years came spilling out. Tears streamed from his eyes like water gushing out of two full bottles. A deep, billowing wail from the darkest bowels of his soul burst out of his mouth into the still, silent night. His body quaked as he cried like he had never done before.

Jesus stood up, walked over to Michael, sat down next to him, and held him tightly in his arms. For over five minutes,

Jesus silently comforted Michael and let him get every last bit of sadness and regret out of his body. When Michael finished squeezing out the very last tears, he looked up at Jesus and somehow summoned the energy to speak with a shaky voice.

"Jesus, please forgive me. Everything Lucifer said about me is true. I was weak and gave in to the temptation of money. In doing so, I gave up on God, and on You."

Michael hung his head in shame, and if he had any tears left, he would have started crying again.

Jesus said, "Michael, despite your sins, you're a good man. You have a good heart, and you mean well. Sometimes temptation can be extremely powerful. Lucifer tried to tempt me in the desert, and it was hard to resist. But I looked to my faith in God, and I found the strength to fight it. And you can too."

Michael added, "In the future, we honor how You fought off temptation in the desert in a religious event called Lent. For 40 days, we give up something important to our daily lives out of respect for what You went through."

"Jesus, don't let him fool you," Lucifer interrupted. "For Lent, all they do is give up desserts or their favorite food. They don't understand real sacrifice."

"Of course, I don't believe that," Jesus responded to Lucifer. Then He turned to the reverend and said, "Michael, it sounds like your future world is full of temptation. And it's probably very easy for a person with no faith to succumb. But look more closely at these people around you in your life who have the money and possessions you want. On the outside, they may seem happy and fulfilled with all their material things, but on the inside, they can only truly be happy and fulfilled with God in their heart. People have all sorts of problems they try to hide behind their possessions. They falsely think that if they have more things, then their problems will go away, and they'll be more content. But that's not how life is. We all have our own troubles, no matter how wealthy or poor we are. As you phrased it so well earlier, we all have our cross to bear."

Michael managed a small smile before Jesus helped him to

his feet. After his knees buckled for a few seconds, Michael regained his strength and was able to stand up straight and tall.

Jesus stood directly in front of the reverend, put His hands on Michael's shoulders, and said, "If you are truly sorry for your sins, God will forgive you. Do you feel better now about your faith in our Father? Has your experience here in this garden helped you?"

Michael replied immediately, "It definitely has. I already feel my faith building inside me. I just wish I had a second chance to make up for my mistakes."

"How can you be getting your faith back?" Lucifer challenged. "You don't even believe this experience is real. You still think it's Purgatory or a test to get into heaven. You can't believe what is right in front of you."

Michael fired back, "It doesn't matter what this place is or if He is Jesus or an angel or whatever. All that matters is that I can feel my faith coming back. And you can't do anything more than you've already done to prevent that."

Lucifer elevated himself to an upright standing position, seemingly without having to move whatever legs might have been hidden underneath his robe. He glared silently and angrily with his red eyes at the reverend. A moment later, Michael felt a sharp, intense pain pulsating between the temples of his head. He grimaced in agony and raised his hands to press against his forehead, trying somehow to relieve the pain. He sensed a warm wetness on the skin of his forehead, so he wiped his right hand across his brow and held it up into the moonlight to get a good look. It was covered in blood.

14 THE AGONY AND THE ECSTASY

For the first time ever in her life, Beth Thomas wasn't at church on Christmas Eve. Instead, she was lying half asleep in a reclining chair in the hospital room of her comatose husband. The rhythmic beeps from the medical monitors were turned down to a low setting, their metronomic repetition making it easy for her to drift off to sleep for a few seconds at a time, despite her high levels of stress and worry. The door to the room was a few inches ajar, but since it was the night before Christmas, there was no activity at all in the hallway to cause any kind of noisy disturbance.

Even though her husband was right there next to her, Beth Thomas was essentially alone with her thoughts and her dreams swirling around together in a murky mixture of semi-consciousness. In between brief periods of waking when her drooping head bobbed her from her slumber, she experienced a shallow dream of her and her husband enjoying a sunny, summer day at the ocean. She was lying underneath a large umbrella and reading a book, while Michael dove into the waves as they crested and before they broke onto the smooth, sandy beach. It was an idyllic day, and they were happy and in love like when they were first married.

Just as a cloud passed overhead and darkened the sky,

Michael was pulled out to sea by a strong rip current. Beth jumped up from her chair and raced to the water's edge, but an invisible force field prevented her from jumping into the ocean to save him. She could only stand there and watch helplessly as he drifted farther and farther away from her.

The intrusive sounds of the hospital door creaking open and a pair of women's shoes clacking on the linoleum floor pulled Beth out of her sleeping nightmare and into a living bad dream. She looked over toward the doorway and was shocked to see Betty Woodson standing there in her fur coat and designer dress and shoes. And judging from Betty's expression, she was obviously just as surprised to see Beth.

"I'm so sorry to wake you," Betty apologized. "I didn't think you'd be here this late after visiting hours."

Betty was starting to turn around to leave when Beth replied, "It's OK. You don't have to go."

Mrs. Woodson hesitated for a moment to decide if she really wanted to stay and then figured she might as well since Beth was probably not going to be away from the room anytime soon and she wanted to see how Michael was doing.

"Thank you. I think I will," Betty graciously acknowledged before she walked over to the left side of Michael's bed and looked closely at his face.

The reverend's eyes were still taped shut, and the bandage on his head was stark white from a recent changing. This was the first time Betty had seen him since her party before the accident, and she was shocked at how many casts, slings, bandages, and tubes were on and in his body. She reached down to touch his right arm, and her eyes began to fill with tears.

"Is he going to be alright? How bad is it?" she asked his wife while pulling out a tissue from her purse to dry her eyes.

"He's been in a coma for a few days now, ever since the accident. They operated on his shoulder, leg, and arm, but they can't do anything about the injury to his head. He has swelling in his brain, which caused the coma. He's still alive, and the rest of his body is functioning normally. All they can do for now is just wait for his brain to heal itself."

"Would it help if we brought in a specialist? If there's someone outside Richmond who can help, I can get him here right away. Money's no object. I'll take care of that."

"That's OK, Betty. He's getting the best care available. Money won't help him get better."

Betty took a good long look at Michael and then walked over to an empty reclining chair near the foot of the bed and only a few feet away from Beth. She slipped out of her fur coat, tossed it onto a metal chair near the door, and sat down in the more comfortable reclining chair. She opened her purse and pulled out a tin of mints.

"Would you like one?" she offered Beth, who nodded yes and took a mint from the open tin.

Beth replied, "Thanks. It's been a long day. By the way, how did you get in here this late? It's way past visiting hours, and they only let in immediate family."

Betty smirked and answered, "We give a lot of money to St. Mary's. Next year, they're building the Woodson Wing. So, you know how that goes."

"I wouldn't know about it myself, but I get the gist of it."

"Listen, Beth. I am so sorry about the accident. And I feel terribly guilty that it happened right after you two left our party. I wish we had offered car service or even Uber to our guests. If we had, this probably wouldn't have happened."

"Don't worry about all that. The accident wasn't Michael's fault. A drunk driver veered into our lane and hit us head-on. There's nothing anyone could have done to avoid it, even if someone else were driving. And you don't have to worry about us suing you and your husband. It wasn't your fault."

"Oh, I'm not worried about that, but even so, we'd like to pay for the hospital bills and Michael's treatment after he gets better and gets out of here."

"That's very generous, but his insurance will cover it all."

"Well, at least let us help you with your car. Was it totaled? I'm sure your insurance won't pay much for that old Volvo. We can get you a better one."

"You mean like that convertible you bought for Michael?"

Betty froze at the realization that Beth somehow knew about the Jaguar. She stumbled to find any words at all to formulate a reply.

"Uh, what do you mean?" Betty stammered nervously. "Oh, the Jaguar. That belongs to Richard. He loves…"

Beth interrupted, "Don't bother lying to me. I know all about you and my husband. I've even seen video of you two kissing and going into your house together. And Michael essentially confirmed it too, right before the accident."

Knowing there was now no point in denying her affair with Beth's husband, Betty acknowledged, "You must really hate me."

"I don't hate you. And I don't hate my husband either. But I do hate what you two did to me. And I'm damn sure not going to let it happen again."

Betty was caught off guard by Beth's sudden show of bravado and confidence, which was seemingly out of character from the way Beth had always appeared in previous interactions, and it put her on the defensive, a position Betty wasn't used to being in.

"I wish things hadn't worked out the way they did," admitted Betty. "Believe me, there aren't many good ones out there. So even though I knew Michael was married, I still couldn't resist the possibility of being with him. When you're unhappy in your own marriage and you meet a man who's smart and witty and warm and handsome and you think he feels something for you too, then it's very hard not to fall for someone like that."

"Oh, so you think you fell in love with him?"

"Yes, I did."

"No you didn't, Betty. What you felt was attraction or chemistry or desire or even loneliness. It may have seemed like love, especially compared to what you have with Richard, but it definitely wasn't. Real love takes time. It takes trust. It takes two people who are willing to build a relationship together that will withstand the hurdles and challenges of life.

"I've had a lot of time to myself here in this hospital to think about what Michael did and whether or not I was going to forgive him. And if I thought for even one second he had stopped loving me and loved you instead, then I would stand aside and let you two be together. But I know that's not what happened.

"He's been going through a lot of personal struggles lately, and they all stem from one thing. He's lost his faith. The drugs, the alcohol, the gambling, the cheating — they all happened because Michael stopped believing that God is with him. Looking back on it now, I realize he was unsuccessfully trying to fill this void in his soul with things that don't really matter at all. And I also realize you became attracted to Michael because you were going through the same thing. In Michael, you saw yourself, and in trying to fix him, you were trying to fix yourself."

Betty was finally beginning to see how messed up her relationship with Richard really was and conceded, "But the main difference for me, unfortunately, is that I don't have a spouse who's willing to work things out together. Did you say you saw a video of Michael and me?"

"Yes. Your husband showed it to me at your Christmas party. He was quite insistent on revealing your affair to me. He said he hired a private investigator to follow you around."

"That two-timing, backstabbing, double-crossing, lying, manipulative, snake in the grass!" Betty exclaimed a little too loudly in the midnight quiet of the hospital. "He's got some nerve to have me followed, especially after all the women he's slept with. I've put up with him for far too long. This is the last straw."

"Betty, despite what you did with my husband, you don't seem like an evil person. Richard, on the other hand. Anyway, don't you deserve to be with someone who loves and respects you completely? I don't know, maybe you can work it out with Richard. Maybe not. But that is something you have to decide for yourself."

"You're right. You're exactly right. And all along, I've

probably known it deep down inside. I do deserve better. It's a shame it took an affair with a married man, a car accident, and Michael almost getting killed to figure it out."

"I guess what I tell Michael all the time is true. Things always happen for a reason."

They both smiled at each other, and Beth reached her hand out as a sign of peace to the other woman. Betty responded by holding her hand out too and gently grabbing Beth's. After a couple seconds of silently rejoicing in their newfound friendly truce, an alarm on one of the medical monitors was triggered and began to emit a piercing, pulsating blare. Both women jumped out of their chairs and scurried over to the right side of Michael's bed.

"Michael! Michael!" Beth cried out to her unconscious husband.

"Nurse! Get in here now!" screamed Betty toward the partially open door.

A nurse immediately ran into the room and over to the left side of Michael's bed. She checked the blaring monitor, turned off the alarm, and leaned down to look more closely at the bandage on Michael's head, which was now partially soaked with fresh red blood in the middle of his forehead.

The nurse turned around and yelled toward the open door and down the hallway, "Get Dr. Thurman now! Tell him it's an emergency!"

"Nurse, what's happening?" Beth pleaded, desperate for any information at all.

"He's hemorrhaging in his brain. The doctor will have to examine him to tell you more."

Three additional medical staff members burst into the room, one pushing a red cart full of high-tech equipment and medications. The two women looked on helplessly before stepping back away from the side of the bed to give the medical techs room to work. In shock at seeing her husband possibly dying right before her eyes, Beth covered her gaping mouth with one hand and her chest with the other. Betty closed her eyes, clenched her hands together, and began to pray.

"What are you doing to him?!" yelled Jesus.

Lucifer calmly responded, "Don't blame me. I wish I could do something like this to a human. But alas, this is God's doing."

Michael dropped to his knees in agony, trying to shake away the pain. Jesus knelt down beside him and placed his right hand on Michael's forehead and began to pray silently. After a few moments, the pain began to dissipate, and Michael was able to raise his head. A few more moments later, Michael felt normal again. He touched his forehead with his hands and then checked them for blood. Both hands were completely clean.

The reverend shook his head to make sure the pain was completely gone, grabbed onto Jesus' arm for support, slowly stood up, and said, "What in the world was that? I've never felt pain so intense before. How am I still alive? Am I alive at all?"

Lucifer responded, "That was fun to watch. But just as things were getting interesting, Jesus had to jump in and ruin everything. You're such a buzz kill."

"Are you feeling well enough to stand?" Jesus compassionately asked Michael while holding his shoulders for support.

Having tested his legs and feeling that he could stand up on his own, Michael answered, "I'm fine now. I don't know what happened, but thank You for healing me."

"Apparently your faith is coming back," Jesus commented.

"What do you mean? How do you know that?" Michael asked.

"Because you were healed," Jesus pointed out.

"What?" Michael uttered with a confused smirk, still shaken from the entire painful episode.

Jesus patiently explained, "If you had not believed, you would not have been healed. Without faith, I can do nothing for you."

Michael let out an ironic chuckle and said, "I tell my

parishioners that all the time, but somewhere along the way, I stopped believing it myself. If you have faith that God is looking out for you, things tend to work out. Thanks for reminding me."

Michael was normally an aloof and standoffish person. He believed that men should act like men and not get carried away with public displays of affection. But this entire experience had been so moving and emotionally draining that he began to feel much more open to expressing his feelings. It was as if all the bad emotions had been purged out of his system, allowing good and honest ones to fill up inside him. So he put both his arms around Jesus and gave Him a huge, warm bear hug. Jesus hugged him back just as tightly, and Michael could feel his entire body begin to feel lighter, like he was full of helium and ready to float away into the air.

"You two are making me sick," commented Lucifer, trying to ruin the moment.

After finishing the hug and pulling away from the embrace, Michael saw a look of grace and peace in Jesus' eyes that he hadn't noticed earlier. He wished he had a camera or a cell phone so he could take a picture and capture this moment forever. But since he didn't have any modern technology with him, he forced himself to concentrate on every detail of Jesus' face so he would always remember it. He took a photograph with his eyes.

Jesus' face was calm and relaxed. The edges of His mouth were slightly upturned, giving off a gracious and content smile. The moonlight reflected off His gleaming, welcoming eyes. Michael had never seen such a peaceful and radiant person.

After enjoying this moment for a few seconds, a cloud began to pass in front of the moon, and darkness temporarily engulfed the three of them. About 15 seconds later, the cloud finished passing by, and the moonlight reappeared, illuminating the entire garden again like an orbiting spotlight.

After Michael's pupils adjusted to the brightness once more, he was surprised to see that Jesus' expression had changed completely. Now, Jesus' eyes were bulged wide open, full of fear and pain, and tears dribbled down His cheeks and into his beard. For the first time since he had arrived at the garden, Michael felt afraid.

"Jesus! What's wrong?!" Michael cried out nervously, trying to figure out if there was anything he could do to help Him.

Jesus threw His hands up to the sides of His head, pressing against them in a futile attempt to relieve the suffering.

"Help Me over to the rock," Jesus muttered between the intense throbbing jolts of pain to His head.

Michael knew Jesus wanted help getting back to the grey slab of rock where He had been praying when the reverend first saw Him in the garden, so he put Jesus' arm around his neck and carried Him like dead weight the 30 or so yards over to the flat rock in the shadows off to the side. Michael's legs and knees buckled under the weight, but he summoned all his strength and kept moving forward. Lucifer stood still and watched without helping. Once they reached the rock, Michael gently lowered Jesus down so that He was able to kneel on the ground and put His elbows comfortably on top of the flat, stony surface at the exact same place where He had been praying earlier.

Trying to ignore the pain and with His hands clenched strongly together, Jesus began to pray, "Father, please forgive them. Father, please forgive them."

He continued to pray the same words constantly over and over again. Michael knelt down in front of the rock to the right of Jesus, waiting to see if he could do anything to help Jesus' suffering. Jesus seemed to be locked into some sort of focused trance, so Michael leaned against the large stone slab to get more comfortable, where he noticed two slight recesses in the rock, one on each side of Jesus, about two feet apart forming a U-shaped section. A few moments later, Lucifer arrived and sat on top of the rock to the left side of Jesus, facing both Jesus and Michael.

"What are you doing to Him?" Michael angrily shouted at Lucifer.

"Why does everyone blame me when something bad

happens?" Lucifer responded rhetorically. "Like I said before, Michael, people make their own decisions, and they have to live with the consequences. In this case, God is providing the consequences."

"What are you talking about?" Michael asked, frustrated and confused at Lucifer's talking in circles.

The Devil answered, "Come on, Michael. You're supposed to be an Episcopal priest. You should know this one. Didn't you just talk about it in one of your pointless sermons not too long ago?"

Michael thought back to his last sermon and suddenly remembered what he had talked about — the Agony in the Garden.

"Finally," Lucifer mocked. "Yes, the Agony in the Garden." He pointed with his small, bony hand at the olive trees across the clearing and said, "Well, there's the garden." Then he pointed at Jesus and said, "And here's the agony."

Michael looked at Jesus, who was still praying the same words repeatedly and suffering visibly, and asked, "Is He really doing it? Is He taking on all the sins of the world?"

"Yes, He is," replied Lucifer. "Your rector was right. For every sin that any person has ever committed in history, Jesus is paying for it. Those are the consequences of the path He has chosen to take."

"But it's His destiny," Michael rebutted.

Lucifer facetiously asked, "Didn't you learn anything from your discussion earlier with Him? Destiny is not carved in stone. It can be changed. He can choose to follow a different path. He doesn't need to follow through with this meaningless suicide mission."

"Of course He does," Michael fired back. "The future of the world depends on it."

"That's completely ridiculous," Lucifer retorted. "You know fully well that man would be much better off without Jesus or any false Messiah at all. Think of all the wars and deaths in His name that could be prevented if Jesus isn't crucified."

Michael replied, "You're wrong. We need Him. He's the most important man who ever lived. And died. So if you think His death isn't important or meaningful, then why are you trying so hard to prevent it? Certainly not out of the goodness of your heart."

Lucifer sat silently on the rock, not being able to refute the reverend's final statement. Then his constantly flashing faces suddenly stopped, leaving an empty black space where his face would normally be. His two red laser eyes still pierced the darkness of the edges of the garden that were shaded from the moonlight.

The Devil leaned down closer to Jesus, who continued His repetitive prayers, and said, "Jesus, this suffering can end. You don't have to go through with it. Isn't it obvious now that Michael was sent here to show you how pointless Your death would be to the future of humanity? If you die on the cross, millions of people will die in Your name. Now you don't want that to happen, do you?"

Michael leaned over to Jesus' other side and said into His ear, "Jesus, he is wrong. Evil men will always do whatever they want, no matter what. Whether they claim to worship You or someone else, they will always justify their evil actions to themselves. Evil men can always find a reason to kill.

"Your death is anything but pointless. What You're about to do is the single most important thing anyone has ever done."

Jesus looked over hopefully at Michael while continuing His prayers. He grimaced in pain and had to close His eyes and look back downward to absorb the overwhelmingly oppressive emotions being forced into Him.

Lucifer, seeing Jesus vulnerable for the first time ever, continued his assault and said, "These selfish, greedy humans are just using You. They proclaim to follow Your teachings and live righteously, but over time, Your influence fades. They fall into debauchery and vice. Even priests in Your church, claiming to be celibate in Your honor, force themselves on innocent children in vile and disgusting ways."

Michael leaned again toward Jesus' right ear and said, "I'm sorry to confirm that's true. Some evil men in the church did succumb to temptation and violate their oaths to serve You. Evil is able to infiltrate any institution, even the ones with the best intentions. And evil did find its way into the hearts of those priests, but it was Your spirit in good men and women that helped stop them.

"What's even more important is how Your spirit helps lift up the hearts of billions of people over the next two millennia. When I first met You earlier this evening here in the garden, I told you I had been in an accident after leaving a party with my wife. But what I didn't tell You was what the party was for. It was a Christmas party. Christmas is what we call the celebration of Your birth. It's the most important day of the year all over the world. Billions of people celebrate the day You were born among us."

"Christmas, Christmas, Christmas," Lucifer jeered into Jesus' left ear. "Let me tell You the real story about Christmas. These Christians celebrate Christmas, the supposed day of Your birth, during the winter solstice. That's more than eight months after Your real birthday in the spring. And the reason they celebrate it then is because the early Christians in Rome wanted to blend in with the pagans' winter celebration so they wouldn't be arrested by the emperor. Oh, the pagans. Next to atheists, they're my favorite group of all. Anyway, I digress.

"Over the centuries, Christmas turns into nothing more than a greedy, self-serving holiday. They take an ancient story about a man who gives presents to the needy and turn him into a fairytale called Santa Claus. In Michael's time, people care more about Santa Claus and what gifts he's bringing them than the real reason for Christmas. Everyone competes with each other over who gets the nicest, most expensive presents. People spend more money than they have to buy things other people don't really want or need. They get into fights at giant stores over pieces of junk that are made by oppressed workers living on the other side of the world. It's so bad that every year I'm getting to like Christmas more and more."

Michael countered, "Of course you would see it that way. While it is true that Christmas is celebrated in the middle of winter instead of the spring, what really matters is the spirit of this most important of holidays. Jesus, we give presents to each other every Christmas in honor of the Magi who gave gold, frankincense, and myrrh to You at Your birth. Sure, some people do get carried away with accumulating expensive presents. But most understand that Christmas is a time of giving. We give money to charities, and we volunteer our time to help the homeless and hungry. We spend time with our families, and we include those who don't have any families at all.

"Some people, like Lucifer just did, try to turn Christmas into a shallow, commercial holiday. But real Christians don't fall for that trick. For us, Christmas is the most special time of the entire year. We have Christmas church services, pageants, parties, and parades. It's a season of joy and optimism. People everywhere come together to celebrate Christmas in honor of the ultimate gift that God gave us — You."

Still shaking and trembling from the overwhelming pain and suffering He was experiencing, Jesus turned briefly toward Michael and was able to force a slight smile. But His smile quickly turned to a grimacing clench of His jaw, and more tears began to trickle down His cheek.

Michael, concerned for his new friend and worried if He was going to survive this crushing experience, gently asked, "Jesus, is there anything I can do to help You?"

Jesus was barely able to summon the strength to raise His right hand and point at a goatskin water bottle lying in the grass next to the rock He was praying on. Michael immediately stood up, walked over and picked up the water bottle, brought it back over to Jesus, kneeled back down beside Him, opened the leather top of the bottle, held it in front of Jesus' mouth, and poured some water onto His lips. Jesus did His best to lean His shaking head back and let a few drops into His parched mouth. Seeing how much Jesus was struggling, Michael held the back of Jesus' head and steadily guided the water gently to His lips.

Once Jesus had drunk enough, Michael poured some water onto a corner of his own robe and tenderly dabbed the damp cloth on Jesus' face. After he finished tending to Jesus, Michael pulled the corner of his robe away from Jesus' face and caught a glimpse of something on the cloth. He held the damp material into the air to get a better look in the shadowy moonlight. On the surface of the light brown robe, Michael could see small spots mixed in with the water-soaked cotton. The spots were dark, slightly darker than the brown pigment in the material. Michael recognized them instantly. They were drops of Jesus' blood.

Michael looked over at Jesus' anguished face and, despite the shadows in the moonlight, could see beads of blood dripping like sweat on His cheeks, nose, and forehead. He raised his right arm and wiped the bloody sweat off Jesus' face with the sleeve of his robe. Some excess droplets fell onto the surface of the rock just a few inches above the right recess of the U-shaped area and directly on top of a thin, white vein in the rock that resembled a "Y" with a small loop at the bottom. Michael wiped away the bloody sweat with his hand and noticed tiny, reflective crystals embedded in the stone that looked like a miniature celestial constellation.

Drained entirely of His strength, Jesus dropped His head down and rested it on the rock in the middle of the U-shaped section. His legs and arms collapsed limply against the ground.

He strained to turn the right side of His head toward Michael and uttered weakly, "The spirit is willing, but the body is weak."

Still on his knees, Michael put both his arms around Jesus' shoulders and pulled His exhausted body up from off the rock and the ground and leaned Him with His back against Michael's chest. Michael then wrapped his arms around Jesus' chest and held Him tightly and securely like a father protectively holding his child.

Lucifer slid across the rock until he was directly facing Jesus, ready to pounce on His weakened condition, and said,

"Isn't it clear to You by now, Jesus? Your dying on the cross won't help mankind. Instead, Your death will cause even more pain and death. Your own people, the Jews, will be persecuted and killed for millennia because of this. Your church will become corrupt and blinded by power and earthly riches, and it will extort the innocent and exploit their fears. And many wars will be fought, and millions of people will suffer and die because of evil men acting in Your name.

"But it doesn't have to be this way. Michael came here to help You. Let him take You down the mountain and away from this terrible place. Right now, there's a ship docked nearby on the Mediterranean coast in Joppa. It has a full crew and plenty of food, water, and wine. You can go anywhere You want.

"Michael, take Jesus away from here, and you'll be able to visit all those ancient places you've always dreamed about. Imagine seeing Athens and the Parthenon before they've been withered away by time. Like you asked Jesus to do earlier, go to Rome and see the eternal city in its prime. You can even go to Egypt and see the pyramids as if they were just built yesterday. And don't forget the great library and the lighthouse of Alexandria and the hanging gardens of Babylon. You can see things man hasn't seen in two thousand years and no modern man has ever seen. The possibilities are endless. All you have to do is save Jesus from an abominable fate He doesn't deserve."

Michael looked over his shoulder, across the garden, and out to the dark horizon, dreaming of all the places he could visit and experience at this time in history. For a few seconds, he was extremely tempted to take Lucifer up on his offer. But just then, Jesus struggled to raise His head up toward the sky and weakly cried out to the heavens, "My Father, everything is possible for You. Please, take this cup from Me."

Tears flowed from Michael's eyes when he heard Jesus' plea for help. Lucifer sat on the rock and stared silently at Jesus, waiting for Him to give up on His destiny. Through the blurry haze of his tears, Michael saw Lucifer looking at Jesus and knew exactly what he was hoping for.

The reverend wiped away his tears with the right sleeve of his robe, reached over to grab the goatskin water bottle, swigged a gulp of water, took a deep breath, and shouted at Lucifer, "Leave us now! You've had your say, now go!"

Lucifer, taken aback at the reverend's sudden bravado, silently stared at Michael with his red eyes before calmly replying, "That's not your decision. It's all up to Jesus now."

Michael looked down at Jesus and saw that He wasn't completely conscious. His eyes were darting back and forth as if He were watching an imaginary bird flying in zigzags in some alternate reality. Jesus was trembling all over His body, and His head wasn't able to stay upright on its own without bobbing against Michael's chest.

Michael shifted Jesus' head so that it was resting more comfortably between his arm and his chest, leaned down, and gently said, "I know You're feeling weak and vulnerable right now. And those millions of sins You're suffering for so that we can be redeemed, it's impossible for me to imagine what You're going through. But I want You to know this agony is not all in vain. God sent You here for a reason. You're here to save us from ourselves. Without You, we have no chance of being forgiven by God. Our salvation depends on Your sinless life and Your atoning sacrifice on the cross.

"We're flawed. We're imperfect. We're weak against temptation and prone to commit sins. But You aren't any of these things. You're the perfect example of what a person can be. And Your life, Your teachings, even Your death, we look to them as examples of what we can do to lead better lives and be better people.

"Before You, the world was a harsh, unfair place with different classes of people ranging from slaves to kings where the strong took from the weak. And we had to endure and survive it until we died, which most people thought was the ultimate end of existence. But after You, we see the world as the beautiful creation God intended it to be. We know all people deserve to be treated equally. We know charity and compassion for the poor and sick are traits of strength, not weakness. Christianity shows us we should help each other instead of trying to conquer each other.

"And in the future, Christianity follows through on its belief of how important it is to care for one another by helping end slavery and segregation. Christians stand up for and help protect the rights of unborn lives. There are thousands of Christian schools, orphanages, charities, hospices, and hospitals all over the world that care for the needy and the sick. In fact, I was born in St. Mary's hospital, a place of healing and care named after Your own mother, Mary.

"And then there's the cross. Right now in this time, the cross represents pain, torture, suffering, and death. The Romans line their roads with crosses as warnings to people who might dare consider breaking their oppressive laws.

"But after Your ultimate sacrifice, the cross becomes a Christian symbol of compassion, love, and everlasting life. The cross is placed on thousands of buildings and churches all over the world. Millions of people adorn themselves with the cross as a mark of our belief in Your teachings of charity and forgiveness and our appreciation for Your suffering.

"Jesus, what You're about to do matters more than anyone can possibly imagine. Your resurrection shows us that death is not the end. We know that, through You, we can be forgiven by God and share in His everlasting grace in heaven. You are the reason we have hope. For all Christians over time and around the world, You are our hope."

Michael waited to see if Jesus showed any positive reaction to what he had just said, but He was still stranded in a state of semi-consciousness. Jesus' eyes stopped darting back and forth, which gave Michael hope that He was ready to break out of His trance. His eyes and mouth opened widely in pain, as if He had been stabbed in the gut with a knife, then Jesus' eyes closed shut, and He went completely unconscious.

"Jesus! Jesus! Come back!" Michael yelled, hoping to snap Jesus back awake.

He put his fingers on Jesus' neck and felt a faint pulse, but

Jesus wasn't responding at all when Michael gently slapped Him on the face and shook His head trying to revive Him. Seeing Jesus just lying there motionless sent Michael into a panic. Chills ran up and down his entire body, and he looked at his left hand to see if it was trembling like it had been doing recently whenever he was under stress. But to his surprise, his hand was calm and steady. And then he realized his left hand had not trembled even once since he woke up after the accident.

The reverend, both frustrated and terrified at the same time, did the only thing he could think of that might work. He prayed to God.

"Dear God!" he called out to the sky, "Please help Jesus! Or else, please help me to help Him!"

Feeling weak and more exhausted than he had ever felt before, Michael let his head fall down on top of Jesus' shoulder, and with all his tears seemingly used up from his earlier breakdown, he sighed helplessly to himself, "I don't know what to do. I can't do this alone."

The garden was completely still and silent. No breeze could be heard or felt, and the tree branches and leaves sat motionless. Even Lucifer sat on the rock without moving, waiting to see what would happen to Jesus next. All Michael could do was bury his head into Jesus' shoulder and hope.

Jesus' upper body suddenly bolted upright and pulled away from Michael's grasp. He inhaled a huge, deep, loud gulp of air like someone who had just been resuscitated after drowning in water. Then He took in several smaller gasps until He was able to regulate his breathing.

"Oh thank God," Michael exclaimed. "Are You all right?"

"I will be fine," Jesus reassured him. "Thank you for comforting Me."

"It was the least I could do," the reverend replied. "But it's nothing compared to what You've done for me."

Now feeling refreshed and full of energy, Jesus quickly stood up off the ground, turned to face Lucifer, and demanded, "Away from here, Devil! It's time for you to go."

"I've made my point with you, Jesus," Lucifer snarled. "Now that You know what the future holds, there's no way You can go through with being crucified. If You do, the blood of millions will be on Your hands. And all for what? In Michael's time, more and more are denouncing the very existence of God. They are trading in their faith for material wealth, just like Michael did.

"But that's fine with me. Because if they don't believe in God, then they can't believe in me either. And that makes my job a whole lot easier."

Lucifer's face began to flash again with images of dozens of people per second, then he turned to Michael and said, "See you again soon, reverend."

The Devil seemed to float across the ground as he glided toward the shadows on the opposite side of the garden clearing. Just as he reached the darkness, his evil laugh reverberated through the air. A few seconds later, both he and his laugh dissolved into the inky black murkiness.

Michael turned back to see that Jesus was looking into the night sky, and His hands hung down by His sides with His palms facing forward. This pose was familiar to Michael as he had seen it countless times in classical paintings and stained glass windows from throughout history.

"My Father, thank You for sending Michael here to comfort Me," Jesus prayed aloud. "I am ready now. As always, not My will, but Your will be done."

Off in the distance across the valley and to the right of the Temple's great walls, a couple dozen flickering torches were grouped together and moving steadily toward the garden.

Jesus turned back to Michael, placed His hands on the reverend's shoulders, and said, "This is the end of our time together, Michael. Where I am going now, you cannot follow. You must choose your own path from here on."

"But I can still help You. I can help carry Your cross."

"That is someone else's task."

Jesus leaned in closer, gently placed His right hand on Michael's cheek, and said, "You are being given a second chance. Do not waste it."

"I won't, Jesus."

Jesus smiled a content and blissful smile, raised His right hand off of Michael's cheek, and covered his forehead with His palm. Michael's vision of Jesus' tranquil, radiant face faded to black.

15 YOU TELL 'EM, GEORGE

"Michael! Michael!" Beth Thomas screamed out in excitement as she felt her husband's fingers finally moving on their own against her right palm. "Doctor Thurman! Come quickly! He's waking up!"

Without letting go of her husband's hand, Mrs. Thomas jumped up from sitting in the chair next to his hospital bed, leaned down closely to his face, pulled off the tape on his eyes with her free left hand, and softly said, "Michael, wake up. Open your eyes. It's time for you to wake up."

His lips slowly separated, allowing an incomprehensible whisper to escape from his mouth. Beth couldn't make out what he was trying to say. She could only detect four syllables being murmured over and over. After eight repetitions, the words finally became clearly audible.

"I won't, Jesus. I won't, Jesus. I won't, Jesus. I won't, Jesus."

Michael's eyes then slowly opened, and he saw a golden aura in the shape of a person to his left. He blinked his eyes a few times to clear his vision, and the blurry image of his wife slowly came into view.

He smiled at her, and a single tear fell onto his cheek. He tried to lift his left arm so that he could touch her face, but sharp pains in his left shoulder, left arm, and left leg shot through his entire body. He looked down and saw the tubes running into his right arm and the casts on his left arm and leg. The shocking realization that he was in a hospital started to sink in.

Beth kissed him on the lips and said, "Oh, honey, I'm so glad you're awake. How do you feel?"

Michael deliberately cleared his dry throat and managed to answer, "Like I've been hit by a Mack truck."

Mrs. Thomas grabbed a cup of water off the tray table and held it closely to his lips. He took a few sips of the cool, refreshing water through the flexible straw and cleared his throat again. Now it was much more comfortable for him to speak.

"Where am I?" he asked his wife, trying to get his bearings.

"You're in St. Mary's hospital. We were in a car accident. Do you remember that?"

"Yes, unfortunately I do. Are you OK?"

"I was lucky. I just had a slight concussion, but now I'm fine. I'm sure part of the reason I wasn't hurt worse was because you foolishly dove over in front of me right before the other car hit us. That's how you broke your leg and arm and separated your shoulder."

"And it could've been much, much worse," Dr. Thurman interrupted as he walked into the room. "Hello, I'm Dr. Thurman. Reverend Thomas, just as your wife was beginning to tell you, you suffered a dislocated shoulder, a torn rotator cuff, a broken leg and arm, a fractured skull, a hematoma, and a cerebral edema. How does your head feel?"

"Like it's been hit by a Louisville Slugger."

The doctor chuckled, nodded his head, and said, "That's very understandable. The trauma of your head hitting the dashboard during the accident is what caused the frontal fracture of your skull, the hematoma, and the swelling of your brain inside your skull. That brain swelling, or cerebral edema, is why you went into a coma."

Michael then remembered about the accident and asked,

"What about the person in the other car? Are they OK?"

"He didn't make it," said the doctor.

"I'm sorry to hear that," the reverend replied solemnly.

Being careful not to pull any tubes out, Michael slowly raised his right hand up to his head and gently touched the bandages. He felt a dull, medication-numbed pain when he pressed his fingers lightly against his forehead.

"How long was I in a coma? What day is it?"

"It's January the 11th, honey," Beth answered. "It's been about three weeks since the accident. You missed Christmas and New Year's. I'm sorry."

Michael smiled and replied, "I didn't miss Christmas. I just celebrated it in an unusual way."

"What do you mean?" Beth asked with a perplexed look on her face.

"I'll tell you all about it. It's a long story."

Dr. Thurman took a small flashlight out of his white coat pocket, went to the right side of the reverend's bed, shined the light into his patient's eyes to check the pupil dilation, and asked, "Do you have any blurriness or double vision?"

"Just my normal 20/100 vision. When can I get out of here?"

Dr. Thurman replied to his impatient patient, "You've been in a coma for almost three weeks, so you need to stay here at least a few more nights for observation. Your brain experienced severe trauma, and I'd like you to take a series of cognitive tests to check if any permanent damage occurred and have another CT scan and MRI, just to be on the safe side."

Having completed his examination of Michael's eyes and finding they were responding normally, the doctor started to test Michael's skull and said, "Reverend Thomas, you're a very lucky man. Because of where the hematoma was in your brain, we couldn't operate on it. It was touch and go there for a while. But somehow, the exact combination of medication we gave you, your body's strong healing ability, the unique shape of your brain, the fortunate location of the hematoma, and the fact that your skull fracture hadn't healed yet, which allowed the blood of your hematoma to be forced out, all contributed to the swelling in your brain going down and you coming out of the coma. The odds of all those happening together successfully so that you survived were astronomical. Or to borrow from your profession's vocabulary, it was a miracle."

"Doctor, you work in a hospital called St. Mary's," the reverend remarked. "If a miracle is going to happen, it may as well be here."

"I get your point, Reverend. You must have powerful friends upstairs."

"We all do," replied Michael.

Dr. Thurman left the room with a smile on his face and even more questions on his mind. Beth, still having not let go of her husband's hand since he had awakened from his coma, reached over with her other hand, pulled out a manila envelope from her purse, and emptied its contents onto the bedside tray.

"Here, I thought you might want your things back," she said while handing him his eyeglasses and family-crest ring. "This is your extra pair of glasses. The others didn't do so well in the accident."

Michael used his good right hand to put on his glasses, and he could now see his wife's face clearly. She looked tired and worn out with dark bags under her red eyes. It was obvious she had cried a lot recently.

"How are you feeling, honey?" he asked gently.

"Tired, but happy now that you're awake."

"Have you been here the whole time?"

She nodded her head yes, held his left hand with both of hers, and said, "Don't worry about me. We need to focus on getting you better."

Michael smiled and thought to himself how beautiful she looked, even with greasy, straggly hair and no makeup.

After picking up his family-crest ring so he could slide it onto his left hand, he noticed a new, tiny indentation in the gold on the edge of the crest. He knew it obviously had happened during the accident.

Holding the ring up to show his wife the mark, he joked,

"Apparently my head isn't the only thing with a dent in it."

Beth simply shook her head and rolled her eyes in response to her husband's corny sense of humor.

Then he looked down at the tray table and saw a folded piece of paper nestled between his wallet and keys. His mood instantly changed from humorous to somber.

"Please pass me that piece of paper," he asked his wife, who handed it to him without unfolding it, already knowing what it was.

He grabbed it with his good right hand, slid it down so his left hand could hold the opposite edge, and ripped the check from Betty Woodson for fifty thousand dollars into tiny, little pieces.

"Beth, we need to talk about a few things. First of all, do your parents have seventeen thousand dollars I can borrow?"

"If they don't, we'll get it somehow," she said with tearful eyes. "Together, we'll figure it out."

The low, dim rays of the setting winter sun streamed through the leafless trees and diagonally into the reverend's hospital room. Even though the waning daylight signaled the end of a short January day, Michael felt like a new life was just beginning for him. And he was determined not to blow it.

Over the next two months, Michael healed quickly from his broken bones, shoulder injury, and skull fracture, and no further symptoms of his head trauma resurfaced. He told Beth about his surreal journey to the garden, calling it a near-death experience, but he didn't want anyone else to know about it just yet. He was still processing what had happened and didn't want people to think he was crazy. He would tell them when the time was right. Beth thought it was a great story, but the part about the Devil creeped her out.

He was able to get the seventeen thousand dollars from his in-laws. In fact, they were honored he had come to them for help. Michael had always tried to be as self-sufficient as possible and had never asked them for anything. They didn't like what Michael had done to get himself into this kind of trouble, but they were glad they could help him get out of it.

Once the bookie was paid, Michael stopped gambling completely. He also quit drinking and cocaine cold turkey. When he got stressed out about something, he didn't feel the slightest temptation to resort to alcohol or drugs, and his left hand didn't suffer any more tremors. He couldn't explain his sudden ability to overcome his previous vices, but he didn't question things too much either. Life was getting a whole lot better for him, and he didn't want to mess that up.

Since the accident was ruled to be the fault of the drunk driver and Michael's blood alcohol level was well below the legal limit, no charges were made against the reverend. But due to the traces of cocaine found in Michael's blood from previous use and to satisfy the District Attorney's and St. Andrew's concerns, Michael did agree to go to counseling for his drug and alcohol abuse problems, even though he never felt the urge to get drunk or snort cocaine again. At the church's request, he also voluntarily submitted to frequent and random drug tests. He valued his career so much now he would do anything the church asked to keep his job. St. Philip's forced him to take a leave of absence from teaching until the following school year, when he could come back providing he passed all his drug tests.

He also opened up to Beth completely about his affair with Betty Woodson. What she hadn't already been told by Richard Woodson, Michael filled in the rest. He was also sure to let her know that he did not sleep with Betty during her Christmas party. That fact was of little consequence in the big picture, but at least it did help clear up one of Richard Woodson's lies.

Michael spent many nights in the guest bedroom so Beth would have some time to deal with what he had done and, to a lesser extent, so she would be able to sleep through the night while he recovered from his injuries. He agreed to go to counseling at the St. John's Center with Dr. Ted Yost and started his sessions within a couple weeks of leaving the hospital.

Their marriage had been pushed to the limit by Michael's

infidelity and addictions, and these two months after the accident were full of tears, admissions, and introspection. But Michael made sure he was always completely open and honest with her. She knew he was sincerely trying to heal himself and their relationship, and his perseverance, along with her knowledge that he still loved her, is what helped her hang in there and work through all the problems.

Betty Woodson got in touch with Michael a couple times to see how he was doing, but she didn't try to continue their relationship. He suggested she seek counseling herself, and one day at the St. John's Center, he ran into her as she was leaving a session. After the shock of Michael almost getting killed in a car accident and her enlightening discussion with Beth in the hospital room, she finally got the strength to leave her husband. She realized she deserved better and didn't need to settle for the way she had been treated by Richard. Michael was glad to see her take charge of her life and begin to fix it. Within a few weeks, she had a new boyfriend, a real estate developer out in the far west end of town. Once in a while, she still went to church at St. Andrew's, but not every Sunday religiously like before.

By the end of his two-month sabbatical, Reverend Thomas was anxious to get back to work, so the rector scheduled him to lead the services and give the sermon on the third Sunday in March. Word quickly got out to all the church's parishioners, and the popular priest's first service back was expected to be in front of a full house.

Michael was putting the finishing touches on his sermon about an hour before the early service when he heard a knock on his closed office door.

"Unless it's important, I can't talk right now," he called out to the unknown person on the other side of the door. "I'm in pre-game."

"It will only be a few minutes," a man responded from out in the hallway.

Recognizing the familiar voice of his boss, the rector,

Michael quickly replied, "Oh sure, sorry. I didn't know it was you. Come on in."

The rector opened the door and, as Michael was awkwardly trying to stand up on his previously broken leg, said while entering the office, "No, please don't stand up. Save it for the service today."

Michael felt a slight jolt of pain in his leg, so he stopped trying to stand up and dropped back down into his desk chair.

"Are you going to be alright out there?" the rector asked as he sat down in the leather sofa next to the desk.

"I may have a slight limp down the aisle, but I'll be fine."

"Will you and Beth still be able to lead the spring break trip next month to Israel?"

"Definitely. The doctor cleared me to fly. We wouldn't miss it for anything."

"It looks like it's going to be a full house today. Are you nervous?"

"For the last ten years or so, I didn't get nervous. But today feels different. I guess I am a little bit jittery. I feel like I'm fresh out of divinity school again." Michael leaned down to open the door in his desk where he used to hide a bottle of bourbon, but instead he pulled out a bottle of Coca-Cola and offered, "Care for a glass? It's the good stuff, Mexican Coke. They use real sugar instead of high-fructose corn syrup."

The rector smiled and accepted, "Sure. Why not?"

Michael pulled out a clean glass from his desk, poured some soda into it, and handed the drink to his guest.

"Cheers," they both toasted in unison as they clinked their glasses together before each taking a sip.

"So what brings you by?" asked the reverend, sliding back comfortably in his chair.

"Just some quick church business I wanted to take care of before things got too hectic around here today. First of all, I wanted to tell you how glad I am and all of us here are that you're back and feeling better. Your turnaround from before the accident has been nothing short of miraculous."

"Thank you, sir. I guess it's true what they say about

encountering your mortality. It makes you examine your life more closely and identify what's really important. St. Andrew's and the church are definitely important parts of my life that I can't imagine losing."

"I'm glad to hear you say that, Michael." The rector pulled an envelope out of his jacket pocket, handed it across the desk to the reverend, and said, "Since you didn't make it to our staff Christmas get-together this year, I wasn't able to give this to you until now. It's our way of saying a belated Merry Christmas and welcome back."

After he slid open the sealed envelope, Michael pulled out a rectangular, grey piece of paper. He immediately recognized it as a check, and it was made out to him from St. Andrew's in the amount of 28,334 dollars.

The rector added, "After taxes, that should come out to right at 17,000."

The reverend stared at the check for a few seconds, and then tears began to well up in his eyes.

"I don't know what to say," Michael managed to get out of his mouth without breaking down.

"You don't need to say anything. You've done a great job of getting your life back together. Your actions have said it all. This should help tie up any loose ends so you can focus on the future without having to worry about the past."

"So I guess Richard Woodson isn't trying to get me fired then."

"Mr. Woodson and his family have been very good to St. Andrew's over the years. And when he was so generous to us at his Christmas party in front of so many of his friends and fellow members of the church, well, let's just say he's very motivated to keep his promises. Since any relationship between his family and St. Andrew's is now completely professional and appropriate, there's really no reason at all why the Woodson Foundation's considerable donation shouldn't be fulfilled."

"Again, sir, thank you. Beth's parents were so nice to help me out, but they certainly aren't well off enough to be able to spare this kind of money easily. This will help all of us a great deal."

"You keep doing what you're doing and stay clean, and everything will work out OK. In fact, I'd even bet on it."

Both men smiled at the irony of the rector's last statement, and then each took a sip of their glasses of soda. Michael paused for a moment and decided it was the right time to bring up something he had been thinking about for weeks.

The reverend said humbly, "I am truly grateful for everything you and St. Andrew's have done for me, not just now, but over the many years I've been here. And I don't want to push my luck, but I had an idea regarding the Woodson Foundation gift. What do you think about using some of the money to fund more programs for the poor, sick, and homeless? I know we already help them, but we could be doing a whole lot more, especially with so much money available now."

The rector responded, "Richard is determined to have a huge wing here with his name emblazoned all over it, but I don't think we need anything that large here. Worthwhile programs like the ones you have in mind are much more important to the church than a big new building. I'm sure I can persuade him to see that too."

The rector put his empty glass down on Michael's desk and said, "Nice idea. We'll talk more about it later. I'll let you get back to your work."

Once his boss left the room, the reverend folded up the check and put it in his wallet for safekeeping. After glancing over his notes for the sermon, he realized they were as complete as they were ever going to be, so he put them down on the desk, finished his last sip of Coca-Cola, and stared out the window in anticipation of being able to get back into the pulpit.

Usually the middle of March is a slow time of year for most churches. After the high point of Christmas, many Christians wait until the Holy Week around Easter to get back into the spirit of going to church. But this year at St. Andrew's was much different than usual. Reverend Thomas was going to be back for the first time since his accident, and every seat in every pew was filled in appreciation for everything the popular priest had gone through. Many had heard rumors of his experience after the accident, and now they were eager to hear about it directly from the source.

After the readings of the daily lessons and the singing of the hymns and the partaking of the communion, Michael slowly but surely limped up the four steps to the pulpit, nervous but excited to be back where he belonged. Once he reached the next-to-last step, the anxious parishioners all began to clap as they raised up from their seats and gave him a standing ovation. He certainly wasn't expecting this kind of a warm reception, and he had to spend a few moments to collect himself before beginning his sermon. All he could do was stand there and smile at everyone's kindness toward him. Eventually the clapping ended, and they all sat back down in unison, with the shuffling of shoes and the creaking of the wooden pews echoing throughout the cathedral.

The reverend's strong, authoritative voice reverberated between the four-story walls of the chapel as he enunciated clearly into the microphone on the pedestal, "Thank you all for that warm welcome back. I'm so happy to be here, I could do cartwheels down the middle of the church. But the doctor says I have to wait until at least Easter for that, so see you in a few weeks."

The congregation laughed and applauded again for a few seconds. Then Reverend Thomas continued.

"First of all, I'd like to thank everyone here at St. Andrew's for the kind words you've passed along to me in the form of phone calls, texts, get-well cards, and letters. I'm trying to return all those well wishes, and it may take me a little while longer. But I will get back to each and every one of you. I can promise you that."

Michael then looked toward his wife, who was sitting in the middle of the right side of the chapel, and said, "And also a huge thank you to my wonderful wife Beth. Without your support both before and after the accident, I wouldn't be standing here right now. You're the best."

Beth smiled and acknowledged the polite claps from the churchgoers seated all around her, and then she smiled back at her husband standing proudly at the pulpit.

"As many of you know, Beth and I were involved in a car accident a few months ago right out here in front of St. Andrew's. Fortunately Beth only suffered minor injuries, and I'm extremely grateful for that. But apparently I'm not nearly as tough or as strong as my wife, a fact I've known for quite a while now, and I ended up going into a coma.

"Now the reason I mention this is not to get your sympathy or pity. I'm here today, and soon I'll be as good as new. I'm telling you this because while I was in a coma, I had an amazing experience that is directly relevant to why we're all here together.

"Some things are still a little fuzzy, but if I remember correctly, my last sermon was about Jesus in the garden of Gethsemane and how He temporarily asked God to make it so He didn't have to be crucified. I think I also talked about Jesus suffering this agony in the garden because he dreaded the physical pain and torture he was about to endure.

"Well, I have to admit to all of you right here, right now, that I was totally wrong."

The congregation sat completely silent, waiting to hear what the reverend meant by this bold statement.

"A few months before I was born, my grandfather was in an accident. His car was hit by a train, and he was in critical condition when they rushed him to the hospital. He was injured so badly that he was clinically dead for several minutes. Fortunately for my family and me, he regained consciousness and went on to live happily for twenty more years.

"When I was old enough to appreciate it, I read my grandfather's handwritten account of what he encountered while he was temporarily dead in the hospital. Right after his accident, he wrote down every detail he could remember about his near-death experience.

"It was very similar to the classic near-death experiences we've heard about involving people all over the world from different cultures and time periods who have died and come back to life. He floated out of his body. He followed a bright light. He saw his relatives and friends who had died before him. He even met with Jesus, who told him he had to go back to Earth to complete some unfinished part of his life.

"My grandfather talked openly about this experience, and no matter how many doctors claimed it was just the brain making endorphins right before death, he held firm in his belief that it really happened. He said all the sensations and images were too clear and too realistic to be anything other than reality.

"When I was in a coma, I also had an interesting experience. It wasn't like my grandfather's at all, though. I didn't leave my body or follow a bright light to heaven. And I didn't see loved ones who had previously died. But it was extremely vivid and realistic. And I did get to meet Jesus. In fact, I met him in the garden of Gethsemane on the night after the Last Supper.

"Now before you say I'm losing my mind and call in the psychiatrists to put me in a straightjacket, I admit that what I experienced couldn't have possibly really occurred. But regardless of what is or isn't possible, what's important to me is something I learned during that experience about Jesus and what he did for all of us. And it's why my last sermon was completely wrong.

"When we read or hear that Jesus suffered for our sins, what does that really mean? Most of us assume it means that He suffered the shame and frustration of people not believing in Him. Or that He suffered from the torturous beatings and floggings He received from the Romans. Or that He suffered the ultimate pain and humiliation of the crucifixion.

"While it's true He endured all that physical pain during His time here on Earth, the most important suffering He experienced was much more intense. While He was in the garden of Gethsemane praying to God to 'take this cup away from' Him, he didn't mean the crucifixion. What he was referring to was the real Agony in the Garden. Jesus was sent to Earth to suffer for our sins and redeem us to God. And that night after the Last Supper while His disciples slept in the garden, he suffered for our sins literally. God took all the sins that any human had ever committed, and He dumped every one of them onto Jesus.

"All those evil deeds, mistakes, slips into temptation, emotional outbursts, and irrational acts of violence. All those murders, lies, abuses, rapes, and betrayals. For thousands of years, man committed countless sins against God. And God placed them all on Jesus, all at once.

"Can you imagine just how much emotional and physical pain Jesus had to endure that night? It was so overwhelming it almost killed him. After He survived it, His inner strength made it possible for Him to follow His destiny and be crucified. He died valiantly on the cross so that we can follow Him to heaven one day. But what He endured in the garden, when He was so stressed mentally and physically that He sweated blood, was how He suffered so our sins can be forgiven.

"So with Easter coming up in only a few weeks, this is something I hope you all remember about why Jesus' sacrifice for us was so significant and how it extended far beyond the cross.

"Now on a personal note, it's no secret I was going through some very difficult times in my life before the accident. I had problems with addiction, and I made mistakes in my personal relationships that almost cost me everything I hold dear. I'm sure there are plenty of rumors going around, and based on my previous actions, I deserve that.

"During this experience I had while I was in a coma, I call it my visit to the garden, I realized that all my personal problems resulted from one central reason — I had lost my faith."

The congregation let out a muffled murmur of surprise and then quickly hushed themselves so they could hear what was coming next.

"When you live without faith, you feel like you have to do everything all by yourself. There's no God to guide you through life, so you reach out for anything you think is going to fill that void and help you survive. For some it's alcohol, or drugs, or gambling, or someone new. Sometimes, it's even all of these.

"Losing my faith didn't happen instantly or overnight. It happened over time. Over the years, I began to focus more on earthly things like material possessions and money and less on important things like my relationship with God. I can't pinpoint the exact date or time when my faith was gone. And I'd like to think there was still some of it left even right before the accident. But whatever amount of faith I did have then wasn't anything even close to what it is now. And that's because my visit to the garden helped me get my faith back.

"So my point is, if you're struggling with your own faith, and you're not sure if it's possible to get it back, I can tell you from firsthand experience that yes, it's always possible to find your way back to God. He's always going to be there. And He'll be glad to take you back.

"There's much more to my visit to the garden than I can cover right now, and if you want to talk to me about it one-on-one, or if you want to discuss your own faith, I'd be happy to. Just remember though, the doctors had me on a lot of serious drugs in the hospital, and the brain can do all kinds of funny things when it's affected by trauma. But even if it wasn't real, my visit to the garden is something I'll never forget."

"How do you know it wasn't real?" an unknown male voice called out from the crowd.

The entire congregation gasped in surprise. No one had ever had the nerve to speak out in the middle of a sermon at St. Andrew's before.

But Michael kept his poise and asked, "Excuse me, what was that?"

An older gentleman sitting in the middle of the first section on the left stood up and said in a deep, booming voice that carried throughout the entire building, "Your experience in the garden. How do you know it wasn't real?"

Michael squinted through his glasses to get a better look at the man, and after a moment he recognized him. It was the older man Michael had met in that very same chapel before Christmas when he had been praying for help.

Reverend Thomas said, "I remember you, sir. It's George, right?"

The man nodded yes.

Michael continued, "Well, George, I just can't presume to believe that I was suddenly sent back in time to two thousand years ago on the other side of the world while being in a coma in a hospital here in Richmond?"

"Why not?" George persistently asked. "Miracles happen every day. A person suddenly finds out their cancer has gone into remission. Two people randomly meet and fall in love. Someone gets a job right as they're running out of money. Those are miracles, right? And they happen all the time."

When Michael had been drinking and using drugs, his patience wore thin very quickly, and he would have been rather annoyed if someone tried to hijack his sermon in front of the entire church. But now, he didn't feel the least bit bothered or upset at George. And he didn't mind having such a serious discussion in front of everyone. No one in the congregation seemed to mind either.

"Yes, those are definitely miracles," responded the reverend. "I agree with you. Miracles do happen all around us every day. And they're wonderful. What I experienced was wonderful. And yes, maybe it did really happen. Who knows?"

George followed up, "You just talked about how you got your faith back. And that's great to hear. But don't forget. Faith in God means more than believing He exists. It also means believing in what He does, however incredible it may seem."

"That's very true, George. I will remember that. Maybe we can discuss it further sometime."

"Sure," George replied before he smiled at Michael and sat back down in his seat in the pew.

Most of the people sitting nearby George gave him some curious stares after he sat down, but from then on, the rest of the service was more conventional. After the closing processional, Michael limped over to the main exit door facing Grove Avenue to say goodbye to many of the parishioners who had come out to see him. There were a lot more than usual, so it took a long time for everyone to speak a little while with the reverend on their way out of the building.

Michael hoped he would be able to say goodbye to George and plan some time to meet with him again in a more personal environment, but he didn't see the older gentleman leave the church. There were several other exits he could have taken, and Michael assumed George had left through a different door. Maybe he would see George again sometime soon, he hoped.

16 TRIP OF A LIFETIME

Early April is a very popular time of year to visit Jerusalem and the rest of Israel's religious sites. Tourists from all over the world go there before and during Easter to celebrate Holy Week in the Holy Land. Beth and Michael Thomas had the honor of being chaperons for a St. Andrew's spring break trip that took 32 young members of the church, along with several parents, to experience in person many of the locations referenced in the Bible.

Michael had always dreamed of going to Israel one day to see these famous churches and landmarks himself, and Beth was very happy to be able to share this special experience with him. Their marriage was much stronger now than it had been in a long time, and they looked at this trip as a way to help make their relationship even better, regardless of if they had to babysit dozens of kids and parents along for the ride too.

For such a large group, the church rented a full-sized tour bus that could fit all of them together for their visits to sites in Galilee, Bethlehem, Nazareth, and Jerusalem. A local Israeli tour guide also provided interesting historical background to each of the places they visited, which included the Church of the Nativity, where Jesus was born; the Basilica of the Annunciation, where the angel Gabriel told Mary she was going to be the mother of Jesus; the Church of the Holy Sepulchre, where Jesus was crucified, buried, and resurrected; and the Church of All Nations, where Jesus prayed during His Agony in the Garden.

Michael added the visit to the Church of All Nations to the busy itinerary just a few weeks before the trip, so the only time available to fit it in was on the last day. Due to his visit to the garden during his coma, he thought it would only be fitting to go to the original site where Jesus prayed after the Last Supper. And thanks to good weather and no travel delays during the weeklong trip, they were still on schedule to make it to Gethsemane right before lunchtime on their final full day in Israel.

"It's beautiful," Beth Thomas commented from inside the white, Greyhound-style tour bus as it pulled up in front of the Church of All Nations. "That mosaic on top there. It's gorgeous."

Three tall arches were lined up along the width of the front entrance to the church, and a brightly colored mosaic of Jesus acting as a mediator between God and mankind covered the top section of the church above the arches. The entire exterior of the traditional Roman basilica, including the façade, steps, columns, and walls, was covered in rose-colored limestone that had darkened slightly over the decades due to weathering and pollution buildup. Ornately designed stained-glass windows containing circles and crosses filled in the archways to the left and right of the main entrance door.

The tour guide led everyone off the bus and to the left side of the building, where they showed their tourist passes to the guards and proceeded over to the main door of the church. Michael and Beth stood just outside the door and let the guide, the parents, and all the kids go in first. While they were waiting, they both turned around to take in the beautiful, expansive view of the Old City of Jerusalem laid out before them. Tall, ancient limestone walls rose up on the other side of the Kidron Valley, crowned by the shiny, golden Dome of the Rock.

"How does it look? Is it the same as you remembered?"

Beth asked her husband, referring to his visit to the garden while in a coma.

Michael answered, "It's a beautiful view, and it's very, very similar. But it's not exactly the same."

"Is has been a couple thousand years, you know. Things do change."

He smiled at his wife and said, "You really do think my experience was real, don't you?"

"Why not? God can do anything. Plus, I've always believed in you, Michael."

"I know you have, even when I didn't deserve it."

He gave her a tight hug and kissed her on the cheek, then he turned back to face the city and said, "I know the walls have aged over time, and the Holy Temple isn't there anymore. But I mean it also looks different from this viewpoint. The way I remember it, the angle was different. Standing right here, we're lower and more to the left of where I saw it during my visit."

"Do you think they found the wrong rock?"

"I doubt it. I mean, what's more likely? After centuries of archeological studies, they found the right place. Or they found the wrong place because some guy goes back in time to a different spot for a visit with Jesus. I think they probably got it right."

The last of the kids filed into the church through the front door, so Beth and Michael followed right behind and entered the dimly lit front nave and vault. The polished-stone floor and Corinthian columns reflected what little sunlight was able to penetrate the stained-glass windows. Once his eyes adjusted to the darkness, Michael was astounded by the beauty of the blue-and-gold painted ceilings inside each of the 12 domes of the church. As the group made its way along the center aisle of the chapel, he could faintly hear the tour guide up ahead speaking English in her Israeli accent.

"The Church of All Nations gets its name from the 16 countries, including your United States, that donated the money to build this Roman Catholic church back in 1924. The first church to be built on this spot was a Byzantine basilica in the fourth century, which was later destroyed by an earthquake in 746. Then in the twelfth century, a small chapel was built here by the Crusaders. But that was abandoned in 1345.

"As we move along to the front of the church, notice the low interior lighting levels that represent the nighttime when Jesus prayed in the Garden of Gethsemane. The columns are Corinthian in design and…"

The guide's voice faded out as Michael's attention was drawn to the painting on the wall in the vestibule behind the high altar in the very front of the church. The midnight-blue background was set behind olive trees on the left and right, with Jesus kneeling on a round rock directly in the center and an angel floating in the sky above Him. Michael rushed toward the painting to get a closer look, leaving the rest of the group behind. Beth stayed with the group and let her husband have this moment to himself.

Once he drew closer to the altar, a two-foot-tall, stone wall with a wooden door in the center became visible. Only a handful of people were milling around inside the walled-off area, so he walked right on in and knelt down on the polished stone floor in front of a one-foot-tall metal fence that surrounded a coarse section of light tan limestone measuring fifteen feet square. Michael noticed the detail on the metal fence and realized it looked like strands of thorns interlocked together, representing the crown of thorns Jesus wore when He was tortured and crucified.

His upper body leaned over the short metal fence, he laid both his hands flat on the rough limestone, and he began to pray to God and Jesus, thanking them for his visit to the garden and for helping him repair his life. A few moments later, Beth knelt down beside him.

She waited for him to finish praying, and then she asked about the rock, "Does this look familiar?"

"This is completely different," he replied. "The rock I saw was grey with small, shiny reflective crystals mixed in, almost like quartz, and thin, white veins running through it, like that "Y" with the loop I told you about. This is all one solid piece of tan limestone. And it feels totally different too."

"I'm sorry, honey. I know you hoped it really happened. But maybe this isn't the right rock. Like I said, it's been two thousand years. How can they be sure this was the actual rock where Jesus prayed that night?"

"You're sweet for trying to cheer me up. But it's OK. What's really important is how my experience helped me find my faith again. It doesn't matter if it wasn't real."

The rest of the tour group joined the Thomas couple a few minutes later at the Rock of Agony, and each person knelt down to touch it. They all said prayers, and when they were done, they filed out of the church and into their tour bus parked in front of the building. It was now lunchtime, and the group headed to a nearby park where they could enjoy a picnic before they would have to go to Tel Aviv to catch their flight back home. The scenic garden of ancient olive trees next to the Church of All Nations was closed to tourists, but the guide knew of a nice, relaxing spot just a few blocks away where they could relax and enjoy their meal.

Five minutes later, the tour bus arrived at the park. Everyone filed out of the bus and walked about a hundred feet into a field with patches of thick grass amidst larger patches of bare dirt, interspersed with a few young olive trees. Some short, dense bushes nestled up against a relatively new white cement wall that separated the back side of the park from a housing development on the other side.

Beth and Michael helped the tour guide spread out blankets on top of a patch of tall, unmown grass in the shade of one of the olive trees, which was much more comfortable than lying on hardpacked dirt and rocks. After passing out all the food to everyone, Michael enjoyed a turkey sandwich before quickly moving on to an Elite candy bar, a brand of Israeli chocolate he had grown fond of during the trip.

"You picked a nice spot for us," Beth said to the tour guide. "Great view too."

"I'm glad you like it," the tour guide replied. "It's one of my favorite places in Jerusalem. Something about it is very peaceful and relaxing. Fortunately, not many people know about it."

Having been sitting with his back to the Old City of Jerusalem while he ate his lunch, Michael spun around slowly, careful not to hurt his newly healed leg. He had felt great during the trip, but he didn't want to tweak anything while he was sitting with his knees bent. Beth got up, walked across the blanket, sat down next to him, and enjoyed the view with her husband.

"This has been a great trip," she admitted. "Too bad we have to go back tonight."

"I know. I've always wanted to come here, and it's been the trip of a lifetime. But I also miss our bed."

"And air conditioning. And lots of ice in our drinks," Beth added.

Michael nodded in agreement and kissed her on top of her head.

"You know, this view is much more like the one I remember from my dream," he said as he turned back and looked out across the valley at the ancient walls of Jerusalem. "The way the walls line up from here is pretty much exactly the same."

"Hey Reverend Thomas, want to throw the football with me?" a young boy's voice called out from behind them.

Michael looked over his shoulder and saw Billy Howard, one of the kids from St. Andrew's, holding a faded-orange and worn Nerf football.

"You probably should. You need to work off some of that chocolate," ribbed Beth.

The reverend slowly stood up, walked toward Billy, and said, "Let's go over there to the back of the park near the wall so we're not bothering these people still eating lunch."

The boy and the man walked together past a couple olive trees, some tall grassy patches, and a rough and rocky ditch before they reached a level area where they could throw the football parallel to the short bushes that lined the white cement wall. They set up 30 feet apart, and Billy threw a tight spiral to the reverend.

"What are those over there?" Billy asked, pointing at five gold, onion-shaped cupolas, each topped with a cross, towering above the tree line a few blocks away. "They look like something at Disney World."

The reverend turned around to see what Billy was pointing at and then responded, "That's the Church of St. Mary Magdalene. It's Russian. See those domes on top? They're very similar to the domes at the Kremlin in Moscow. Have you ever been to Russia?"

"No. My dad says it's too cold there. He wants to go to Hawaii on our next family trip."

"Between you and me, I'm with your dad on that one."

They threw the football back a forth a few times, and Billy said in between passes, "I enjoyed your sermon a few weeks ago. That thing that happened to you when you were in a coma, it sounds pretty cool. Why don't you talk about it more with people?"

"It's just something that happens to your brain sometimes when you're in a coma. It was a very surreal experience, that's for sure."

"I've heard about people on drugs having these weird things happen to them. I think they call it tripping. Is that what happened to you?"

The reverend couldn't help but laugh out loud before he replied, "No, that's not at all what happened. And don't do drugs. They're very bad for you."

"So if it wasn't like that, and it felt as real as you said it did, then why don't you think it really happened? Like that old man said during your sermon, miracles happen all the time."

"Billy, it was just so weird and completely out of the realm of possibility. I know they say anything's possible. But I was there, and I seriously doubt it really happened. We can talk about it more sometime if you want. Feel free to stop by my office whenever. I know you live close-by the church, so you can just drop in anytime. I'm almost always there. OK, enough serious talk for now. Aren't you a Redskins fan?"

"Yes! Hail to the Redskins!" Billy yelled back.

"Alright. Good. Then run over there to your right, and I'll throw you a deep-corner route like Theismann throwing to Art Monk."

"Who's Art Monk?"

Michael shook his head and said, "Never mind. Just go deep."

Billy ran away from the bushes that lined the tall cement wall, and Michael threw a high arcing spiral that landed perfectly in the boy's outstretched arms.

"Nice grab!" Michael called out to the boy after he made the catch. "See if you can hit me over here!"

The reverend ran gently on his tender leg toward the bushes and watched the football fly straight and high, right over his head and into the dense greenery at the base of the wall.

"Nice throw," he called out to Billy. "That was my bad. I guess I can't run as fast as I used to."

Michael trudged deliberately into the dense shrubbery to find the lost football. Billy started to run back to join him in the search, but once the reverend was just a few feet into the bushes, the boy lost sight of him. He could only hear the snapping sounds of the reverend pushing branches back to clear his path and the occasional "ouch" caused by a thorny branch scraping his skin. As Billy drew closer to the spot where Michael had entered the dense shrubs, he noticed that all the sounds from inside the bushes had suddenly stopped.

Worried that something had happened to the reverend, Billy shouted, "Reverend Thomas, are you all right?"

There was no reply.

"Reverend Thomas?" the boy yelled again.

After a few more moments of silence, the reverend called out in a shaky voice, "Billy, I'm OK. But please, run and get my wife. It's important."

Without taking any time to respond, Billy took off running back toward the rest of his tourist group who were still finishing their lunch in the middle of the park. He sprinted as fast as he could past the rocky ditch, past the tall grassy patches, and past the olive trees until he slid to a stop on the blanket where Beth Thomas was sitting.

Out of breath from running at full speed, Billy gasped, "Hurry! Reverend Thomas needs you! He says it's important!"

"Where is he?!" she exclaimed.

"This way! Follow me!" Billy told her before he took off running back to where the reverend was.

Beth jumped up from sitting on the blanket and started running right behind Billy.

"Is he OK?" she shouted worriedly.

"I think so, but he sounded like something wasn't right."

In the relatively short distance she ran to find her husband, dozens of different scenarios ran through her head. She worried that maybe he has having a relapse related to his edema. Or maybe he broke his leg again. Or maybe he was having a stroke or a heart attack. Every bad possibility she could think of, she thought of. After what seemed like a marathon, Beth and Billy finally reached the bushes.

Beth called out first, "Michael, where are you?"

"I'm OK, Beth," the reverend responded. "But you need to come in here now."

Beth turned to Billy and told him, "Listen carefully. Stay here. Do not follow me in there. Do you hear me?"

Billy nodded his head yes. Beth looked back at the bushes, walked up to the nearest one in the direction where she had heard her husband's voice, and spread out the thick branches with her hands. She ducked down, walked in a few feet, and then spread apart the next set of branches.

"Michael?" she yelled out, hoping to adjust her course through the thick greenery.

"This way, Beth," he answered.

With her heart racing in her chest and sweat beading up on her face from worry, she forced her way through another ten feet of dense shrubs, where she came upon the sight of her husband kneeling on the ground with his back to her and the football lying on the ground at his feet.

Hearing her right behind him, he turned his head around while still kneeling on the ground and said in a trembling voice, "Beth, come see this."

Still bent over at the waist, she took a couple more steps and kneeled down just to the right of her husband. He pushed back some heavy branches with both his hands to reveal a dark grey slab of rock that rose about a foot off the hard-packed dirt ground. She looked closer and saw two slight recesses about two feet apart forming a U-shaped section. Just above the right recess, which was directly in front of where she was kneeling, could be seen a white vein in the rock in the shape of a "Y" with a small loop at the bottom. She gasped in amazement.

"The 'Y' with the loop," she whispered, out of breath from running and shock. "It's just like you told me."

Michael turned to his wife and, with a smile and watery eyes, exclaimed, "It was real! It really happened!"

The two hugged each other tightly and began to laugh loudly. From outside the bushes, Billy heard the laughter and was able to stop worrying, but he still didn't know what was going on.

"Are you two OK?" he called out.

The laughter stopped, and a few moments later, Michael and Beth emerged from the bushes with huge smiles on their faces.

"What was so funny in there?" Billy asked.

Michael replied, "The rock from my visit to the garden, it's real. It's right in there. That means my experience actually did happen."

Billy asserted confidently, "Of course it was real. I never understood why you doubted it, Reverend Thomas. Like we said before, miracles happen all the time."

Having rushed over to see if the reverend was safe, the rest of the tour group arrived at the bushes concerned and out of breath. Once he told them what he had discovered inside the shrubbery, they all circled around and gave Michael and Beth and each other huge, joyful hugs. With a single tear rolling down his cheek, Michael looked up into the clear, sunny, warm, bright-blue sky and smiled toward the heavens.

17 EPILOGUE

After the discovery of the rock in the park in Jerusalem, Reverend Thomas told the Israel Antiquities Authority how he believed that was the actual place where Jesus suffered His Agony in the Garden. An excavation was completed, the rock was protected, a more permanent shelter was built, and further investigations were conducted to check its legitimacy. But due to limited references in the Bible and the lack of historical documents about the Rock of Agony, no one was willing to change the official site to this new location. For hundreds of years people had worshiped at the rock in the Church of All Nations, and that was going to continue. But to a priest, his wife, and a group of tourists from Richmond, Virginia, it didn't really matter at all. They knew the truth.

Betty Woodson completed her divorce from Richard and received a large settlement in exchange for her discretion. She gave generous amounts to worthwhile charities and continued supporting the St. John's Center in appreciation for how they helped her. After making the real estate developer sign a prenuptial agreement, she married him in a small ceremony at St. Andrew's. Reverend Thomas was very happy for her, but he made sure another priest performed the ceremony.

Michael and Beth Thomas continued to work on their marriage and Michael's addictions. He successfully avoided any future temptations of alcohol, drugs, gambling, and adultery, and he passed all his drug tests, which allowed him to go back to teaching at St. Philip's. The student who supplied him with cocaine, Paul, never got a college recommendation from the reverend.

Michael was finally able to find peace and contentment with his financial status in life. Since his Volvo had been totaled in the accident, he bought a newer used Volvo wagon, but this one was grey. Yet on those rare occasions when he saw a Jaguar XKE roll by, he did imagine how nice it would be to own one.

After another decade of loyal service to St. Andrew's while steadily expanding the church's programs to help the poor and sick, Michael was promoted to rector when his previous boss retired. Rector Thomas maintained a close relationship with his old mentor and friend and continued to visit him for advice for many years.

Michael never saw George, the older gentleman, at St. Andrew's or anywhere else ever again. He always hoped he would run into him someplace so he could tell him about the rock in Jerusalem and how his words in the church that day during Michael's sermon ended up being true after all. But since the story about the rock quickly became big local news, he figured George probably heard about it somehow. There was no way to be sure, but Michael had faith.

ABOUT THE AUTHOR

After more than 20 years as an award-winning copywriter and creative director in advertising, Jeff Carleton decided to pursue his real passions: films and novels. His film experience includes co-writing and co-producing *The House Behind the Wall*, a movie based on a famous ghost story at Ft. Monroe, Virginia.

The Man in the Garden is the first of what he hopes to be many novels that entertain and educate readers about modern society. When the weather is nice in Virginia Beach and Jeff isn't writing, reading, or watching films, he can usually be found on a golf course. He dreams of one day being able to play golf as well as some of his characters do.